Molly & the Cyclops

This book is dedicated to my family—Mum, Dad, Leonie,
Orna, Sorcha, Breffni, Caoimhe, and Ayesha—
my friends, and the people of East Timor and Palestine.

Molly & the Cyclops

AILBHE KEOGAN

First published 2006 by
HAG'S HEAD PRESS
www.hagsheadpress.com

Copyright © Ailbhe Keogan, 2006
Flick cartoon © Joe Dixon, 2006

All rights reserved. No part of this publication may
be reproduced in any form or by any means without
the prior permission of the publisher. A CIP record
for this title is available from The British Library.

10 9 8 7 6 5 4 3 2 1

ISBN 0 9551264 1 X
ISBN-13 978 0 9551264 1 3

Printed in England by MPG Books, Bodmin, Cornwall

0:1: Telephone Transcript

In Search of Infinite Relief, C.W. Sisle
Contracted to Diggin Media Group
Subcontracted to Employee 03
Recorded at 11.23 a.m. on 07/01/****

E03 Hello.

C213 Hi Laurence. It's Annie.

E03 Hi Annie. How've you been?

(Caller 213 coughs)

C213 I'm really good today. I wanted to tell you about something that happened yesterday. It really brought home everything we've been talking about.

E03 Wonderful, Annie. I've been working on a piece all day and it's going nowhere. Go on. Tell me. Take my mind off it.

C213 I met this girl yesterday—well she's old, same as me. Not old, but I went to school with her. I don't know why I insist on calling grown women girls. Anyway, Luca—that's her name—Luca and me were always in competition at school, not over books because I was interested and she wasn't, but with our looks. Up-front to you, Laurence, we were the two best-looking girls in our term. It was obvious to everyone, not that we were in competition but that we were literally the two most—anyway it was just the way things landed—so we meet and we do the hellos and after we're both still standing there. And I have to say she's still a handsome woman. So am I. I mean people don't look so much as they used to but I still get a wayward eyeful. A man walks by with his little beady eyes peeping over his mask, he's taking us in and then my old rivalry stops by again. And while I'm trying to gauge how I fare now against Luca, she turns to me and says, pointing to her breasts, –They're fake, she says. You still with me, Laurence?

E03 I'm listening, Annie.

C213 OK. So as I'm thinking—grudgingly, *At least she's honest about it*, she puts her hand into her blouse and pulls out this plastic thing. –The Sickness, she says, twice, and swoops in to rescue the second one. She's standing there with her entire chest in her hands. I don't know what to say to her. So I show her my dead hand, I'd show it to you but ... I show her my hand and say, –My son. Remember I told you about that?

E03 Platt—I remember. The iron.

C213 Yeah. So then she says, –Thanks Annie. –For what? I say. –For putting your hand up to lost beauty, she says. –Excuse me, Luca, I say, there's been no beauty lost here. My pride swelled, Laurence! See that. How I just jumped in defensively. Anyway, she says, –No, there hasn't—and insists on taking me out to lunch. It's the best afternoon I've had in years. Wasn't that—

E03 Listen, Annie, how long have we been calling each other?

C213 How long have I been calling you, you mean? I'm teasing, I'm teasing. Over ten years I guess. I remember calling you on my thirty-seventh birthday because in my house they forgot. So definitely, at least ten years.

E03 Over ten years, that's right. Annie, I know we've never talked outside the lines before, but you're my longest caller. To be honest, I think I need your ear today more than you need mine. I know you're paying but ...

C213 Oh, just tell me.

E03 They've sold my number. I didn't know they could but they did. A new house has the contract. I don't know who got it, what he's like.

C213 What does that mean exactly, Laurence?

E03 It means I don't have a job, but scarier still, it means that someone else will be playing Laurence.

C213 I don't want anyone else.

E03 Neither do I. This wasn't a job for me. It was something else. Something I don't want to put words on. I'm very cut up.

C213 Can't I still call you? Can't we still be friends outside any of this crap?

E03 Course, Annie, but what about all my other callers?

C213 Maybe we could all contribute something and keep you on a wage of sorts? I don't know, Laurence. We can think of something.

E03 I don't know either. I don't even know why they sold the contract. I'd a steady trade.

C213 You were good at it too. More than good, you know that.

E03 I was good at it, Annie, because ... Annie, I wrote the book. I wrote it after my wife died. I really am a musician. I really do believe what I wrote, what we've talked about. I believe mankind may—one day, outsmart the Wanting, Annie. I really believe we can. On the good days I think we will.

(Caller 213 begins to cry)

C213 I ... I ... I just thought you were really good at it.

E03 My replacement is the one who'll have to be good.

C213 It won't be the same.

E03 He might be better.

C213 Shut up, Laurence. When are you going? Will you be there next week?

E03 Yeah. Let's leave our goodbyes till then so.

C213 OK. Bye for now.

E03 Bye, Annie.

End of transcript

1:1: Mr. ****

I work solidly until lunch. I'm good at my job. Most people think I'm a genius at what I do, I don't argue with them because I agree. I'm one of the longest-serving employees here in the shed. I could go with a bigger house uptown in the Library District but I don't feel the inclination to move. I suspect it's because I enjoy feeling superior in this shoddy hole. Fathead knows this and plays on it by dumping compliment after compliment at my feet, and I in turn enjoy watching him play a game I umpire from behind my desk.

It's quite easy to be good at this game but true greats are a rarity. Everyone gets so far but few get past the end post. I spend most of my time at the end post, waiting for everyone else to tread on the ribbon I have left in tatters. People say I should be on screen, but people say a lot of things that I tongue from my teeth and swallow without tasting. I don't want to be on screen. I like what I do now from my cubic office with its cubic corners full of cubic people stuffed into their shoebox lives. I just jump into the stint and leave it begging for life at six. I never care to bring it into my house. That's why I'm still here.

I'm about to leave for lunch when Davy comes to my door.

–Dennis is going over, he says excitedly.

He is young. It's his first time. (Davy, not Dennis. Dennis is old, but it's also his first time and probably his last.)

–How do you know? I ask. Hunted. Weary.

–He's wearing a suit for one, Davy says.

I look at him in abstraction, standing there in my doorway. Panting. Excited. I do not say anything.

–He's never got dressed up before. Has he?

–No, I say.

–And he gave me a business card. Look!

He throws it down on my desk. I nod. I see his point. Excited. Puppy. Davy, not me.

–We thought you should call someone.

–Why?

–Because you probably know someone up at the house. You've been here the longest—well, except for Dennis, but he can hardly make the call.

Davy starts to grin shyly but I dunk him in a look that leaves his nascent laughter limp and soggy. I look at him for a minute, then pick up the phone.

They come to collect him an hour later. They tell him they need him to oversee some project up at the house. He goes believingly. Davy comes back down to my office to savour the excitement with a cohort. I tell him I'm leaving for lunch and brush past him on the way out.

I would've liked to watch Dennis go over. He would have been a good one. But it's likely he'll be reclaimed and end up working as a house administrator.

I'm not hungry but the City gurgles beneath me. I pass Fathead on his way in. He is indicative of the slob-like-shiny-lapel practice that passes for a work ethic here. Our shed is just about floating above board. Our house does not condone personal engagements, but some of its employees do them. There are some sheds that open all night but their clients, employees and services reek of sex and shadows—the personal touch is meant quite literally. I know men here who do personal engagements. They do it for the money or because they get off on it or because they have no lives waiting for them by the door. These are the ones you have to watch. These are the characters most likely to go over but you can never really tell who is going to slide.

I knew one character that kept on a stint for over thirty-five years. He is the nearest thing to a professional I have seen passing down these corridors. He had a family and a personal life. He took time off twice a year, called home between stints, called you by your real name at the water dispenser. The others here called him the Switch. *One day he short-fused on the wrong side.* That particular quote wafted from the canteen some days after. It amuses me to use it now. He short-fused on the wrong side! The men here are lacking in everything but a sad want to be. They wear watches that drip and hair oil that smells of past horrors. The Switch went over. His wife brought him down to the shed. She ran from room to room, shouting, calling us thieves. I enjoyed the spectacle. It broke up my day, gave it fractions. Most times I swallow a day whole. The Switch sat outside in the car. He was still in his pyjamas, kept tapping the window screen and talking into some contraption he'd devised.

I have already bought a paper from Gonzo this morning but I see Freddie and buy a rag. The powers are still in negotiations with the Global Security Council. The pictures are of fully dressed men sipping mineral water; they have not found their way to the front page yet. Locked away behind wooden doors and teak politics, WAR has not yet made itself accessible to the masses. There are no images yet, no blood, no handsome generals to inspire the khaki swimwear collection. Instead, a pop star has hijacked the front page. LESS OF THAT CHEEK MR. PONDLEPASS the headline screams in a block typeface that grins inanely. A picture shows some mindless ass-grabbing at an awards ceremony.

I walk down the street, silently sidling up to the City. I pass a woman that smells like the Ghost and I grimace. *Marriages don't tend to sit comfortably on this game.* I'm smirking now, thinking of the boys in the canteen and the narrative of faux bravado and world-weary resignation that lives amidst their stained teeth. But these are the best moments. Mostly, we just come, take our assigned stints, go through the preliminaries, sit by the phone, and wait for the calls to come. Come. Take. Go. Sit. Wait. Pretend.

Somewhere I stop for food. When I have finished eating I walk back to the shed and heckle the day until it eats itself. After work, I go to my house and watch the Ghost watching me from the corner of her lifeless vision. My bed calls to me and I surrender without a fight. Another yelping day put down.

I live an hour away from work. I like the time this journey takes off my hands by necessity. I have no choice but to give away these hours and this affords me a certain pleasure. I only buy my paper from two vendors, route and mood dictating: Gonzo and Freddie. My two papery friends.

Gonzo is small and fat and has sold papers for over half a century. He sleeps with his heavy ink-stained hands. The first thing he does each morning is smell his fingers. He has volunteered this information. I have never asked nor ever wanted to. I find this gesture obscene, but for Gonzo it's a ritual. He told me that to smell the print on his fingers helps validate the why*s* of his existence.

–What if you were a fishmonger, I'd said, and you smelt fish on your fingers?

–I would know I'm in the wrong profession, he'd told me, I was born to sell papers.

–Do you see yourself as an important part of the global chain of communication? I'd asked—to be a cunt and to mock his simplicity.

–I don't claim to be part of anything other than the greater good.

He'd said this in recognition of me being a cunt. I'd acknowledged this and said nothing as I'd handed over the money. I remember him shouting after me to keep on the right side of the road. I knew what he was trying to tell me. I'd raised my hand over my shoulder to confirm that I'd heard but I didn't try to catch his words. Purposely, I'd let them fall. There—on the ground—they had found their end, like the words of so many others, stepped on and dirtied, abandoned, incomplete.

I buy a rag from Freddie this morning. I glance down at the front page. TOO LITTLE, TOO LATE. TREEHOUSE VOICES OPPOSITION TO GSC RESOLUTION. I don't bother reading any more. I know what is to come because I have understood the motives from the beginning. I can't believe Treehouse's claims to liberation—his PR people fucked up weeks ago when they shifted priorities and namesakes around a lacking diplomacy. Stupidly they exposed the festering motives beneath.

Freddie sells his rags because he wants to be a writer and claims this is the best possible vantage point from whence to court his subjects. From whence. Ha! I know he sells papers because he'll never be a writer. I know that he can't write because he tries to feed me his daily revelations with a pride that belies their naturalness. His revelations are observations. He is half-blind with two good eyes. Then again, Freddie is only thirty-two. I didn't ask. He volunteered the information as if I cared. Me. The kidney dish. But

Freddie has time to live one story that will choose him to tell itself. Maybe then he'll be lucky. But if I were a story I would not choose Freddie to speak for me. He is sloppy and wears a medallion on his wrist. He disgusts me and I enjoy him for this very reason. I can't believe he can afford so many smiles.

The City's rumbling. Everywhere, these hairy clumps of people amassed on the City's hind. I put them in cages—it helps me to digest their existence. Drifters are drifting, carried by their slow intent to finish each day and start another. They have stopped asking questions; they have stopped caring. They are content to be carried by the life that lies beneath them. You can find a Drifter anywhere because they never stop to turn around and assess their mileage.

Fighters are fighting to find themselves. I see it all the time. Battling with the City to reclaim their identity. To know who they are. In a city teeming with millions, the Fighters adorn themselves with symbols of who they are, who they believe themselves to be. They walk in their respective traditional dress, laden with badges asserting their beliefs, their war cries. Probably not the worst thing in our game—knowing or thinking you know who you are or where you have come from.

I don't work with many Progressives. Any Progressives in this game are uptown. Progressives fight for themselves, they fight to get ahead, they fight to get richer, they work with the Media to their own ends. They spend their time glancing over their shoulders whilst looking ahead to their future. They progress. With elbows greased to wind you on the way into the lift. The honest Progressive is a perversion to City normalcy. But they do exist. I have seen them walking on the stairs.

Searchers do not drift or progress quickly because they are looking for something. I can see it in their eyes, a constant watching, a constant urge to know what it is they are looking for. They know that some piece of them is missing yet they do not know where to begin their search. That is why they are everywhere, in every crease of this existence. I can't bear to look a Searcher in the eye because they shamelessly look to me for answers and this offends me. This is how desperate they are. They look to me as if they think I care.

I'm bored now thinking of people and their rumpled lives. There are countless groups and countless more that have sprung from countless others. Everybody is a hybrid of everything else. Even this industry, this fictional life by the phone, has created a subsection of society that sits down beside the Lost and Forgotten. It's only a small minority. Yet it will not be long before the Media takes them—only to give them back to a world they have created and a family that no longer knows who they are.

1:1: Telephone Transcript

In Search of Infinite Relief, C.W. Sisle
Contracted to Gleeson Media Group
Subcontracted to Employee 12
Recorded at 11.53 a.m. on 13/01/****

E12 Hello?

C213 Hello? Laurence?

E12 Hello, Annie.

C213 Shit! You're the new guy. Does my name come up on a screen or something?

E12 Annie!

C213 I don't mean to be rude but I don't want to do this with you. I knew Laurence a long time. I can imagine you'd appreciate that. And I appreciate you've got to do your thing so maybe if you can just give me Laurence's number.

E12 This is Laurence's number, Annie.

C213 Have you a manager I can talk to?

E12 Annie …

C213 Fuck. Sounds like you're begging me now. Don't talk outside the lines, don't talk outside the lines. Is this recorded?

E12 We were friends, Annie.

(Caller 213 shouts)

C213 If anyone listening to this has any scrap of humanity left, could you please call me with the old Laurence's number? Thank you. And thank you, new Laurence. I know this isn't really your fault. I'm just cranky 'cause I lost my friend.

End of transcript

1:3: Molly

I'm sweeping the floor with a hunger to see it clean, knowing all the while that—tonight—my hunger is inspired by my thirst. I want to get finished up here and get sitting down. I want to share close of day with a drink.

–Molly! Molly!

I follow the shouts to find Lucon yelling at me from the door.

–We're putting the rubbish out now. Have you any full bags up there?

–No, I say, this is the last pile. I'll throw it in behind the bar.

When I turn again to the task at hand, I find Monkey curled up in the industrial-sized dustpan. He is pretending to be asleep but I can see the smirk seeping slowly out of the corners of his mouth. I laugh to myself and motion for him to get out of the dustpan. A smile floods his face as he rolls out slowly and keeps rolling until he hits the Clap's bar stool.

I look over at Augusta. I look at her and love. Quickly. All at once. I look back at J to tell him that I love him and he tells me with his eyes that he loves me too. I try to find Lou's eyes to pass on the message, but she's screaming at someone to keep the door shut, her eyes aflame. I turn back to Augusta. Her hair is scraggy and I remind myself to bring in the conditioner that Isha bought me. I wonder who the man is. She likes him enough to rest her head on the counter and look up at him. When Augusta doesn't like someone she keeps her body rigid in protest. I throw the rubbish in the bin behind the bar and then go over to them and pull up a stool.

–So where the hell did you come from anyway? I ask.

Tying my hair back and grinning.

–I've been out of the City for a while, he says, I used to come here all the time when I lived here. I know the Clap.

–Well, I say.

–Well what? he says and smiles.

–Well then, tell us a story.

–About what?

–I don't know, I've been working all night while you've been drinking. I deserve not to be bored on my own time.

I say this smiling. He knows that I'm not being offensive. He knows I have recognised him enough to sidestep routine introduction and not waste any time asking questions I don't care to know the answer to. In this city people come and go so it's important to get right in there while you can—especially here in the bar. You learn who to dive with and who to swim with.

–Direct me, he says.

–Do you remember the first time you realised your mother didn't know everything? Augusta asks out of nowhere. She says it lazily into her hands.

–Fuck, Augusta, I say, that's a cracker. What bottle are you on?

–Eighteen.

–Break open your last one then and hope this man has a good answer.

–In my bag there, she says motioning with her head.

I find her bag wrapped around my stool. I take out a baby bottle and pour it into her glass. I smile at the man. He is wearing a handkerchief around his neck. To what avail I can't really tell. I like it. I think of him laying bricks. I think of him building things with his hands. If I ever got a job laying bricks I'd wear one just like it.

–So, I prompt.

–No, he says.

–No what? I ask.

–No, I can't remember.

–What? You still think she knows everything?

–No one knows everything, he says, but I never knew my mother. Can I volunteer my father's ignorance instead?

And I smile to tell him that yes, he can and that I never knew my mother either. The motherless find their own because our hollows overlap. The gaping wounds fall to a warm recess. A dirty smirk skirts the rim of my senses. I ignore her. Not tonight. Tonight I am loved and brave.

The man lights a cigarette.

–When I was ten, he says, my dad took me to the sea. He was seeing this lady called Monica and she was mad for water. I don't think my dad had that much interest in it himself but he really liked her so he got someone to pull some strings and got us all a travel permit for the day. I think he just wanted to be with her. So the three of us took a journey. I used to drive my dad mental. It was a big thing for him to be taking the risk of getting me excited because I drove him even more mental then. My enthusiasm used to annoy him against his will. I was always howling with excitement. Literally howling. I was chubby and excitable. This little ball of fat rolling around our quiet house, squealing or howling at one thing or another. Like when my favourite cartoon came on I'd whoop and squeal. Dad would say, –Could you scream into a cushion, or not scream even? And I'd say, –Sorry Dad, but I just love this show. And I didn't just say love. I used to drag the word out until it was on the verge of snapping. You know the way teenage girls say, *Oh I looooove so and so*. That's what I used to do. I used to collect wind from the bottom of my gullet and then let it out as I was saying it. Dad always knew I was about to say I loved something because I'd take a huge breath. And then I'd be off. –Oh Dad, I loooooooooooooooooooooooooooooooove this song. –Oh Dad, I looooooooooooooooooooooooooooooooooooooove burgers. –Oh Dad, I loooooooooooooooooooooooooooooooooooooooooooove Shaggy the Cat.

The man with the handkerchief exhales a childish enthusiasm. It relives. Augusta is smiling at his diversion. I am too. We both trust that it will come to good. He puts out his cigarette and continues.

–And the thing with my dad was, he knew he shouldn't dampen my enthusiasm. He was a good man. He just wished I'd had volume control or had been born a mute. I'm exaggerating a little there. So we came up with this thing that if I had to say I loved something I'd say it into the crook of my arm. I spent a lot of time with my arm in my mouth. All my jumpers had saliva patches on the inside of the elbow. So, we all go to the sea. Dad looks at Monica when I get my first view of the ocean. He shakes his head happily as I take a huge breath and dive into my arm. Monica is laughing at my muffled shouts. We take a long walk. Dad and Monica are holding hands ahead of me—actually it was the first time they held hands in front of me but that's not really important. Anyway, I just walk behind them, looking out into the sea, nearly biting my arm off with excitement. We must have walked for two hours. We get to the next town. Dad and Monica want to go and have a coffee. We find this little place overlooking the sea. Dad asks, –What do you want? This bit isn't technically relevant, ladies, but it still makes me laugh. So Dad says, –What do you want? I say, –Orange. –Orange what? Dad says, looking for my manners. I say, –Orange juice—as if it's the only obvious answer in the world and Monica laughs so much she crosses her legs.

The man with the handkerchief pauses. We rest our smiles on his shoulders.

–Can I take one of your cigarettes there?

–Sure, I say. I give each of us one for the story's end.

–Later Dad turns to me. –Well, he asks, what do you think of the sea then? –Oh Dad, I say—gathering momentum. –Oh Dad, I say—taking a deep breath and I can see him bracing himself. My arms are rigid by my side. My head is tilted to the skies. –Oh Dad, I loove the sea.

Then I pass out because I've forgotten to breathe. When I come round Dad is standing over me. I'm slumped in a chair. He shakes his head. –You can't love anything that much, he says. And that's when I knew that he didn't know everything.

Augusta and I exhale. I panic because I may never see this man again and I already have a thousand questions for him because I think he has something I want. My panic finds a voice.

–Where are you living? I ask.

He knows what I'm saying and almost apologising, says, –I have to go again tomorrow.

–Go where?

–To the coast, he says.

I think about moving to the sea with him but I know how ridiculous it is. So I think about moving to the sea without him, but again ridicule finds me. *I'm not going anywhere*, I think to myself. I buy us a round of drinks. There is a musky chatter floating overhead, lifted every now and again by odd puffs of laughter. Everyone is warm and humming. We are happy, enlarged, conscious. A song knows this and opens itself to us. Somebody beats out the rhythm on a tabletop.

I feel brave tonight. Brave enough to be happy without looking over my shoulder, brave enough to pick up my pen even. I look at this stranger before me. He has something that milks quiet contentment from an eye's smile.

Qualify, Scribe prompts, *qualify*.

His eyes smile first thing in the morning. He is contented.

OK, Scribe says, *sometimes your tongue is loose and fanciful.*

Sometimes, you don't have one fucking word ready for me, I tell him.

Then I apologise because we need each other and I love him even if he is a little lacking. I know that he wants as much for me as Isha does.

I drink loads that night. I'm extraordinarily happy. I have been so for a good while now, long enough maybe to trust in it, to make plans from it. I think about my life, the people I know, the friends I have, and Isha at home sleeping. I get the shivers, sitting there, thinking about every small wonderfulness that makes up my existence. I get so excited I have to wee. I can't wait to go to the toilet so I will miss what I can come back to. I do that all the time here. Go to the toilet so I get to come back to the beautiful hum I have left by the bar. Testing its reality. I go and take my time. I look in the mirror and imagine I'm smiling at the sea.

We're not going lowly again, I tell us ... I promise. I've got it all wrapped up. It's pretty simple. I can't believe we made such a fuss about everything the last couple of times. Here's our plan, I think. Smiling. *We're going to keep it steady, Scribe,* I shout over the well-wishing rowdiness of the Villagers. I see him sitting at his anvil. Drunk.

You and I will be a lot busier tomorrow, I say to him, *we're starting tomorrow. I'm going to clean out my desk, there'll be no timetables, no highlighters. We're just going to get our sleeves rolled up and start banging it out. Iron hot,* I tell him. *Iron hot!*

I call the rest of the Villagers to attention but I'm not stern. I send my thoughts out dancing.

Hear ye, hear ye, I cry—my voice raucous, drenched as it is in a robust excitement.

Tomorrow, I tell them, *we start to live!*

A cheer ignites and is carried, pulsing, by the music. We are lords to none other than ourselves. We will not fall again. We inhale our resolution deep. We draw it in and away from doubt.

Feel it in your bellies, I cry, *and lodge it there. We will not forget this victory!*

I let the Villagers back to carnival, and as appointed leader, I retreat to my quarters to make some practical notes for our future's happiness.

One. I'm not going to smoke ... in the mornings.

Two. I'm going to buy new socks and underwear.

Three. I'm going to eat fruit and buy vitamins.

Four. I'm going to wash every day. And moisturize.

Five. I'm going to start reading the newspapers and watching the news.

Six. I'm going to get dressed before I go downstairs in the morning. Like Isha.

Seven. I'm going to look up words before I forget them. *Scribe!*

Eight. I'm going to compile a birthday book.

Nine. I'm going to start Baby Mac's music collection.

I exhale.

Ten. I'm not going to sleep with anyone unless I'm sober. Maybe I won't sleep with anyone at all. Or maybe a man like the stranger outside. Not him, but one like him, when it's my turn.

I smile in conclusion.

I think we've made some important decisions here tonight, Molly, I tell myself. *I think we have,* I say and exhale.

I go into the cubicle and sit down on the cold ceramic seat. Monkey sticks his foot under the door, points his toes and moves it from side to side, for no other reason save to make me laugh. I throw my head back and a volley explodes in the cubicle. It rebounds on all sides before tumbling down my back. My spine giggles. I can hear the echo of a cheer as it rebounds off the walls of the bar and into the bathroom. I can hear the Clap clapping.

He has the loudest clap I've ever heard. It's truly remarkable. He makes construction workers jump. Isha did not believe me when I tried to show her with the dictionary. Thwack. Thwack.

The table shook before her head did.

—No one's clap is that loud, she'd said.

—His is, I'd told her, thinking of his hands.

He always says that he was born to applaud. I always say he was born to applause. And then he always applauds me on my word play. I like this exchange. It's very important to me.

I inhale as I open the bar door back out onto our existence. I panic when I see my motherless man with the handkerchief putting on his coat.

—Where are you going now? I ask. Stay and we'll go for breakfast.

—I can't, he says, I have to be somewhere.

—Where? I demand.

Augusta shakes her head and says, —Somewhere that's not here, Molly. Would I be correct?

The man smiles and nods.

—I fear for my life and my liver, he says, and I'm working to the deadline of a promise.

He looks at me and his face unfolds before me. I think about running at him and tackling him to the ground, knocking him unconscious and stealing his identity so that when he comes round he believes himself to be nothing other than my friend. I tell him this calmly.

—You're the smallest psychopath I've ever met, he says.

He brings me forward and upwards in a hug. He smells of salted cotton. He lets me down and leans over to kiss Augusta. She demurely offers him her cheek.

—Well, look at you, I say to Augusta, being kissed.

—Yeah, she says, it happens occasionally.

I walk him to the door to make sure it's closed properly behind him. No one must know we are still here. We officially closed four hours ago. At the door, he turns and gives me a book.

–Read this, he says, you'll love it.

–What is it?

–A book, he says, I looooooooove it. There's a number as well. Maybe give it a call.

–Not yours?

–No, it comes with the book, he says, but he's good. He's really, really good. Been with it for over thirty years. He's just a really good man to talk to—about anything.

–Have you met him?

–No. You don't need to meet him in the flesh to understand what I mean. He can smile with his voice. He often does.

The man with the handkerchief says all this to my face and then leaves me with an empty doorframe. I pull the bolt across the door and go back inside.

Augusta is arm-wrestling with the Clap. She's using two hands and her hip wedged under the table for leverage. J is talking to the Clap about 'our interests' as Treehouse sees them. He is excited and his hands are angry. They lash out at the air around them; they try to free themselves from J's frustration.

–We need a new order, J says.

The Clap nods his head like he always does.

I don't really know what J is talking about. I don't even know if I care. I know the music is mine tonight and that everything is how it should be. I laugh at Augusta. J rants and she keeps pulling. The Clap moves his arm every now and then to let Augusta know that he is aware of her hanging from his hand. I laugh because Augusta is one of the maddest people I know, without being mad at all. She's simply and completely uninhibited by the restrictions of normality. She's only undignified to those who do not really understand dignity at all.

I think of Matron so I instruct the men to put the thought away before it unfolds me. Before the night becomes as other nights before. I hear someone snort behind me. She'll not find me here tonight. *I'm too strong*, I tell myself—and her, if she's listening. I'm too strong, too brave, too happy. I won't be getting sick again. *I'm going to grow up*, I tell her, *so you needn't worry about looking after me anymore. And I won't be getting sick again.*

You are sick, she says, *you're only fooling yourself if you think otherwise.*

Lou passes by and winks at me on her way to the toilet. The Matron is wrong, I tell myself as I follow Lou. I go to the toilet again. I see that the scrunched-up toilet paper in my hand may just as well be a white flower. I push open the door and show it to Lou. She agrees as she hands me the joint.

–Make a couple, she says, and we'll bring 'em out.

–Joints?

–No, flowers, she says.

So I do.

We rejoin the hum that is our home. We give everyone we love a flower. The women aah and the men make burly noises before offloading theirs on each other. The Clap ends up with a heap of soggy paper next to his glass. I think about bringing one home to Isha but some things don't last too long outside of here so I think about making a call instead.

2:1: Mr. ****

Another day, another collar.

I walk to work, weaving my path through the clashing monitors that pedal the pulp of a new generation. A child with a snake wrapped around his neck skips by with his mother. The Media more or less put it there. This amuses me. I don't particularly like the Media, but I enjoy watching it at play, juggling the wants of the masses with a reckless abandon, walking the tightrope above the addled throngs with a clinical precision that belies their sequined smiles. I admire its genius—as vulgar as it is. I take my hat off to it every day whilst spitting in its shadow. In turn, it salutes me whilst laughing in my face. We're old enemies relying on each other to survive. I get bored thinking about it and thoughts of work sidle into this crack. I've been assigned a new stint. The lines opened two days ago.

That Cranky-Annie-No-Life.

–I'm Laurence, I'd said.

I feel something now, just thinking about her reaction, and I suspect it's a kind of excitement. This stint will be a challenge. That is why they offered it to me—it's why I accepted. I don't really care what drove our house to secure this contract; it's unlike anything else they have done. It speaks of wisdom before or beyond the Media. I'm told the book itself is out of print but the line has a steady trade. My challenge is to keep it this way.

I think about the brief on my desk. *In Search of Infinite Relief*, the title laid out in bold on the crisp white sheets. I picture some buff-nailed secretary gathering them together in her hands, bringing them upright and in line, finding their collective edge on the desk. Clack, clack. Stapling the neat white rectangle before laying it to rest in her out-tray. A flat, leafy shape that details the man I'm about to become for eight hours a day. Laurence. Nestled as he is amidst the collection of adjectives gathered for him by the house profilers. *Kind. Constant. Funny. Imaginative. Articulate. Intelligent. Compassionate. Empathetic.*

He is a good listener, they note. *He has a great understanding of people*, they write. *He cultivates a near intimate rapport with all his regular callers*, they report. He does and so will I. The lines open at 9.00. He'll be begging for life at 6.00.

I take in the City unwillingly as I walk. Not the people, the monitors or the traffic, but the City itself. This stony-grizzled giant that tosses in his sleep beneath us. Someone down an alley calls for the attention of a suit. I turn to see that he is looking at me.

–What? I demand. Unphased. Superior.

–Come here, he says.

I turn to walk on.

–It has to be you or else there's no one.

I turn to him again. I can't see his body. Just his head sticking out of an old fridge like a rotting turnip with glazed eyes. He has said this to me before. He has said this to countless men that have passed by his lair. Today, I'm easily distracted. I think I may even be seeking distractions. From work, perhaps.

Empathetic, they stress.

–What is it you want? I ask, although I already know. I have heard him bartering with others.

–I need a rib, he tells me, I have to grant life.

I say nothing. I let him expound. He does so by climbing out of the abandoned fridge. He is naked. His chest is a patchwork of skin grafts. I can't locate his nipples.

–None of my extractions have proved fruitful, he explains.

–You have no nipples.

–They are superfluous to my needs. I only need a new rib.

–I'm not interested, I tell him.

No one is anymore. CH33 did a piece on him years ago. Now he is nothing more than a momentary distraction for those who give him an ear instead of a rib. Two people gave him both. Searchers. Hopelessly hoping that this might be their way. One rib less, both dead and now forgotten, lost to the disinterest that grows afresh from the new attractions that sprout endlessly in a city that kills for thrills. Perhaps even he has forgotten—this hysterical madman I choose to walk away from.

I continue my journey to work. I keep walking, head down, neck dusted by the City's dirty breath. I see a man walking backwards. He is standing on his shoes, not in them. He drags his feet to keep the shoes wedged between the ground and his ragged socks. A lady with floral sleeves and a snub nose asks him what he is doing.

–You can never have a truly individual thought here in the City, he says, because somebody else has had it for you.

–But why don't you just put your shoes on? she asks.

–We've got to learn to think outside the box, he says, everybody gets *in* their shoes and walks forward. Now me today, I got on my shoes and I find the only way I can walk is backwards. One new thought a day helps us think outside the box, even if it's just for that moment of wondrous clarity.

The lady looks confused but polite. –You'll ruin the heels.

–They've ruined our minds, he says, I can afford the leather.

She frowns at him and walks away. He continues forward by walking backwards.

I reach the shed. I meet Davy in the corridor.

–Have you heard any news on Dennis? he asks.

–No.

I say this to close all lines of communication that Davy thinks Dennis's Trespassing may have opened between us. I hope my curtness feels like a slap.

I make it to my desk a little before the lines are opened. I paw through the brief again. Something about this book makes me feel sick. There is a mawkish claim lodged between its humane sincerity and its powers of articulation. It speaks of a higher consciousness and a law bestowed upon mankind. It talks of freeing the self from all claims made by the ego—there is even talk of happiness. I wet my lips and wait for time to serve up my first caller. Something deep within me is dying to try out these new words. I sit there and mouth the word 'JOY' over and over again, hoping none of it will stick to the walls.

The first call comes at 9.12. I take it as I take all the others that flood my phone line that day. At 6.00 I get up and leave, stepping over the life now slumped by the door.

Bits of the walk home get lost somewhere between my imaginings of the evening to come and my conscious digestion of the day just passed. Vileous Kussock's face smiles down on me from a monitor. It relieves me—not him, but the context he currently inhabits. It speaks to me in eager appreciation. The other and us. The administration is fuelling a fear that will fuel a WAR. I think of all the hopeless hours that will be spent in mediation with a power that made its decision years ago. I'd laugh if I felt like it. Instead I walk home. Unsmiling.

The Ghost is in my house. She lives there and has done so for ten months now. I don't know her history. I've never asked. She arrived on my doorstep early one morning as I was heading out to work.

–What do you want? I'd demanded.
–To live with you, she'd said.
–Why?
–I've been looking for you for over eighteen months.
–Why?
–I'm not intrusive.
–Who are you?
And so she had told me her name.

She had walked past me then and put her bag next to my chair.

I've never asked her to leave. I've never asked her to stay. I've never asked her to do anything. She just floats around my house. I don't know what she does during the day. I don't care. She used to make me food in the beginning, but these nights I eat mostly in my restaurant.

I know why she came. She seemed eager to tell me and disappointed to know.

–I read your poem, she'd said that first night.
–What poem?
–The poem you wrote on the wall of Eddie's toilet.
–I don't write poetry, I'd told her.
–You wrote your name and city after it. The poem about the Boy.
–Where's Eddie's? I'd asked.
–Eddie's is the bar at the end of the Scraggy Walk.

I remembered then—going to the bar, getting drunk and writing my name. I do that sometimes. I get drunk and write my name on the wall of toilet cubicles. I don't know why I do it. A small gesture to who I am maybe. I find it pathetic in sobriety. I've often winced in recollection of a recent scrawl but I don't beat myself up over it. There are worse things I could do. I could've written that poem, for one.

–I didn't write the poem. You've found the wrong man.

–I'm here now, she'd said.

–Get up, I'd ordered, you're in my chair.

She had got up then and walked into the spare room, now her room, if ownership has any place in a house that does not care.

So when I get in from work she's there. Sometimes she sits on an old cushion she found on the street. Sometimes she goes out walking or goes over to the woman across the street she's made friends with. Sometimes, when I'm in my chair—sitting among the falling motes of dust, she'll come to me and put her head in my lap. I don't stroke her hair. I don't reciprocate this gesture in any way. I don't do anything, bar sit with stony thighs and reticent hands. She has never asked me for more. Not very often she comes to my room. We have sex. It's a silent exchange that affords me minimum pleasure and maximum satisfaction. The sex is for my relief. I know this and have made her understand this by directing her hips with my hands. Forcefully I put her back on my path if I think she has fallen to her own. She lies in the bed for a small time after the exchange. She knows to leave then. She's neither attractive nor unattractive. She's nothing more than a Ghost.

Someday I'll banish her. Someday, but not tonight—tonight I have other things to attend to. There is a casual appointment I have to keep.

2:2: Telephone Transcript

In Search of Infinite Relief, C.W. Sisle
Contracted to Gleeson Media Group
Subcontracted to Employee 12
Recorded at 9.12 a.m. on 15/01/****

E12 Hello?

C78 Hi, a man gave me your number. He's gone to keep a promise.

(Caller 78 hiccups)

E12 And you're keeping your promise to call me?

C78 No. I never promised him anything but I probably would have. He was ... one of those people.

E12 A natural salesman eh? One of those persuasive types.

C78 Not like that. That makes him sound cheap, like those guys you see advertising acrylic balls or easy-fit pants. No. He had a handkerchief round his neck. Do you know him?

E12 I don't know about the handkerchief. It's hard to figure these things over the phone.

C78 Anyway. He told us—that's me and my friend, Augusta—a good story too. About him and his dad and the sea. He told me you could smile with your voice. Go on. Let's hear you smiling. On the count of three. One, two, three, SMILE!

(Caller 78 hiccups)

E12 Well, how was that?

C78 I don't know. My ears are not too attuned to smiles. Maybe you should say something as you're smiling. Like ...

E12 Well what's your name? At least let me throw your name back at you with a smile.

C78 Molly-Mae. Molly, I suppose.

E12 Hello, Molly. You sound tired.

C78 That *is* good. I know what he means now.

E12 I think smiles are invaluable. I can remember when the masks came in, you know. I know they protect us but ... I don't know. The City is deprived of nearly all its smiles and those who don't wear them don't care and their smiles are just empty hollows where their voices used to nest.

C78 That has to be from the book. Is it? I'll tell you now—what do I call you firstly?

E12 Call me Laurence.

C78 Well, I just want to be up-front with you here. One, I just got the book tonight, this morning even. Two, I'm very drunk. Three, I'm not in the habit of making calls like these. And four, which is actually like three, mark two, I think it's a little pathetic. I was surprised our man did it. And four, I've kind of got free use of a phone so I may very well call again after I read the book.

E12 Well thanks for being so up-front, Molly. I've a couple of things to say to you. One, please do read the book. I think you'll like it. Two, please call again because I think you sound like good fun. You sound sharp even though you're drunk which is not exactly three but two, mark two. Don't call again so drunk. And three, who are we to say what's pathetic and what's not? We can never know how far people have come or where they have travelled from to reach a level someone else steps on as pathetic. We just can never know. Especially in this city.

C78 Now I feel suitably shit. Thank you, Laurence, or whatever it is you're called in your own time.

E12 Molly, I never asked you to call.

C78 That's true. I don't really know why I am. Maybe it's because my friend's asleep and I'm bored.

E12 Well then, Molly, tell me something. Tell me something about your day.

C78 I work in a bar. I'd a really good night tonight.

E12 Why did you have such a good time, Molly?

C78 I really don't mean to be rude but could you stop saying my name after every sentence? You sound a little …

E12 OK. Go on.

C78 I want to be a writer though. Even though I love the bar.

E12 Yeah? What are you going to write?

C78 I don't really know. I outgrow my writings by the paragraph. I write something then look at it the next morning and I actually cringe for myself. But I suppose I like people best of all. I think I would write about people. The best things I've written are for other people.

E12 People still astound me. They're super. Although I have to say it's good for the spirit to get away every now and again.

C78 Yeah, I do too. I think it's important. But it's hard to be without people. It's hard to find a place. They're everywhere.

E12 I know but—

C78 But I'm really loving people these days, Laurence. I probably sound like a pervert now, using your name after every sentence.

E12 Is that what you thought I sounded like?

C78 Yeah, but that's 'cause I saw it in a film once. I can hear his voice now. Kept on saying their names. I don't think you're a pervert.

E12 Thanks, Molly.

C78 Anyway. I don't want to talk about perverts. I'm too happy.

E12 Good for you. What has you so jubilant?

C78 I like your word, Laurence. I just feel really … I'm going to match that word of yours if it kills me. I'm supposed to be the writer here. Ehm. I feel … I feel … I just feel really good.

E12 Wow, Molly. Sorry, can't talk, running to the dictionary.

(*Caller 78 laughs*)

C78 I'm being very cleverly profound there. It's all about understatement these days. Seriously, I feel really good.

E12 Feeling good's a serious business.

C78 Don't kill the pig for the one-liners, Laurence.

E12 How do you mean?

C78 It was a hammy line. Feeling good's a serious business. It sounds like a concept wronged by the lads up in advertising.

E12 I was being deadly serious though.

C78 I know. And underneath this cynical façade is a girl already sold to the idea.

E12 So what has you feeling so good anyway?

C78 Everything. Sometimes everything is in the right place. I feel like I know what's what and it's all good. I can safely believe it. I feel alive too. Do you know that feeling? Like pulsing. I feel like I'm living every second, absorbing every wonderfulness I can see or find or hear and I know I'm drunk but it's not the drinking. It's because I feel like this that I'm safe to go drinking and not end up crouched on the tiles.

E12 Is that what normally happens?

C78 Not really anymore. I'm getting better at judging myself. That's why I feel so good now. I feel solid but still floating. I've been like this for ages too, for a good while. I feel like I've finally got the hang of this thing.

E12 What? Life?

C78 Yeah, I suppose. Life. I think I've got the whole thing figured out. I feel like maybe I've grown up. Maybe all the other stuff was just like teething problems and I overreacted, you know. These days I keep thinking to myself—fuck, how lucky am I? I'm gonna work in the bar, get up early in the mornings, eat fruit, do the crossword, then sit at my desk and write. I think I'm ready to write a book. I'm going to moisturise every day and get my hair shining. I'm going to spend quality time with Isha and my friends. I'm—

E12 Who's Isha?

C78 She's my grandmother. She's like my manager. I can tell her anything—well, I wouldn't tell her everything because some things might upset her but if ever I have a problem, I can just go to Isha and she'll tell me what to do. She's infinitely right, she knows me better than I know myself. Everybody loves her; she's like a mother to everybody who knows her. Even people her own age.

E12 Wow, Molly. That sounds good.

C78 Yeah. I think so. I think I really might have grown up. Hang on—what sounds good? The book or ...

E12 Isha, everything.

C78 I'm very excited about life. I said to my friend today—I was in behind the bar and I just got this massive surge of excitement— and I said, –I'm very excited about life. I get them a lot. The surges. Like these waves of sheer excitement and well-being and bravery and invincibility and possibility all rolled into one.

E12 Wow!

C78 I know. It's unreal. And I said to him—he's hilarious, you should meet him, he's got class—anyway I said to him, –Lucon, I'm so excited about my life that I literally can't wait to live it. And even this morning, I looked at my feet, you know when they were just sitting in the bed looking at me and I thought, *I LIKE my feet*. I've never liked my feet but now I do. I think they've grown up too. And I keep running everywhere because I'm so happy, I can't contain it in a walk. I just have to run. I put on my headphones and just start running. And as well I think I may be gathering momentum from the people I meet. Friends and strangers. I just keep finding everyone so wonderful—amazing even. It's like I get a real energy from being around people. I want to hear everything they have to say. I want to devour it and really talk to them because sometimes we don't really talk at all. I mean people in general. We don't communicate, not really. We just present facts. Chivers says everyone announces things these days, they don't listen so much anymore. We just announce things. He thinks it's because we're always in competition with the box. You should meet Chivers, he's incredible. I mean, talk about people blowing you away. He does it but quietly. It keeps dawning on you that you're talking to one of the most special people ever, and no matter how long you know him, he keeps dawning, like a perpetual sunrise. Wow, that's good. I'll have to tell him that tomorrow.

E12 Who is Chivers then?

C78 He's Isha's best friend. One of them. But he's like my friend too. Isha and me are really more like friends these days.

It's really good. Like we're on an even par. She talks to me. Anyway, enough about you, let's talk about me.

(*Caller 78 laughs*)

E12 That's some laugh, Molly.

C78 Standard issue, Laurence. You should hear how the deluxe fires. It's impressive. Actually, it's scary. The boys at school used to call me AK47. Seriously though, enough about me. How are you?

E12 I'm good too, Molly. Solid. Like you say. I like hearing someone being all excited about life. Excitement's contagious. I could be infected.

C78 I hope you are. Maybe we could be each other's viruses. Infecting each other and others beyond. Fuck! That doesn't sound good at all—especially now with this second wave. We'll have to find a different metaphor.

E12 We could be each other's friends.

C78 Laurence, you're good.

E12 Is that cynicism creeping down the phone line?

C78 Nah. I'm just teasing. I think it's a little funny, talking like this. That's all. I'm a little self-conscious. Cynicism is a defence mechanism we employ when our hearts want to believe but our heads think they know better. *Dr. Dreyfus*. Last Tuesday's episode. A special called *The Hurt Within—Childhood Wounds that Never Heal*.

E12 I don't really watch the box that much.

C78 I have to say, some of it's pure genius. Not Dr. Dreyfus obviously, although I do have a soft spot for him. At least he's not doing specials about men in love with dolphins. Ceptus did that the last day. But you do have to wade through so much crap. Isha reckons it actually causes clinical depression.

E12 Yeah. She has a point there. Molly, when we talk, if you feel self-conscious, maybe try suspending your disbelief. That's what you'll want your readers to do. Sometimes people can grow into their pretences. That's why you should smile when you don't feel like it. Most times your face grows into it and then your heart can't help but follow suit.

C78 I know. It's just a little weird. It's my first time. And I hate when people tell me to smile when I'm not up for it. I feel like telling them to sling their smiles over their shoulders and fuck off. Not often but sometimes you literally can't smile. People have to respect that. I'd smile if I could. Anyway, I don't need to pretend, Laurence, I'm smiling down this phone line. I hope you can feel the glow on your face.

E12 I can, Molly. Thanks.

C78 I'm gonna go now. Be good.

E12 And you. Keep running, but stop when you get tired.

C78 Well hopefully the tiredness won't come again. I've it all in the bag. Bye.

End of transcript

2:3: Molly

At some hour we are ejected from the night. I leave Augusta's house and walk home. I find half a newspaper playing the wind off a lamppost. There's print of a failed resolution, of bio-bombs hidden in mountainsides, of denials and calls for time. It's laden with names I can't even pronounce. I throw the paper away, promising to read the next day's instead.

I wake up to find a sausage in my bed and Isha at the curtains.
 –I wish you wouldn't bring food to bed, she says.
 –So do I. Baby Mac keeps eating it before I wake up.
 –Get up, Isha says, lunch is ready.
 I smile to myself as I watch Monkey attach a pillowcase to his head and pretend that it's hair. He flicks it from side to side with a girly wrist action. He makes the face of a pompous teenager from the pearled brigade.
 I turn to Isha.

–I met this man last night, I say, I think you would have liked him.

–Well, tell me at the table, she says, at least then I've some chance of making a getaway. The backdoor's on the latch.

–No, not a man like that, I say, an *old* man.

I put my face in the pillow.

–I don't feel like telling you now, I say.

–What?

I lift my head up just enough to allow the words to escape, –I said I don't feel like telling you now.

–Bring that sausage down with you, she says.

I live with Isha. She's not cute, but robust and sturdy. We don't hug or kiss. Ours is a home where all tactility is mobilised by function or humour. If I'm feeling particularly affectionate towards her I will wallop her across the arse. People say, *Don't hit your grandmother like that*, and I say, *Don't mind her*, she's as sturdy as an ox. If she's feeling particularly affectionate towards me she'll oil my scalp. I will sit between her knees for an hour and when she's finished she'll wallop me on the head and tell me to make her tea. I never tell her I love her. She never tells me that she loves me. This is our quiet reserve. There is no want for these words here. I did tell her once as she was cleaning out her tights drawer.

–I don't need to hear it, she'd said, but you should say it to others.

–Your tongue is too old and your limbs are too frigid, I'd teased.

–My past is too stubborn to allow me to change, she'd said sadly.

And I'd wanted then to let her out of herself.

Isha has had a hard life but she's brave; what she can't do for herself she'll do for others. So because she's nearly always right about everything I have started on this lark. Now I do tell people I love them. And every time I do I think I'm saying it for Isha as well—for every time she couldn't. That is how we work. I live an extension of her life and she lives an extension of mine. We pool all our resources and try to survive the City. Together we have eighty-six years behind us. When everything is lowly I remember this and march on. Well that's what I plan to do from now on.

No more stopping and starting for our Molly.

We live in a cul-de-sac. I love the fact that it has only one entrance and one exit. That's rare enough in these parts. The whole City is open to everything. It's a sprawling labyrinth of cement and noise with exits and points of entry in constant battle for traffic. At least with a cul-de-sac there is no fighting and both roads run to a common goal. It seems like a calmer place because of this.

Isha moved here late in life. I don't sleep in the same bed my mother used to sleep in. Isha had to move here when she thought she'd all her moving done for a lifetime, so a lot of things here are not what they were in the old place. All my memories start here. I don't remember being a child. I don't know where my memories have gone, but I know the Village was only a settlement then. Lots of artefacts have wandered astray. Sometimes I think they were stolen. Or I must have been elsewhere. Isha will sometimes recognise the small truths of my childhood as I tell them—re-imagined, re-formed and re-modelled as I want them to be in a world I have made my own.

I'm sorry for Isha that she had to move. I know she thinks about the days that came before, the life she knew before me. I know she thinks back and wonders how things would have been if it had been different. But she has faith in life and living; her retrospection is armed with a deep acceptance that all things are as they should be in a life that was never truly her own. She's the strongest woman I know. Everyone says we are very alike. Sometimes when I talk to her old friends, they catch my arm mid-sentence, turn to each other and shriek and squeal that it's like talking to Isha when she was young. I smile and try to remember what it was I was saying. I'm very eager to be heard. Most small people with big words are.

We live in a boxy house squatted amongst ten others. We are no odder a household than any of our neighbours. Family units based on marriage and childbirth are still common but they are hanging on by a thread. Isha reckons lasting marriages will very soon be a forgotten romance. She tutted all day when the powers that be saw fit to include a named and optional third party on each side in the civil nuptial agreement.

–How can they know what real love is, she'd asked, when we are fed all these alternatives by the Media? Everybody thinks they're missing out if they're not constantly in love. You can't live your life if you're constantly in love. You would die of hunger for one or drop dead of exhaustion for another. You'd spend your time over the toilet bowel.

–I don't know what type of love you had then, I'd teased.

–I'd the best of it, Isha'd said, but I knew to stay put when the new love died and the quiet love came. Everything has a time and a place. Nobody knows a quiet love anymore—everything has to be thrilling. Thrills don't last, they have to die to make room for the next. It's just the way things work.

Isha has said this more than once and sometimes I think she may be right but I'm a thrill-seeker—much to our dismay.

Isha has managed the new modernity well because she's never stopped growing. She has a good life, she's kept her friends. She's not lost to her husband's death nor her daughter's. She still gets sad but gives it space to breathe, live and die again. Sometimes I think about Isha dying just so I can feel something real. I think about it and I cry and then I go downstairs when my eyes have dried and love her all the more. I've never told her this because I know Isha does all her crying in her own time. Maybe she imagines me dying and cries about that.

Maybe a part of me hopes she does.

I want to be a writer. Isha hopes I will be, but she has issues with the fact that I do not write at all.

–If you wrote as much as you drank, she says, you would've written a tome by now.

Isha is not creative or particularly imaginative so I tell her that she doesn't understand the creative process. This aggrieves her because she believes in a process inspired by progressive development. She believes in sweat and routine, even on the artistic journey. She's not so romantic as I about my future. Isha is a realist, but in my world so am I.

–I have to live first, write second, I tell her.

–Well you could at least make a couple of notes while you're at it. With the amount you drink you won't remember anything. You'll be writing about crap.

–Nah, I tell her, I have a plan.

But I don't. I'm scared of writing and secretly fear that I'll be nothing but a bundle of empty ambitions. I don't tell her this in case she believes it. If neither of us believe then we'll have nothing. So I tell her that one day I'm going to write a novel that will make her proud.

–Most of it will be way over your head, I tease, but I'll still bring you to the launch because you'll enjoy the finger food.

—It'll be nothing but a 300-page beer stain with a coughed-up lung splattered somewhere in the middle, she says.

—Wait till you see, I say as I light up another cigarette, have your frock ready.

Serge drops Baby Mac round in the mornings. I'm usually in bed and some days when he isn't done with sleeping, he'll crawl into my bed and finish his lot. Isha gives out that the child is inhaling my toxic breath. She tells me that she has to sober him up after these naps. She pulls my curtains open at 1.00, not every day but most days.

—You'll look beat when you're thirty, she tells me.

—I've ten good years to go then, I tell her.

If I'm really hungover she'll feel sorry for me. She'll feed me water and fruit and look on as my mouth bows lower than she would like. But I'm happy now. I'm strong, like her. And anything I do as a drunkard these days is fuelled by goodwill or a harmless recklessness. The Village has not been plundered for some time.

I'm glad to be home. Before this I'd stay in a wet lifetime for months on end. I'm happy now. I don't want the tablets. They glaze you up, cover you over in a transparent wrapping. Neither of us want the tablets for me again and I'm grateful that Isha doesn't want the quiet life at any cost.

Isha and I always take a long lunch. I watch her eat and she gives out about my smoking first thing in the morning. I've gotten into the habit of drinking a glass of milk in front of her before I light my first cigarette. This visibly relieves her worries a little. She actually tilts her head back in collusion with mine. It's my concession to the life she would like for me. Baby Mac lives among our legs for these hours. Our conversations are punctuated by his antics.

I say to Isha that this tribal gathering is very healthy.

–Look at us, I say, three generations brought together by food and music.

–You're full of shit, she says but I know she silently and practically appreciates the sentiment. She does not say shit in front of Baby Mac. She pushes it out through her teeth and sends it to me over the kitchen table.

I say, –Baby Mac, Isha has just said SHIT at the dinner table.

She laughs despite herself. She always does.

–I feel like doing something constructive today, I tell Isha.

–You could tidy up that mess in the sitting room, she says.

–Mmmmmmm, I muse, not really what I'd in mind.

–Or else finish it, she says. One or the other. I can't keep stepping over it.

–It's good exercise for you, I say.

She goes to the bread bin and leaves me to look out into the sitting room. I can see a mannequin's torso lying prostrate on the floor, half covered in clay. I do that all the time. Get really excited about starting something, run out and buy everything I need, run home, dive into it, and then lose the excitement that should get me to the finish line. I don't know where it goes; I must lose it somewhere on the dive down. But I seldom find it again. I spend more time looking for it than actually trying to cope without it. Isha says I should forget about the excitement for a bit and keep on but she always ends up saying this to my back as I'm climbing rocks, looking for my flyaway thrills. I go out and stand over the torso for a bit. Tickling it a little with my toe.

–I might go into town and look for some clay to finish it, I say.

Isha nods her head.

–Put it in your room then, she says.

She doesn't believe I'll finish it, nor do I, but now I really want to go into town in shoes, not runners. Visit my butcher, my cobbler. Play the lady, don't you know.

I sit down and share my hopes for the afternoon with another cigarette.

–I might head into Chivers later, Isha says.

Chivers is Isha's oldest friend. Whatever his health, his mind is perfect. I understand why they get on so well. He is as wise as his past but he's never stopped growing, just like Isha.

–Everything about Chivers makes me swell, I'd told her. If I ever meet a man like Chivers, I'll marry him.

–You could start by living your own life first, Isha'd said.

–I *am* living, Isha. I'm living a great life. When was the last time you saw me down? I've never been happier in a job. I'm not leaving the bar until the book's finished.

–Fair enough, Molly, she'd said—and then went on to say absolutely nothing more. She does that, Isha does. She stops talking and leaves a huge hole for me to fill in. Or fall in. I'm not sure which but I always head straight for it. I can't stand things being left unsaid. I don't think it's right.

–It's like you're waiting for me to fall, I'd said.

Unfairly, probably. Molly-like.

–Don't be so dramatic, Molly.

–I'm not. I just wish ... nothing.

–What? she'd prompted.

–Nothing, I'd said because there is too much to say that can't honestly be wrapped up in a smile. If things aren't right with Isha then things aren't right at all.

Baby Mac spits his food on the floor.

–Tell me about this man then, Isha says.

I'm reluctant now, especially as I have just remembered making the call. I can't tell Isha about the man if I don't tell her about the book and I can't tell her about the book if I don't tell her about the call. And for some reason I'm embarrassed. I know what Isha will say. She'll tell me that I have better things to be doing with my time, or worse still, she'll say nothing.

The phone rings. Puckie tells us that Chivers has taken a bit of a turn. Puckie is the lord of understatement so Isha leaves her toast.

3:1: Mr. ****

It's been weeks now since I started this stint and I've yet to fully discipline the phrases that insist on following me home and into my chair. *Sometimes people can grow into their pretences.* These words scramble playfully around my mind, they spill over into my mouth and with their taste recalled, I grow queasy. I stand up and put on my coat.

Head down, I bore a hole through the pulsing throngs only to spy my restaurant at the other end. Nobody there knows what I do. I go there to get fed but also to play draughts with the Dishwasher out back. Casual appointments I have to keep. They feed me in a way the restaurant cannot. He doesn't finish up till 11.30 so I have to mull over my food for four hours.

I like the Dishwasher as much as I like anybody that does not speak to me or ask about my life. Maybe a little bit more. Raven-eyed and sullen, he does not smile. I distrust those that try to confound me with their smiles. In fact, they repulse me. This is the reason I'm finding my current stint more challenging than expected. I've spent my life sidestepping callers like these. They're

a different breed. They make me sick. Searchers. I've had them for two months now. Two months too long. This is why I need to play draughts with the Dishwasher. I need to get my mind off work and back to a place it can call its own.

I've often spent five hours at my table. I pay rent on it—I pay for two meals instead of one. But I get all my coffee for free. There are four waitresses. I've been through them all and have made clear my preference for one. She has served me now for over six years. She was the smiliest of them all. That's why I picked her. I've taken her smile, which affords me a great deal of satisfaction, and in a way I have restrained her laugh, often the harder of the two to contain.

People tend not to laugh in my presence. I heard the waitress laugh once, on a smoggy night, outside the restaurant. She was talking to a girl and laughing. I had to do nothing but approach. She inhaled it, sucked it back in and held her breath. I studied the menu outside even though I knew it by heart and had already eaten. I wanted to see if she would choke on her own laugh and suffocate. She survived by walking away, dragging her friend by the arm.

A woman I once knew said that to laugh in my company was to contaminate the essence of joy. When I smiled she had walked away. I have not seen her in eleven years. I have never missed her. There was never a lack, just a space, filled with time, duly eaten by its passing.

Tonight, I order lamb. My waitress is suitably withdrawn. For the first time I see that she is pregnant.

–You're pregnant, I announce.

–Yes, she says. Bringing her hand protectively to her belly.

She hurries away before I can say anything else. I don't want to say anything more. I just want her to know that I know. More often than not this is enough to serve a purpose.

The owner comes in. He is an enormous man, not fat but bloated. Like someone has injected a huge amount of ill-health under his skin. He salutes me dutifully. I nod my head in his direction. My coffee cup is refilled in his presence. I look at the clock. It's 11.30. Other eaters are picking their teeth and putting on their coats. The owner wedges his body between table and chair and the takings are brought to his fingers. This is my cue. I go out back and find the Dishwasher laying out the board.

We don't talk much but every now and then he'll lay something more than draughts on the board. Always I'm held by this possibility. We are equals at this game. I win or he wins every other time and this brings me pleasure. We start to play.

–Anna's carrying twins, he says after a silence.

I nod my head in receipt of the news.

–There'll be fighting, he says.

Again I nod and we continue to play. I win three. I lose three. Sleep beckons and I submit eagerly to the call. I'm a slave to it. I get up and walk to my house.

The Ghost is not in the sitting room or the kitchen so I presume she's asleep. Although she may have a nightlife I don't care to know about.

I lie down. I don't dream. I never dream, not even on waking. Dreams have no place in this, my hungry sleep.

I take Freddie's route in the morning. Not because I want to see him but because I feel like throwing him a bone. I feel particularly cuntish this morning. I woke up with a taste for it. When he sees me approach he gets my paper ready. I pay for it.

–Exhibitionism is a way of attracting people's attention away from one's self, he announces.

–Interesting, Freddie, like the fact that when you try to exhibit your prowess as a writer and sage it only draws attention to the fact that you will never be either.

–Fuck you, he says, you ain't smarter than anyone else—intelligence is relevant.

The wind carries the last of these words to me. *Relative, Freddie*, I smirk.

I enter my building. I'm early so there are only a couple of people about. I climb the stairs to the third floor. I meet no one. I sit down at my desk and wait for the phone to ring. Come. Take. Go. Sit. Wait. Next time I look up I see lunchtime so I look down again and cast my gaze over the rag.

A human trafficker is caught supplying dwarves to an aging actor that still lives in the hills. Two of the dwarves had died in transit. I smile at that one. I wonder what else I could order if I knew the right people. I close the rag. A picture of Wilkes sharing a podium with Treehouse spreads itself slovenly across my desk. WAR is now near enough to be front-page news. It's now big enough to break down into bullet-point-proof. Celebrities will have to grow an opinion to keep apace with the headlines. Global politics lather, all the players speak in bubbles. With or without Wilkes' transoceanic diplomacy, there will be WAR. Let it come. Let the pie charts start charting and the box graphs start graphing. And while the best men on the front line are given up to facts and figures, polls and politics, contracts are being signed in the back bedrooms.

I look out my window. On the monitor across the street, I see Treehouse's doe-eyes smiling over the City's clatter. I look at him but think of the men behind him and the system behind the system that brought him to power for a reason. I push the rag aside as I rise up from behind my desk. A nameless colleague appears in the doorway.

–Did you hear about the evaluation? he asks.

–No, I say. Sitting back down.

–In reaction to last week's piece on Trespassers on CH6, he says.

–I didn't see it, I say.

–What? he asks. Incredulous. Invasive.

–I don't have a box.

He is now even more incredulous and I'm bored by his face, his surprise, his person. I will him gone.

–It was pure brilliance, he gulps, the heads up at the house are going mental. The Switch's wife was interviewed, showed the Switch talking into his contraption, calling his wife 'Ellen'.

Reluctantly, he pricks my interest.

–Did it name our house? I ask. Re-inhabiting myself.

–Yeah, we came out badly, he says, apparently the houses uptown do this evaluation test before anyone signs any contracts. Which is lies according to Rigo, but still, they were quick enough to save face before broadcast.

–When is the evaluation? I ask.

–Next week, he says, some top psychologist—they spared no expense for this damage control.

–Did they talk to anyone from our house? I ask.

–Yeah, Salisburg, he was dynamite. The we're-all-consenting-adults routine—there are no victims, merely players. He came off well in the circumstances. Made some good points, downplayed the hysteria. Turned it round, said we play an important role in people's lives. Healthy escapism. Promoting culture. Might have even mentioned your stint. Not sure.

I make a move to get up from my desk a second time. –Can you tell whoever's on that I won't be back after lunch? I have to go to the doctor's.

–Yeah sure, he says, see you tomorrow.

I don't feel hungry. I feel like walking so I do. I go to see if the man is still in his fridge. He isn't. I'm being held by the idea of the evaluation and its grip is uncomfortable. I need to pass myself over to different hands so I decide to go to Kitty's Laundry. I never wash my clothes there but she lets me sit among the machines when I feel so inclined.

Kitty is the largest woman I know in every respect. Physically, she's a monstrosity, and the ground plan of the Laundry accommodates her size at the expense of the machines. She has only five washers, five dryers, where there is room for ten. Kitty is not a Drifter or a Searcher or a Fighter or a Progressive or any other subsection I can identify. She's in the business of souls. An archaic word but it amuses me to use it now. I've never asked Kitty what term she applies to her work. It'd be a small victory to her—and in this war, I am safely entrenched.

Kitty is quite good at her job. Not many people know what she really does for a living; not many people know what I do, so this is our bond. The ties of secrecy. When Kitty looks at me through her huge glasses, I know she sees right through everything. There is a huge relief in being known. Very few people are truly known like I am by Kitty. She doesn't like what she sees but she's an old hand at this game and she's not shocked. Rather she understands me as a doctor understands a disease. Kitty never smiles at me nor I at her. There is a silent acknowledgement between us. I know what she wants from me but will not submit. She knows that if she pushes for it she'll never get it. She knows it has to be by my own concession. She knows that the hours I spend here will either strengthen my resolve or shatter it completely.

As I sit there a young woman comes in. She looks blank and withdrawn. She's been seduced and abandoned by the incubus of the City but she must have some fight left for she's arrived here to Kitty. She has no garments to wash. She holds in her hands the remnants of everything she once was. Kitty relieves her of it. Throwing it over her shoulder like a seasoned swimmer. She directs the emptied woman to the back room.

I've never been in the back room. Kitty hopes that one day curiosity—if nothing else—will bring me to her here. It won't. But I often listen at the door. Kitty knows I do this and it's understood.

Kitty closes the door behind them. I take my position. I can hear Kitty's soft hum. It's always the same tune. I'm not a fan of music so I don't know what it is, but it lactates mother.

I can hear the washing machine going and then the soft sobbing of the girl. They all sob, even the men. I've never cried so I find this perversely entertaining. I'm in its hold. When the spin cycle ends there is always a quiet. They re-emerge. Kitty gives me a look. I throw it back at her. The girl thanks Kitty and leaves. She leaves like all the rest of them that have emerged from this back room over the years. She leaves glowing.

–I saw the documentary on Trespassers, Kitty says.

–Yeah? I say. Pretending to feign an interest of operatic proportions to annoy her, to put her off.

–Tomas Bigg's wife came to see me, she says.

–Who? I ask.

–The Switch.

–There's nothing wrong with his soul, I tell her, it's his mind they have taken. That's the risk.

Kitty looks bored and uninspired by my industry remark. This aggrieves me because I'm not part of the industry—I'm playing it as it plays others. I get up to leave. I get a pronounced distaste for her and her hugeness. It invades my space.

–You're in my shop, she says dryly.

I walk to the door.

–They can spoil the soul though, as well as the mind—they do it quite well. They stain, I say. Taunting her.

–Oh, I know, she says, I've washed the worst of them.

–The worst could not find their way here. I wonder, Kitty, what you have really seen if the worst are lost and forgotten to this City.

–YOU of all people know what I've seen, she says. Finding me.

I walk out the door. She follows me and shouts after me. I turn.

–They are brought to me, she says. Looking me in the eye, negating the distance between us.

–Who? I shout.

–Your so-called lost and forgotten.

She re-enters her shop and shuts the door. I see her put the closed sign in the window.

I tire Kitty. I make her weary and her life heavy. This gives me a certain strength.

3:2: Telephone Transcript

In Search of Infinite Relief, C.W. Sisle
Contracted to Gleeson Media Group
Subcontracted to Employee 12
Recorded at 1.42 p.m. on 19/03/****

E12 Hello?

C78 Hi there. It's Molly. I don't know if you remember me.

E12 Little Miss Molly Mae! Course I do. We were to be friends but then you went and abandoned me.

C78 I did leave some food in the cradle and a lock of my hair.

E12 I know. It's in a locket around my neck.

(Caller 78 laughs)

C78 The food or the hair?

E12 Half a biscuit. I ate the hair. How are you? Still running?

C78 How did you know I was small?

E12 What?

C78 You said 'Little Miss Molly-Mae'.

E12 Hello? Night-vision goggles?

(Caller 78 laughs)

C78 Seriously, did you know or was it just a casual appellation?

E12 I see you with your big words. Small people always use big words. Form of compensation.

C78 Yeah? Well, small women also bite. They take a running jump at you and get their teeth in. Form of survival.

E12 Yeah?

C78 We chew on kneecaps and spit them into tin buckets for pleasure.

E12 Yeah?

C78 Yeah.

E12 I could tell because you're so feisty. Most small women I know are feisty. In a good way.

C78 Not in a loud, vulgar, desperate-to-be-heard kind of way?

E12 No. In a cartoonish way. That's a compliment. The world needs more cartoons.

C78 That's weird. We had this conversation at work the last day. AJ reckons cartoons are the most powerful tool of imagination. He says that when someone creates a new world in literature, every reader creates their own personal impression, imagines the world their own way. But with cinema or filmmaking, new worlds take massive team effort and huge finance, albeit helped along by the digital revolution. They have to physically create new things, sets or software, whatever. It takes an entire workforce. But we get a common vision. We are presented with the same images. Whereas animation can create new worlds without this huge cost and they provide a common vision. Literally anything is possible in a cartoon, there are no restraints. It only takes one man to make a cartoon. Theoretically. If he had all the time in the world. That's not exactly what he said but something like that.

E12 I like cartoons because they never take themselves too seriously. I think man should stop taking himself too seriously. Mankind needs to realise its limits before it can transcend them. We need to see how ridiculous we are.

C78 Look, Laurence—I haven't read the book yet. I hope that doesn't hurt your feelings or anything. I did have a flick through it though but it's all a bit ...

E12 No matter, Molly. Talking's good anyhow.

C78 Yeah, I thought maybe I could ring sometimes and we could talk about other things. The man with the handkerchief said you were a good man to talk to about anything.

E12 Absolutely, Molly! How's your writing going? Is your hair shining?

C78 It's going OK. I haven't really got my desk set up but I will. I've just been busy, you know. Working.

E12 Working or living?

C78 Well—that's just it, Laurence. I think I'm living although ...

E12 You'd know if you were.

C78 I am then. Although ...

E12 Although what?

C78 Isha thinks I should settle a bit. She doesn't really like me working in the bar. She says I'm going to waste away there. She says I should get a real job. She thinks I don't use my head there but I do—in fact, I think my head's after ripening inside there. I've been introduced to things I never would've found on my own. I can't even begin to tell you about all the new music I've heard, stuff that you can only get if you go looking for it. The hunt. I love it. And I can say anything that comes to mind without having to check whether or not it'll make sense to the other person. There's great freedom in that, you know. Isha cuts out advertisements from the papers and leaves them for me. Or she says small things.

E12 Like what?

C78 I'm not going to go into it. It kind of makes me mad at Isha and I don't feel too right being mad at her.

E12 Most mothers—and grandmothers—just want what's best for their children. But then most children eventually know what's best for them. Sometimes there's a discrepancy between the two. It doesn't have to be that big a deal. Don't be personally hurt by it, Molly.

C78 Yeah I know. But ... I feel bad. She's making me feel bad.

E12 No. You're making yourself feel bad. Isha's only doing what she thinks is best. It's your job to process it and make what you will of it. If you were completely at ease with your decision to work in the bar then her efforts to highlight a different path would bounce off your happiness. You'd just love her all the more.

C78 Fuck! Are you going to take her side without even listening to me?

E12 There are no sides, Molly. You're not at war, you know.

C78 Well, sometimes it feels like I am. Not a guns-blazing-make-a-run-for-the-ditch kind of war, but you know, I feel I have to win her approval. It's subtle. Women are subtle. Defensive women from the same gene pool are even more subtle. I'm the same as her, remember. It's a quiet war pockmarked by these great big holes of unspoken judgement. Fuck me—I'm dramatic.

E12 Yes, you are.

C78 I think I'm completely in love with me and my own narrative.

(*Caller 78 laughs*)

E12 Aren't we all?

C78 Anyway, dramatics aside, it's how I feel. I just don't feel as close to her as I used to and that makes me feel fucking awful. I wonder how good anything can really be if it puts a wedge between Isha and me. And for the first time, I think that maybe I don't want the life she wants for me. It just makes me sad, that's all.

E12 If she sees you're happy, then she'll be happy.

C78 I'm happy.

E12 Well then.

C78 Yeah, I know. It's fine.

E12 Don't get in a huff.

C78 I'm not. Do you know something though? I love physical work. I fuckin' love it. I've done the office, I've done college, but it's not the same. I mean if you're in an office, you've got to keep some part of your mind on the job, but there's still time enough to send your mind on small excursions and it'll come back to you with little insights and observations from the bottom of the garden, actually daydreams mainly. There must be loads of them growing down there. I'm ridiculous for daydreams. Ridiculous. But with menial work, cleaning say, you can send your mind off on massive expeditions and it can come back to you with all sorts of insights and revelations. The phone isn't ringing, someone's not asking you for a fuckin' paper clip, your mind is free to go wherever it wants. It's great. I love it. And then, there's the small systems that seem to underlie the work process. The ergonomics, the fluidity of motion, the flow, the circles. Ah yes, Laurence, you have to love the process. Oh, the closing of the circles ... Ahhhhhh. That's me salivating, by the way.

E12 I presume the drugs have kicked in by then.

C78 Hey!

E12 What do you daydream about?

C78 I couldn't tell you that. Needless to say, I'm always wonderful in all of them. Actually, now that I think of it, I daydream about pretty cartoonish things.

E12 Like what?

C78 Ridiculous stuff.

E12 Like what?

C78 I'm not telling you. Anyway, I don't really have one main daydream, it depends on what film I see or the book I'm reading. They're actually quite funny. They're probably more like really bad films. Half a slaughterhouse. I was going to tell you something funny there but I've forgotten.

E12 Tell me.

C78 I will. Hang on. I have to think of it first. Fuck! It was something to do with daydreams except ... oh I have it.

E12 Go on.

C78 I have this little monkey friend. In my daydreams obviously. He's not like a real monkey, he's a cartoon but ... I'm even smiling now thinking about him.

E12 I should have known this wasn't going to be straightforward.

C78 No no, wait. It's funny. Although, you'd really have to see him, which you can't obviously. He doesn't talk as such. It's the way he kind of swaggers about the place that's so funny. And his proportions—his little bum and his knobbly legs. He's irreverent and he doesn't care. He does really stupid things but they're actually ridiculously clever. In my mind, he's a comic genius. It's physical comedy. That's what it is.

He does things to make me laugh. Shamelessly. That's what he does, he makes me laugh. I could be in any situation and he'll swagger into view. He'll walk about the place but it's the way he's walking, he'll pretend he doesn't see me but he knows right well that he's making me smile. He'll stop and pretend to be doing something and he'll make these facial expressions. Not everyone would find them funny but he knows I will. Kind of playing up to me. Anyway, I get good mileage out of that one. He's skinny too. Lanky.

E12 Maybe I should get me a monkey.

C78 I think everyone should have a monkey. That monkey there—for me anyway—is a sign that I'm alive and well. Otherwise the Lows come and the monkey goes. Whichever order.

E12 Everyone does, Molly. It's near impossible to be happy all of the time.

C78 I know that. I'm not stupid enough to imagine I can live up there all the time. I've tried it. I'm not asking for that. I'm not asking for anything. I just like when I'm snuggled up in my world. I've made it a good place to be, for me anyway. But sometimes, the real world gets in and pisses all over it. And Isha says I can't live in my own world all of the time. She's right too. I know that. I suppose that's why friends are so important. They get your world, you can invite them in and they'll take off their shoes.

E12 You've a very lively way of speaking, Molly.

C78 Thanks.

(*5 seconds' silence*)

E12 Have you run out of steam?

C78 Yeah. No. I'm just tired. I haven't slept that much lately.

E12 Why?

C78 Why?

E12 Why?

C78 I don't know. I go through spells where I don't sleep too well. My mind gets a little agitated or I'm uneasy about something. I don't know. This is like therapy, Laurence. You're good to talk to. I don't feel like I'm burning your ears. I am but I don't feel bad about it. It's good. Everyone should have a Laurence. I'm going to freak out everyone at work by starting every sentence with *Laurence says*—it'll be funny. *Laurence says you should befriend your inner rage, take time to understand it, ask it politely to leave. Laurence says you should get reacquainted with yourself every morning before re-introducing yourself to the world. Laurence says—*

E12 Laurence says shut up, Molly.

(*Caller 78 laughs*)

C78 It'll be funny. I'll play it up to the nines. You'll start to say darker and darker things. *Laurence says you should cut off all ties with your family if you ever want to be free—*

E12 Laurence says tell me what makes you uneasy.

C78 I don't know.

(*4 seconds' silence*)

C78 I don't like some of the places my mind goes.

E12 Molly, I'm not going to judge or quantify what you tell me. Describe it for me because I know you can and it's important I understand.

C78 Right, see there, when I'm wiping my glass down and my mind's on an expedition, excursion, whatever, and I'm happy out—I'm not afraid then because there are other people about. If the expedition goes wrong or I see it starting to take a wrong turn, I can call it back. It listens when I'm in the company of other people. I can just turn around and talk to someone, you know, have a laugh, be with other people but when I'm on my own, sometimes my mind goes the wrong way. And it doesn't listen when I call it back. It just keeps on going down the wrong way.

E12 Where does it go?

C78 I don't want to tell you.

E12 OK, but you've helped me to understand some. How's that perpetual sunrise dawning?

C78 You know sometimes, Laurence, when you have a nightmare and it's full of demons and monsters, other worldly things?

E12 Yeah.

C78 But then you have these nightmares where everything seems so ordinary, it's full of people you know and things you use and places you go? And you're in them? You are yourself in them.

E12 Yeah.

C78 They're mostly like them, which are worse. My mind takes me to places like them.

E12 Are you awake?

C78 Yeah but in that half-land between waking and sleep. So I have to keep awake, to try and keep my eyes open or else I'll see the things that are in the bad place. Bad place? That's Dr. Fuckin' Dreyfus taking over my body again. Anyway, more dramatics by Molly.

E12 Molly—

C78 So I basically have to get my mind out of there.

E12 From where?

C78 From there.

E12 Maybe your mind needs to go there for some reason. That's why it's so insistent.

C78 It doesn't.

E12 Maybe it's a thought or memory that needs to be looked at.

C78 No.

E12 OK.

C78 Do you ever get that falling or jump-start feeling when you're lying in bed, just about to doze off?

E12 I'm always falling off a bicycle.

C78 So am I! That's weird. It's funny, isn't it? How we sometimes get the same dreams?

E12 We're all human. Sometimes we forget that. We are all so alike on a certain level.

C78 I know but some people don't act human. They fall either side of it.

E12 Under or over it.

C78 Yeah.

E12 Are you going to sleep tonight?

C78 Yeah. I'll be fine. I'm reading a good book. No offence to yours.

E12 It's not technically mine.

C78 I know. I'm just afraid that they're coming back.

E12 Who?

C78 The Lows. I'm still in solid form but I'm not floating as high as I was. If it's any consolation, I wreck my own head. Sometimes I'm painfully aware of how I'm feeling.

E12 We all are. We're human.

C78 Not everyone. I know people who aren't.

E12 Human? Tell CH23. They pay good money for that kind of thing.

C78 Shut up. I know people who aren't painfully aware of how they're feeling. You know, they just seem to be contented. Just seem to get on with things. They don't really think about themselves at all.

E12 Molly. We're all self-aware. We are conscious.

C78 Do you think that some people are born contented?

E12 We're all born conscious, it's what we do with our consciousness that helps us find a contentment.

C78 Are you content?

E12 I am now. I wasn't always. Before I was so taken with the Wanting that I only ever saw contentment on the horizon.

C78 What did you do?

E12 I took myself to the horizon.

C78 You can't ever be on the horizon because the horizon is always in the distance.

E12 Not if you know the way to it.

C78 You do?

E12 We all do. You do.

C78 This is that weird shit from the book?

E12 Anyway, I've a feeling you'll find your own way there.

C78 What if I don't?

E12 You will and you'll never want to leave.

C78 I'm going to send my mind off on an expedition tonight—to find it.

E12 It might not be a bad idea to send your heart along with it. It's good at reading maps. And before you say it, no animals were hurt compiling that line.

C78 I'd have my suspicions. Thanks, Laurence. I like talking to you. And not just because I get to talk about myself the whole time. I like talking to *you*.

E12 Don't leave it so long the next time.

C78 That's a real auntie thing to say. Anyway, thanks for listening. I know it's what you do. And I think you're really good at it. I think you're sincere. And even if you're not, and you're just sitting there picking at your nails and watching the clock, I don't mind. I'm going to do an Augusta on it.

E12 What's that then?

C78 When Augusta's unsure of someone, she always talks to the person she hopes they'll become. Blindly—with two good eyes. And she has taken a few lashings for it but she does it anyway. So that's what I'm going to do with you. I'm going to address the man I trust you to be, if not now, someday. Well anyway. Bye.

E12 Bye.

C78 Laurence?

E12 Yeah?

C78 You're the only person besides Augusta that I've told about Monkey.

E12 Does he have a name?

C78 No, just Monkey.

E12 Does he wear clothes?

C78 Not for me but Augusta tells me that she's seen him prancing about in a pair of green dungarees. Bye.

E12 Bye.

End of transcript

3:3: Molly

I like watching the box from the rug in front of the fire. I stand there barefoot, committing to nothing, as I try and make my way up the stairs to get dressed. Remote in hand, I watch the channels file by before me one by one. Sometimes, I talk to it, say things to the people on screen, but only when I'm sufficiently lost to myself. When I hear myself talking, I stop. But only after I've finished what I wanted to say. Sometimes, I can hear Isha snorting in the kitchen. Laughing, I think.

When she passes through she says, –You shouldn't stand so close to the box, it'll make your mind go square.

She stole this from a pamphlet I brought home once. I laugh.

An advertisement comes on. The Family Manots figures. I look at all three, neatly packaged together, hours of quality family time spent on the shelves of Wundermarkets and Toyoutletz. Wendy is laughing and if she wasn't twelve centimetres high and made of latex, I'd have wanted to be her. Nestled between mother and father. Matron laughs at me but I ignore her and turn to Isha instead.

–That's good, isn't it? I say.

–What? she asks, coming in from the kitchen.

–That they're sold as a family, you don't have to buy them all separately.

–Well, they probably cost three times the amount.

–They couldn't, I say and turn to listen.

–Come on, we haven't time, Isha says. Get dressed. I can't stand to watch you shivering. You're purple.

Isha and I walk to the hospital. I go because I want to and I'm relieved to notice this. It's been weeks since Chivers fell, or took a turn as Puckie says. He fell and couldn't get up. One of his dogs ran to Arnold, the man Chivers buys his tobacco from, and got help. Amazing really. When I heard it, I really wanted a dog but Isha says I only wanted one because of the story and not because of the dog. Maybe she's right.

Chivers is in the hospital now. In a room off a ward. He won't get to go home again. Isha says she wished she had the money to get him into private care but Chivers tells her to stop. –I like it here, he says but he is being brave.

I wonder if I could, would I give him my youth? I can hear Matron tutting softly, somewhere nearby. I refuse to acknowledge her; she's been hanging around a lot recently. She makes the Villagers self-conscious when she sneers at them through her slit smile. None of us want her around. But I'm safe enough with Isha for now. And Monkey. I have to keep Monkey away from Matron. I'm not sick. *As if you're a good judge,* she whispers so I turn and offer my mind to a conversation that will make her stop.

–Will Puckie be here? I ask Isha.

–I don't know, probably. He normally comes at this time.

I love Puckie and my mind forgets to converse as I silently

think of him. He is Chivers' best friend from his old street.

Puckie is only in the middle of his life. I enjoy their friendship maybe as much as they do. Puckie is gruff and unspoken. He is also one of the kindest men I've ever met. And he smiles a lot when he is comfortable in company. He dresses well for someone as flabby and grumpy as Puckie. All three of them have a touch of class, him and Isha and Chivers.

Puckie owns a small gin mill that seems to run itself. He keeps a huge open fire burning for most of the year. He is a perfectionist. He spends hours shining each glass over a steaming, cracked teapot. He's a long way from home to have ever befriended a man like Chivers. He's from a very specific neighbourhood where the barbers only ever use blades and the tables are bolted to the floor. A place where their own kind are deemed the only kind worth knowing. I admire Puckie for getting out of this world and making his own elsewhere. Sometimes friends from the old days call in to see him. Sometimes he has to ask them to leave, but most leave in good time knowing they were right to call in on a whim. Puckie is everything but whimsy—he is sincerity on all fronts. Puckie drinks a bottle of cop-on a day.

The hospital sits on top of a huge hill that overlooks the entire city. Just as we reach it, an alarm goes off and a recorded voice tells all citizens to stay in their respective apartments until further notice. There has been an incident in Apt. 305. I give Isha a small slap on the arse. She finds these announcements difficult.

We enter the foyer of the hospital. Old people make my eyes sting and my throat hot. And here in these corridors, old age is everywhere. It's reflected in the buffed tiles of the foyer, in the mirrors by the lifts, in the eyes of the smiling nurses. Everywhere, crooked limbs and wrinkled flesh, smelling like the babies they once were. Cabbage and peppermint, chrome wheels and rolling chairs, couples stabilised by each other's hungry grip, a slippered trot, odd socks and bed jackets, the uncomfortable scuffle of men in shoes, rattling the car keys waiting for an end embrace.

Old people, hot throat.

This is as hopeful a place as hope humours.

Humour rhymes with tumour, Scribe says.

Sorry, Molly, don't know why I said that, he says then.

I don't know why you did either, I say, diverting my thoughts back to the hospital.

Here Chivers is everybody's friend, without actually befriending anybody, although Isha tells me the Doctor has started having supper with him. Isha says they talk for hours. I look for a note of jealousy in Isha's face as she says this but Isha is not like that. I am.

An old man runs to us as we cross the foyer.

–Have you gots a cigarette? he screams. I needs another cigarette. I've gots two matches but only one cigarette. Have you gots a cigarette?

I hand him a cigarette. I give him one every time I come here. He only ever has two matches and one cigarette.

I stand at the lift and think about the City growing up[wards]. *Nice brackets, Molly!* Scribe says, trying to make amends. I ignore him and think about vertical concrete and iron girders, manned and travelled by lifts. Fuckin' lifts. It has taken me years to understand our exchange. I hesitate before pressing the button and Isha's hand finds its way into the frame. I'm glad because lifts confuse me. I'm never sure if I'm supposed to press the up button to tell them that I'm going up so could they please come down to get me, or if I press the down button to tell them to come down and get me because I'm going up. I say this to Isha.

–How can you be so confused by a lift, Molly? she snaps. They're not that hard to understand.

–I know, but both ways it makes sense. That's all I'm saying.

The door opens and I'm glad that either way, it has come down to eat us.

Isha is tired. She's worn out, I think. By life, maybe, or by me. I don't know, but she's full of short smiles and thin lips and tight mouths these days. I remind myself that I should try and make her laugh. But she doesn't seem to find my stories as funny as she used to. She doesn't really like my stories from the bar at all. Matron tells me that I, as I am, pollute her world but I don't believe this. *I don't believe you anymore*, I tell her, pushing her away so that she can't claw at my resolve, or unearth any doubts that may afford her more power than she already has. *Isha's just tired*, I tell myself, *it's her turn now. I will be an Isha for Isha.*

Puckie stands before us as the lift opens on the fifth floor.

–Well, he says.

–Well, we say, and Puckie smiles.

–Chivers is in his room, he says, I just have to check something out at reception. I'll see you both in ten minutes.

We swap places in the lift. The door closes and he descends from view. We find Chivers in a new bed. Nearby, his hammock hangs empty. Chivers has slept in a hammock for as long as I can remember.

–I like your new bed, Isha says.

Chivers beams, hoping the largesse of his smile will swallow our pity.

–I've put my back out properly, he says, I'm not allowed sleep in the hammock anymore. You might want to take it home.

–No, I like it here, Isha says and swings herself up into it. We talk for a while. I tell Chivers about the Clap. About how his granddaughter had swallowed a blade she found on the street in front of his house, about how he fell asleep in the sun, about how he gets up every morning and sweeps the streets near his house, about how it's too late because his son hasn't brought his other two grandchildren over since it happened two years ago.

–I'm a great believer in sunshine, Chivers says as I finish and I know that he says this on the overlap of sleep and waking. I turn to Isha and find her swaying gently in the hammock. I can hear her downy snores. By the time I've looked back at Chivers, he too has gone over fully. I wish I'd thought to bring a book. I'm afraid to switch on the box in case I wake them both. A nurse puts her head in the door and finds me sitting on the floor, staring at a blank screen.

–I don't know about the missus in the swing, she says, but that man will sleep through anything.

She retreats, followed by my smile. I flick through fifty channels before I realise that I haven't got the stomach to watch any of it. All the politics are over and now the talk is of WAR. J says there was never really any politics from our side. I keep flicking through the channels. I look at all the shiny programmes that J says help deflect intelligent debate.

–We see something glittering just ahead of us, he says, so we turn and give chase. They've made morons of us all.

I'm afraid to believe J. It means too much should it be true. On the screen a scientist is crawling through the implications of nanotechnology on cell restructuring in the quest for optimum longevity. I'm impressed and I wish Puckie would come back so I can ask him what he thinks. Puckie's always a good man for a sound opinion. He doesn't shout when he's trying to make a point. He can just tell you whether something is stupid or not, even if it's wrapped up clever. As I'm listening to the drawl of the scientist, I spot an old disc under the player. There is just a cartoon sticker on the front. I'm half curious, half bored, so I turn the box off and put it in. I press play. There are cartoons on it and I wonder if Chivers has gone a little senile.

Isha says Chivers used to talk to the box when I was a child. He used to check the listings and find some cartoons. Then he'd get down on his knees and talk into the corner speaker. He used to tell them that Molly had been a very good girl and that she'd like to see some cartoons. Then he'd turn on the box and the familiar logo would appear. I don't remember any of this but I can imagine how I felt. This is one of my most precious memories—fifth, I'd say. The nurse comes in again and puts Chivers' medication on his bedside locker. She watches the end of a cartoon with me, then leaves. I slap another smile onto her shoulder blade.

I can still hear the automated alarm announcing a murder in the apartment across the street. I go to look out the window but I can't see anything except the crowd that has come to watch as the body is taken away. Many follow marked ambulances around the City in search of the next body. I can't understand why they spend their days like this. Isha always says, *Let's hope we never can.*

The cartoons have stopped when I turn back to the screen. Instead there is a clouded image of Chivers playing tennis in his small garden. I laugh at his spindly legs and dapper shorts, at his sweatband and his antique racket. The camera is shaky. I'm intrigued so I pull a cushion up in front of the box and turn it down a little more so that it doesn't wake the sleeping pair. On screen, the ball is lost on Chivers' side of the garden-court. Chivers is standing stubbornly on the service line.

–I can't get it, he says to the Boy, if I do I'll miss your serve.

The Boy knows he's somehow being teased by logic and scowls at Chivers. Chivers laughs and the Boy runs after the ball. The Boy is about four years old. He's wearing a white towel dressing gown held together by an old belt. He throws the ball high and puts it straight into the net, which is being held up on either side by chairs. The camera action breaks and finds Puckie sitting on a couch on the front lawn. He's obviously watching the game. He looks awkwardly at the camera. For three seconds he is a ten-year-old and then he curses for the thing to be taken out of his face. Again the camera cuts. It finds itself indoors. Chivers is lying in the hammock. He is wearing his white linen suit. The Boy is seated at a desk. I remember the room as Chivers' old house. The Boy is drawing. Chivers is snoozing. The hammock gently rocks. The Boy is kicking his legs in time to the music, which escalates to a climax. The Boy responds by kicking his legs fiercely, the hammock goes into uproar and Chivers is begging the Boy to stop. It's only then I see that the Boy's leg motion is moving the hammock through a piece of twine tied to his ankle. I can hear Puckie laughing. The camera turns to reveal that he is sitting on the couch. He is encouraging the Boy. The Boy squeals with delight. Chivers can't speak for laughing before he is finally ousted from the hammock by one swing too high. It's then I hear it—Isha's laugh. Huge, raucous, cackling, absorbing. My stomach forgets when I last heard her laugh like that.

Puckie comes to the door of the room. I'd forgotten all about him. He looks at the screen. It's filled with the face of the Boy.

–Where's Juls? the Boy asks.

Puckie comes over and bends down to turn the disc off. He is dripping and it's a second before I realise he's crying. I can do nothing but look to Isha and hope she wakes up. I'm scared of crying men who do not cry. Chivers bolts up in the bed before his bad back pulls him down. Isha wakes with a fright. They both look to me and then to Puckie. Our faces tell of something that has happened in our waking. I follow Chivers' eyes to the screen and return to find Isha's eyes have followed us both. The Boy's face is on pause. Pulled from the freeze frame by a moment's passing.

–Where's Juls? the Boy asks.

–Turn it off, says Chivers. Sharply.

I do.

–Who is he? I ask.

But they are all three looking to themselves and each other. Nobody has heard my question.

4:1: Mr. ****

Again I go to Kitty's Laundry, and again she helps reaffirm my true nature. This stint exhausts me on a level I've never experienced before. She's my tonic. I watch her huge mass plod and oscillate from one heavy corner of her being to another. I watch from across the street before turning back into the City.

I walk without intent to a place I've not yet found. I think about going back to the shed, throwing the hours to work, but I'm energised by my time spent at Kitty's. I feel like taking on the hours myself. I even think about getting drunk and writing my name on bathroom walls. This is how carefree I feel. I take a risk and walk into the first bar I come by. It's dark and characterless. There are ten boxes surrounding the big screen. *Electrocution* is on. Unusually, all ten images are moving in sync. The bar is either trying to restrict our choice or free our minds a little—I'm not sure which. I sit at the counter. I sit near enough to the other drinkers to listen but not to be addressed. I order a whiskey.

–Any preference? the sweaty barman asks.
–No.

He pours my drink. I put the money on the counter before me. In doing so I have set my preference in service. I will nod and he'll pour. I will put and he'll take. *There is no need for words*, I scream silently over the faux-marble top.

I take in the couple sitting to my right. They are cheap. Every inch of them has been undersold to nothing. She gives me a look that tells me I could have her up against the urinal but the thought makes me queasy. I can see the broken veins through her nylon tights. I think about looking for another bar but there are hers and whores and hims everywhere. Instead, I take on the City again. I walk for two hours. Then my chair calls me back to my house. My chair is the greatest time-killer I know when the climate suits. I go. I sit. I sleep. I wake. I go to work and begin everything again.

I buy a paper from Gonzo.
 –There's little hope now, he says. Sadly.
 –It's a terrible time, I say. Smiling.
 –Did you march? he asks. Knowing.
 –My voice was heard, I say, I'm on the right side with this one.
He looks as if he is about to say something else but then suddenly he looks as tired as Kitty. He says nothing.
 –I'm saving my placard for the next one, I say.
 Bright. Breezy. The Voice-of-the-Future.
 I turn and walk away.

The Doctor is here today instead of next week. I'm not ready. I see him talking to Fathead in the corridor. Soon it will be me.

I go into the room designated for the evaluation test. I'm not comfortable. Neither is the chair. I sit there and answer questions that have not yet been posed. My head is all a-chatter. I don't understand why I'm feeling like this, especially given my work record. And the fact that I don't *care*.

The Doctor walks in. Smiling. Reassuring. Reaching out.

–How are you, Mr. ****? he asks.

–I'm fine, I say.

Expressionless, housing everything I want to say in this.

–You understand the reasoning behind this evaluation, he says gently. I'm sure you've all been going over it upstairs.

I hate him then, I hate him for picturing me with them upstairs, fretting and exchanging answers like giddy schoolboys before an exam. All nervous, excited, puppy-like.

Fuck you, I scream in my head.

–Yes, I say aloud. Strapped to the belly of an afterthought another yes escapes. I inhale myself.

Then for some reason I regain control over the entire situation. My control is steeped in a new wave of apathy that I have missed in recent weeks. I even feel like having fun with him.

–Tell me a little about yourself, he says.

–I'm a native, I tell him, lived here all my life. I'm not married. I enjoy my work. I live a quiet life.

–What about family? he asks. Looking me in the eye. Kitty-like.

–I've none to speak of, I say, my parents died when I was twenty-two. I'm an only child.

–Why do you enjoy your work so much? he asks. What is it exactly that appeals to you?

–Does there have to be a reason? I ask. Smiling.

He smiles back. –I'm asking you for one. Humour me. Give this evaluation some flesh, Mr. ****.

–I guess I like it because I get to use my imagination more than most, and I'm good at it.

–Apparently, he coos, you've been here for over ten years. Why have you not moved uptown? You'd make more money and you're good enough.

–I just never felt the need, I say. I like it here.

–Less stress I suppose, less pressure.

–Maybe, I say.

–Tell me about your stints over the years, he says. Which ones have stood out?

I tell him everything he wants to hear. I tell him about the stints that have challenged me, the stints I have felt some affinity with, the stints that took their toll on me. All lies; or truths, fleshed out like lies, told to appease.

–How do you like your current stint? he asks.

–It's interesting.

–I'm familiar with the book, he says, I read it many years ago. I read it still.

I don't want to imagine the Doctor reading. It makes me uncomfortable. I feel like smacking him across the face for bringing any of this up. We talk some more. He asks questions and takes his notes. I answer them and take my time.

–That's it, he says then, unfortunately our time is up but I would like us to talk again.

–I don't see the need, I say, I enjoy my job. I'm of sound mind. I'm aware of the dangers. I know where the boundaries are. I don't feel at risk.

–I want to talk about your father, he says. Kitty-like.

–What of him? He's passed away, I say. Bristling.

–He's currently a patient of mine in the Assumptia. You signed the admission form thirteen years ago, Mr. ****.

I want to run away.

–I don't want to make you feel guilty, he says gently, I just think you may help me understand him more. I think he can be helped. You can do it from here, from this room or over at my office, in your own time.

I turn and walk out of the room. My back ablaze.

The climate at work is changing. It leaves me unsettled. First the evaluation test and now a follow-up talk. It's revolting and I feel like never coming back to this office. I watch as people who don't give a shit try to look like they do. The place reeks.

I've lost my appetite for work and yet the phone rings and I drink endless coffees at my desk. Everyone in the shed has their own office. It's always been considered the best way to operate, the most effective. It's misleading to call them offices in the traditional sense of the word, in the Progressive sense. There is no leather or view, no comfort or space. They are just rooms, cell-like and functional only in containment. They contain our voices and our phones so we can work in relative silence. Most pricks put things on the walls. Work-related info or pictures of people resident somewhere in their lives. Wives, children, lovers, friends, icons. I have nothing on my walls. What would the Doctor think of that?

FUCK THE DOCTOR.

A man whom I've never seen before comes to my door.

–There's a talk in the kitchen, he says. You're asked to attend.

–Who's giving the talk? I ask.

–The same guy who gave us the evaluation, he says. Disappearing.

–When? I shout after him.

–Now—should only take about half an hour.

I reluctantly make my way out from behind my desk. The phone rings. I don't answer it.

The kitchen is full of men. It's only incidental that we have no women working here in the shed. They pull stints same as us. This gender imbalance is silently appreciated. They don't miss the mating dance around the desk. The men here think they are better than any women who would work here. They seek their prey elsewhere. They have false notions. Disgusting but perversely entertaining all the same.

The Doctor is standing by the sink. It's an undignified place to give a talk but he doesn't seem to mind. He's more concerned with having everyone in view. Like a professional photographer, he choreographs our huddle.

—Karver, can you move out from behind the door?

He already knows all our names by heart and now he wants to address us with our faces in view. I shudder in recognition of the man he is. He looks at me. I stare back but block my line of vision with sheer obstinacy and defiance. I'm challenging him not to look but his eyes tell me that he has already seen.

—Mr. ****, could you hand these booklets out please?

It's not a question. In this moment I hate the man before me with an energy that betrays my apathy. *You prick!* I scream. It ricochets off my skull. I catch it on the rebound and hurl it again with even more ferocity. *You prick!* He and I are the only ones in the room who have heard it. Amidst its reverberations, I dole out the booklets entitled *Trespassing in the Workplace—Identity at Risk.* We stand before him, or more accurately, around him. I don't really listen. Words and phrases find themselves at my ear.

—Never take the same stint for too long.

–Look out for each other.

–Call home during the day.

–Let your wife/partner/family read the job description so they may be more alert to the early signs.

I look down at the floor. I want him to wrestle for my attention. But I know he's clever; I know he'll take me on another time, for different reasons. For now he's content to talk to my co-workers. He knows I'm not really at risk. True to his breed, he'll prioritise instinctively and work in an ordered fashion.

We go back to our cubicles. I finish a day's work. I walk home a lot slower than I usually do. I never actively want to see the Ghost but today I actively don't want to see her. I already know I will eat out and pay double for the meal. I think of Anna's twins.

There will be fighting, he'd said.

There is always fighting.

I've never felt enough for anything to fight for it. It's a good disposition to carry. Earlier, the Doctor had brought me to the ring but I'd turned my back. I tear at his image in my mind. Clawed and tattered, I throw it away. I think instead of Anna in labour. I decide to have pork that night.

The Ghost is not at home. I see her seated in the kitchen of a house across the street. I can see her sitting at the table while Cynthia sorts through a heap of old letters beside her. Lavy Tallulah. This is her old stage name. Her real name is Cynthia Bates. She was a contortionist with a group of body artists in a time gone by. She has slept with over fifty men in her past life, all of them dogged by some deformity or another. I know this because she told me one morning, volunteered the information from across the road, said she had always channelled her compassion through sex but now she'd found education and taught free body expression to the mentally handicapped every Tuesday and Thursday.

–Everybody still calls me Lavy, she'd told me, it's as near to sex as I get these days.

She'd said this over her shoulder as she'd sprinted up the steps to her house. She was wearing leggings and a leotard and it was a Wednesday. I didn't respond. She didn't need an answer. She's an expressionist, a self-proclaimed creative, she needs to share everything with everybody. A blank cheque to her private life lies open on her doorstep. I guess the Ghost decided to cash it in. I smirk to myself. The boys in the canteen would love that one.

I can't imagine the Ghost having much to speak of. But then neither do most people and still they talk on, transferring empty thoughts from their empty heads into the empty space they insist on bringing with them.

The Ghost waves when she sees me coming. I nod in her direction. Cynthia looks up to see who she's waving at. She sees me and shimmies then, as if her salute is fuelled by beans jiggling about in her body. I feel like swatting her like a fly every time she does it. But I nod and walk on.

I go into my house. I take off my coat and sit in my chair. I sit there for half an hour, murdering the minutes. Oh chair, time-killer extraordinaire! I get up again and put on my coat. I realise I'm actually hungry. The Ghost comes in just as I'm about to leave. This, I know, is on purpose. She has something to say to me. The Ghost no longer really wants to talk to me. She has learned to dispatch statements that require my response.

–A man called to see you today, says the Ghost.
–When? I ask.
–Only a while ago, she says.
–What did he want? I ask.
–He said he was a doctor, she says. He said he wanted to talk

to you about something private. He said he'd call again later.

I breathe.

–If he calls again tonight, tell him I've nothing to say to him. Tell him I don't want to be disturbed either here or at work. Tell him this is final. I'm going out.

The Ghost nods. –Are you sick?

–No, I say, the man is confusing me with someone else. I don't want to talk of it anymore. Go back over to Cynthia's. She's going to piss herself if you don't hurry back with the who*s* and the why*s*.

The Ghost looks tired.

–I didn't tell her anything, she says, but she says to tell you that you need to glue your shoes. Your sole is flapping as you walk. She says it looks like a duck talking.

I don't respond. Instead I walk past her and think about pork.

I keep walking till my phone rings. I answer it because I don't know what else to do. My mobile never rings. It's work. A client. I'm confused because somebody must have diverted the office phone. I take the call but keep it short. The Dishwasher is waiting.

4:2: Telephone Transcript

In Search of Infinite Relief, C.W. Sisle
Contracted to Gleeson Media Group
Subcontracted to Employee 12
Recorded at 8.12 p.m. on 01/04/****

E12 Hello?

C78 You still sound the same. Hi.

E12 Why wouldn't I? Haven't bought my new voice box yet.

C78 Assholes needing new voices. I'd never get it done unless I'd a voice like Scott Hybvone. I can't believe someone gave him a job reading the news. What were they thinking? It'd be kindness if someone took him for a few hours each week and taught him sign language. It's Molly.

E12 I know. You still sound the same as well. You sound good.

C78 I am. I'd a weird day though. I think I'm still soaking it all up. Bits of it.

E12 What was so weird?

C78 It's a long story. I think. Actually, I don't even know what the story is. Just that—I put on this disc by mistake when I was in the hospital today. Chivers is in hospital but from the smell of cabbage and peppermint I know his ward is more of a home for the elderly. That's upsetting enough in itself because Chivers doesn't belong in a home. He's always been his own man. They won't even let him sleep in his hammock. Anyway, I was there with Isha. And there was this other friend of ours called Puckie. Remind me to tell you about Puckie. He's a lord. And there was this Boy in the footage. The disc was home-movie stuff. He was asking for something and Puckie started to cry and I heard Isha laughing, I think she was the person holding the camera. But Puckie started to cry in real life. There in the hospital. Chivers told me to turn if off. But I don't know who the Boy is. I don't know why Puckie was crying. I thought I knew everything about those three. Well, not everything, but all the big things anyway. A missing Boy is fairly big.

E12 When did they last see him?

C78 I don't know. The footage didn't look that old. Puckie still wears the same shirt. But then again that doesn't mean much now that I think about it.

E12 What did Isha say when you asked her?

C78 It was awkward in the hospital. She didn't seem to want talk about it afterwards either. I'd to go meet a friend. Isha just said she would see me at home. I asked if the Boy was dead. And she said she doesn't know. I asked her if she wanted me to go with her and she said no because she had to collect something for a demonstration she's giving in my old school. I'm still out. I haven't been home.

E12 Well maybe, just go home and ask her then.

C78 She needs her time. And I don't feel right about just asking her 'cause she was real upset and to be honest, Laurence, I can't believe she never told me about this Boy.

E12 What? You feel left out?

C78 No. Just. Well maybe. I think I feel guilty.

E12 Why do you feel guilty?

C78 I was off doing my own thing although I'm not even sure what that amounts to save the people I met. I was off working. I called home but there were spells when I didn't because I couldn't. I don't know, Laurence. Isha and me have only become really close over the last couple of years. I just never really wanted to be at home. I don't know why. I just needed to get out. I feel shit, Laurence.

E12 Why? Because you do what lots of young people do when they're trying to find their feet?

C78 Your words, as soothing as they are, are making me feel worse. I'm even wondering now if she mentioned him and I just wasn't listening. It's actually frightening how possible that is. My stomach is churning just thinking about it. I'm an awful person. I'm a worse grandchild.

E12 Molly.

C78 Don't, Laurence. If you met Isha—the shit I've put her through. I just can't seem to manage myself. I fly and then I fall. I fly and then I fall. I fly and then I fall. Again and again, and now there is this little Boy that can make Puckie cry. And Puckie never cries. There's this little Boy that they all seemed to love. Chivers was playing tennis with him and rocking in the hammock with him. Everything. And this little Boy went missing sometime and Isha never told me even though we are like best friends. And I don't think she told me because she's a better person than me and she didn't want to worry me. So I go and give her my worries, throw them on top of her like dirty laundry, and she says nothing about her own. I have to grow up. I have to start living in this world. Anyway.

E12 I think you're thinking too much about where you fit in to all of this. Maybe this is one narrative you don't feature in. Maybe you should just go home and sit with Isha.

C78 I know what you're saying, Laurence. And you're right. But it doesn't mean that I'm wrong to feel guilty.

E12 I never said you were, Molly.

C78 I'm sorry.

E12 Can I ask you something, Molly?

C78 Go on.

E12 Why are you living with Isha?

C78 My parents died when I was small. Separately, though. It wasn't one of those car crashes that orphans superheroes. My Mum wasn't ever really with my father. I think they were only going out. Isha says she would have done anything for him but that he was a ladies' man. *A hopeless romantic*, she says, hopeless being the operative word. Always talking about the someday when. Isha says Mum was always a little silly when it came to men. She used to lose her head a bit. She worked for the Goring Group. She was the fastest typist in the City at one stage.

E12 Maybe that's why you want to be a writer.

C78 That's a little far-fetched, Laurence. Even I'm not that romantic. She got the virus, first time round. That's what I mean. Isha's been through the wars.

E12 How did your dad die?

C78 I can't even pronounce it. He died in hospital. I never knew him. I've seen photos though. He was a real looker. He used to wear his hat at an angle. Still looks good in the photo. I don't think Isha was taken with his antics even if Mum was. I wrote a poem about them once called 'The Giggler and the Gargler'. Good title, isn't it?

E12 It's good. Double g. Horsey.

C78 Did I tell you I loved crosswords?

E12 No, but I do. And now, obviously you do.

C78 I love the horses too. I like the smaller races. I don't like this super horse business. It's gone like the cars.

E12 I know. Super man next. But I do like the title. I like it. Who are you like?

C78 I think I'd be really like my mother if she'd actually been my father.

E12 Here we go.

(*Caller 78 laughs*)

C78 I'm not so girly as she was. She was a real girl.

E12 What are you then? A tomboy?

C78 No. I feel half man. I like that half—it's simple but still full of notions, simpler than the other half anyway. It's wise enough too. It's got a great sense of games. I like making games of things. It's the other half that complicates everything. When I'm *with* someone—a man—it's not in good shape. The other half can't even bear to watch.

E12 You're very complicated for someone so small.

(*Caller 78 laughs*)

C78 I've huge hair.

E12 Fair point.

C78 Sometimes the pair of them work it out nicely though. In the right company, I can be truly both. It works. You can't beat the company of those that know you best. It really is nice to be known.

E12 Never heard it put so simply. You're right. They say a friend's eye is a good mirror.

C78 It's reassuring to know that.

E12 It should be nice to know yourself.

C78 I know. It's hard knowing exactly who you are though. Say as a family member, you have a role, be it daughter, aunt, mother, grandmother, in fact, you've multiple roles. There is responsibility. And I believe it's ultimately enriching. As a lover and wife, you inhabit other roles, there are other commitments to make. In friendship, ideally, you are nothing but a naked personality, genderless and free of all roles. Two friends owe each other nothing but the time to enjoy each other's company, time to share their common ideals and passions. Based on choice. Ideally, that is, but often there is role-play or performance. But who are we when we're on our own? Who are we when we interact with our selves? Is there another role for us to inhabit? Do we choose it subconsciously? What the fuck am I going on about?

E12 I don't know.

C78 I don't fuckin' know either. I should go home to Isha. Sign up for a personality transplant en route. I laughed twice tonight and I didn't think I would. See! People really are the way out.

E12 Way out of what?

C78 I'll tell you again. I'm going to go home and slap Isha on the rump. She likes that.

E12 Take care, Molly.

C78 Or as some hippy said to me today, –Give care. I thought it was nice.

E12 Bye.

C78 Bye.

End of transcript

4:3: Molly

We start off through the back passages of the City. Although I've known Augusta for years, I've never shared sobriety with her. She has none to offer. She lives her entire life behind a fuzzy gauze.

–Do you think you drink too much? I'd asked her one morning, leaving her outside an off licence on our way home from the bar.

–Of course I do, she'd said, but I'm old enough to know that I'd prefer to spend the days humming then cold sober. I can't defend my drinking any more than that.

Augusta is humming by 7.10 each morning. She drinks nineteen baby bottles a day at regular intervals. Never more, never less. I like the way that she has contained her drinking. Isha thinks that she's a sad case for applause but I think her capacity to deny bottle twenty is a shining triumph.

–If I was an alcoholic, I'd said to Isha, I would definitely drink as much as I could get my hands on in any one day. There's no way I'd have the discipline to keep the genie in bottle twenty.

–We're lucky you're not an alcoholic then, Isha'd said sarcastically—eyeing the bruises on my knees.

–That was funny, I'd said.

–Oh I'd say it was, she'd said. Thin-lipped.

I'd tried to climb up a billboard the night before. I was trying to get on the featured motorbike.

I'd laughed again at the memory. –Do you not think that's funny? Do you not think it's funny that I was trying to mount an image of a motorcycle?

Isha didn't answer because I was laughing too much to care.

–Anyway, I'd said in mock defiance, moderation is an alley cat in this City. Augusta Ghitz has won.

Isha and Augusta would like each other if one wasn't so scared of the other, and the other wasn't so scared for me. I think about this whilst I'm looking at Augusta and thinking about Isha. I want to go home to her.

Augusta asks me to help her sell the last of her fruit before I go home. I do it halfheartedly because I want to see Isha. I want to see her with so much of my heart that there is none left for vending and Augusta kisses me on the forehead and puts me in a fare.

The driver doesn't want to talk to me. He is listening to the radio.

–You're probably one of them, he says, looking me up and down.

–Who? I ask.

–You're either with them or with us, and if you're with them I won't drive you any further. Least I can do.

–With who?

–You're either with us or with them, there's no in-between or maybes. There's no talk of innocent babies or any of that stuff you women go on about, any of that stuff that gets in the way. There's only really two sides if you stop with all the stuff in-between. If you're not with Treehouse, you're with them. Wilkes just about got that in time. Even though I never liked him.

I stare at the driver because he might be the most ignorant man I've ever met.

–I think you might be the most ignorant man I've ever met.

I say it because something in me is beyond caring. I'm tired of men and war and the everydays that insist on coming one after the next. The driver stops the fare and shoves me out clumsily. He doesn't even ask for the money.

–What the fuck do you know about about war anyway? he snarls.

–Nothing, I say.

And it's true. There is so much to think about that my head hurts. Everything spins. I taste an understanding and grow afraid of hopelessness. I have no cigarettes left so I persuade a street vendor to sell me a single. Scrawled on the side of a building are the words, *To yearn for the absolute is as insane as a pendulum yearning for the other side of its swing.* –Hawkeye.

Wanting, yearning, swinging—pendulums the lot of us.

Isha is watching the box when I get home. I'm conscious that my tipsiness is misplaced. She's not angry but she's weary. She has aged slightly and I left her only five hours ago.

–Do you want a cup of tea? I ask.

–Please, she says and then says no more.

I go sit with her on the couch.

–I'll sit on your feet if you want, I offer and raise myself to allow her feet to clamber in. I sit back down.

–How's Puckie? I ask.

–He's OK, she says, it just took him by surprise. I don't think he realised Chivers still had the disc.

–Can you tell me about him?

–His name is Daniel, Chivers used to look after him.

That's all she says, but my mind is racing with too many questions to stop another falling from my lips. I bite on it as fast as I can because Isha is tired and I've been away drinking and do not deserve to know. But the word 'when' has already dropped from my mouth and onto the couch. Isha looks at it for a while before picking it up to chew.

–Chivers met Daniel on his fourth birthday, she says resignedly, when he found him parked on the street's end, eating his birthday cake on his own. That was typical of his mother. She would buy him cake but forget to eat it with him. She was a complete floater. Daniel was wearing a nurse's outfit that his mother had bought him in good faith but bad judgement. Or maybe not—Serge would disagree.

–She must have been a bit mad, I say.

–Maybe, Isha says, it felt like she wasn't quite all there.

–He looked like a gorgeous child, he'd that creamy skin.

–And brown eyes, and a smile that could swallow a harbour. Chivers' words, not mine.

She smiles to herself sadly, in a recollection that takes her away from me.

–He didn't live with Chivers though, did he? I ask quickly, to bring her back.

–Kind of, Isha says, not straight away. Daniel used to wait for Chivers on the steps of an old factory. He used to spend his early mornings chewing gum and sticking it to the sides of the doorframe. He could be a real odd child. But in a good way. Beautifully odd. He definitely had something that little bit special about him.

I want to ask her if I'd been a beautifully odd child, if I'd had a smile that could swallow a harbour, but I don't because the neediness of the question registers in my stomach and makes me queasy. It would put Isha further away from me. Now is not the time. Matron steals up behind me. She tells me that if I'd been a good child I wouldn't have grown up to be what I'm now. *I try to be good*, I say but Matron doesn't want to hear it. She's sick of me. She retreats and leaves me with myself.

I, in turn, give myself back to Isha.

–Then, when Chivers would come down with the mongrels, she's saying, Daniel would burst through all the gum he'd fenced himself in with and run beside them till he got to school. With all these ribbons of gum hanging off him. Chivers said he was a very fast runner. He could've been an athlete if he'd had a chance. Chivers used to set the dogs after him and Daniel would run just ahead of them squealing and laughing. It was hilarious. So Chivers would bring him to school, then he started picking him up. Eventually Daniel started to stay over. His mother didn't care but Chivers made sure that he did his best to include Daniel's mother. He encouraged her to come over for dinner, come over for drinks in the evening. But she never wanted to. She just spent her days in front of her box, dressed in a Malene copycat dress that she'd found in a market. He stayed with Chivers about twice a week and she was happy enough that he wasn't around so much for her to forget.

–Who would she be like that I'd know? I ask.

Isha thinks for a while.

–No one really, I've never really met anyone like her. It was very frustrating. *She* was very frustrating because she'd nod her head and seem like she was listening and taking it all in. But either she wasn't or she just didn't bother trying. She wasn't all there, I suppose. Mightn't be the fairest way of putting it but it's the best way I can think off. Ask Chivers. He could tell you better. Anyway, Chivers would spend his afternoons in Puckie's. Sitting at the counter, sipping tea and Puckie would prop himself up at his side and chat away to Chivers. Puckie always got a great kick out of Chivers. Chivers used to bring in Daniel's drawings to Puckie. And Puckie was happy to look at them and give an odd grunt every now and again. You can imagine Puckie. He had a different crowd in the old place. And one night someone questioned Chivers' interest in the Boy—one night in the bar, in front of Chivers. Some little shit.

Isha does not say the word through her teeth like usual. She says it angrily. And then drops her head to tell me she can't even remember his name.

–Some little shit, she says again, starts going on about Chivers and Daniel and all the little shits behind him start sniggering and throwing in their own mouthfuls. Spitting insults and accusations at him. They knew he was gay but they probably would have said them anyway. Everyone's a paedophile these days if we're to believe the papers.

Isha is getting upset. In front of me.

–And they didn't care about Daniel, they just did what they always did—watch everybody else slit-eyed to help them celebrate their own miserable lives.

I'm surprised at Isha's eloquence. Sometimes she says things that can be said no other way. I think about telling her this but it's not the time for my observations to float to surface. This is real life and I have to remind myself of all the people that make up this story. Real people that I know and love and my stomach drops to think of Chivers, head bent, at the forefront of this abuse. An anger swells in me and seeps out through my gritted teeth. I want to go out and find the men and run at them and bite them and make them see, but I stay to hear Isha speak of a time I don't remember because I was never really there.

–Puckie asked the men to leave, Isha says, then others started up and he eventually cleared his bar of business for the night.

In this moment I love Puckie for everything I know him to be and for all the simple rights he keeps in his trouser pockets.

–I love Puckie, I say to Isha. Isha says nothing and gets up to make tea.

I get up and follow her and she half laughs when she turns to find me propped at the kitchen door, picking at my nails.

–I hate those men, I say, how could anyone ...

–They came back that night, Isha says, and threatened to burn the place down. And they would've too, would have done it without a second thought, just for the spite and the evening's entertainment. But Puckie did it instead.

She starts to laugh so hard that the tea canister falls from her grip and lands in the sink. I stand there, eyes wide and expectant, hoping she slows down a little to let me climb aboard a laugh that I've never heard as her own. It's sharp-edged and almost angry.

She's laughing still as she says, –Puckie just bent down, got out a container of fuel, came out from behind the bar, closed down the hatch door, and circled the bar, pouring the fuel all over the wooden countertop. Then he threw a match on it and offered Chivers a fare home even though he only lived around the corner. He just put on his jacket, lit a cigarette and left the little shits there. Closed the door after them so they had to break a window to get out.

The laugh dies a natural death. I bury it in sheer wonderment. Isha is smiling proudly because she sees I'm impressed with the antics of her friends. Sometimes Isha is beautifully transparent.

–And that's how those two became proper friends, she finishes, friends in their own time, outside the bar.

–That's not right, I say.

–What isn't?

–Burning down the bar.

Isha starts to laugh again. −Wait. Puckie gets on the phone when they are in the fare and calls someone at the fire station. −Dundin, he says, I'm sorry to ask but I need to call in that favour. I've just lit up the bar. You couldn't get someone down to it?

You can imagine what Chivers was thinking, thought he had a right lunatic beside him. But you should get him to tell you the story. He does Puckie very well. You should see Chivers taking off Puckie as he's circling the bar, laying the fuel. Puckie—all pumped up with bravado, belly out. It's very funny.

−Did the firemen get to it on time? I ask.

−Course they did, arrived with the works, skipped the queued hit points and got straight down to Puckie's. Overrode an order to get down to the Satellite District where CH24's head office was on fire. Puckie gets such a kick out of that. −Midnight in the garden of morons, he always says.

−Was the bar ruined? I ask.

−Well, I think Puckie was happy enough to avoid getting burnt out while he was upstairs in bed, and the other boys left thinking that he was a complete nutter and not really worth bothering about. It's no good burning out a place if the owner's willing to do it for you. Spoils all the fun. And apparently, I only found this out years later, Puckie had helped pay for Dundin's training fees. He used to work with Puckie behind the bar so it came back to him I suppose. In a funny way.

−Everything comes full circle, I say, because I don't know what else to say.

−Not if a piece of the circle is missing, Isha says, mocking herself and looking away.

And I know then that a circle has been broken and I want with all my heart to give Isha back the missing piece but I don't know where the Boy is and I don't know how to help, so instead I start to cry and wish I could be an Isha for Isha and not a Molly that floods her world with tears. From somewhere I reach out and hug her reluctant body and tell her that everything will be OK. Drink talks so much that sometimes it says the right things. Isha tells me to let her go because the teapot is crushing her pelvic bone.

–Everything will find its place, she says briskly. Shaking off the tender atmosphere that weighs in heavy on our moment.

–Everything can be understood with the right understanding, she says.

Strong again for her and for me.

I don't understand what Isha is saying but it brings me relief.

–Do you want me to sleep with you tonight? I ask. Embarrassed, lost.

–No thanks, she says. And I know she means it—Isha has never let me share her sadness.

She makes a cup of tea to bring to bed.

–Empty the ashtray before you go up, she says as she climbs the stairs.

–I will, I say and smile at her.

She smiles back but Isha's not in it.

I climb onto the couch. I turn on the box. I find a programme about Treehouse. I try to remember the names of all the people that slide in and out of his ear. I try to remember secretaries and generals and advisors and chiefs and spokespeople and all the rest of them. I don't want to end up like the driver. I need to know who is really to blame but there seems to be no definite beginning or end to anything. Everything shifts in circles.

I try to understand what or who is at the middle of it all but the warmth wraps itself around my breathing and my system grows disinterested in the cigarettes I insist on lighting, one after the other. I know it must be time to sleep. I watch ten more advertisements, think about buying a revolutionary papermaker, empty the ashtray and go to bed.

5:1: Mr. ****

A man on a street corner asks me to join an ANTI-WAR group.

–I believe in WAR, I tell him, I think a good WAR is just what we need to keep this City's passion burning. I'm proud we're fighting a just cause. If we don't do it, no one will. We're lucky to be living in the greatest City on earth. We're lucky to have our man, Treehouse, in office. I think he'll be remembered as one of the great humanitarians of our time.

I get bored then. I get bored looking at his face, wedged as it is between sadness and horror.

–He's not my man, he says, I didn't vote for him.

–Then you're not our man, I say, although not everyone is smart enough to understand what this City really needs. Can't blame people for stupidity—it's all we can do to teach them.

–I might as well sit here and give myself paper cuts with these pamphlets than try and talk to people like you, he says.

–My man, that's exactly what you should do, spill a little blood for the cause. Show them what stuff we're made off.

–They've fitted cameras to some of the guns, he says wearily.

They want to broadcast the killing from the source.

I can't believe he bothered to tell me this. He is desperate for people to understand.

–That's an idea, I say, let everyone in on the action.

The man walks away.

Something inside me stirs but I kick it in the head. I roar and take stride.

There will be fighting.

Anna is serving an elderly couple when I come in. She acknowledges my presence and brings me a coffee on cue.

–When will you be giving up work to have the baby, or babies …? I ask. Smiling knowingly.

–Not for a while, she says. Afraid.

I nod in receipt of this information and order beef. I leave her go and look at the other waitresses. My mind is uneasy. I want to play draughts now but the Dishwasher is working. Anna can be replaced. He can't. I never fear that I will walk in one day to find him gone. Some people know what suits them. He'll not leave unless he has to. Of this I'm sure.

I look at the other eaters. There is a couple that holds me as they hold each other's hands under the table. They do not speak aloud. I know they are conversing through their hold on each other. She gently massages his hands, each finger individually tracing patterns on his upturned palm. *Fuck him!* I cry out in my mind. *Fuck him there on the table! Dirty the linen! Hang from the lighting! Make us watch! Get out of your world! Come into mine!*

But they don't hear me. They stay as they are, smiling like co-heirs to the same seduction.

I turn my mind off as it has become vocal of late. I order it to be quiet, then sit and eat what I've ordered. Eventually, the bloated owner comes in to sweat over his takings and I go out back to the Dishwasher.

The board is set up. I make my first move. I know as I set down the piece that it's clumsy and wanton. The Dishwasher looks at me. He stays silent and moves his piece. I move again.

–Change is coming, he says. Making his move.

–Good change? I ask. Making mine.

The Dishwasher laughs. Snorts. This is the first time I have ever heard him do this. I don't want to contain it. I want to fly it higher, set my own upon it, have them mate savagely in a wordless understanding. But he is no longer laughing so I ground mine.

–You'll have to fight, he says. Making his move.

–Who? I ask. Making mine.

–You'll have to fight.

–Have you fought?

–I've fought and won.

–How can I win?

–You can't, he says, looking at the board, and I realise that I have already lost. To him.

–I will, I say. Faking fine.

An uneasiness strokes the back of my neck, it breathes wetly on my ear. We play on in silence.

This is the longest exchange we've ever enjoyed.

The sitting room is empty when I get home. I go to the kitchen to get a glass of water. There are two empty cups at the sink. When I see this I go to her room. The Ghost is lying on her side.

–What did he say? I ask her.

–I gave him your message, she says quietly.

–He is not permitted in this house again, he is not to drink my coffee. What did he ask you?

–My name, she says. Dry whisper.

–What else? Tell me what he said.

–We just talked for a while, she says. Turning into the corner, turning her back on me.

–About what?

–About me, about why I came here, my life before—he knows where I come from.

–Did he ask about me? I falter. Nervous. Sickly.

–No, she says to the corner.

–He said nothing at all about me? I bark. Relieved.

–No, he left you a disc. Said you may want to watch it. He left his office number.

–If you talk to him again I'll send you back.

Back where? I muse. I've never asked her where she's from. I think about strapping her to the roof rack of a bus headed for nowhere.

FUCK THE DOCTOR.

–The disc is on your bed.

I leave her to the dark and go into my room. There is no note. Just his name and his number. He is banking on my curiosity. But I've never been the curious kind. He has made a bad investment.

I'm walking through a derelict street. The buildings have no façades, they are empty shells of dust and shadows. From the leftovers of an old bedroom, I hear my father's voice. It's ugly and snarled. He is shouting at me.

–****! Look at me, cold as the day you were born. They fucked us over when they gave us a changeling son.

I look to find my father but he finds me. He puts his hand gently on my shoulder. He is wearing his old golfing jumper. He smiles.

–You're late home, son, he says. Tender.

I'm calm. I'm not afraid. Again his voice sounds from the building across the street. He releases a vicious invective against me. Loud. Bitter. Jeering. Lamenting.

–Dad, I say, you're throwing your voice.

He looks old and confused.

–When did you become a schizophrenic? I ask. Wearily.

–I'm not, he says. Confused.

Again his voice sounds from the building across the street.

–Look there, Dad, I point at the empty building. You're throwing your voice.

We are interrupted by my mother's approach. Her white hair is matted to her neck. Her nightdress is torn. Her tights are down around her ankles.

–Oh, Mum, you haven't gone and wet yourself? I ask.

–No, she says as she hands me her hipbone. The ball is shattered. Can you super-glue it?

–No, Mum, I say. It works around a fulcrum point. Glue won't work.

I take in the two of them—both staring at me, both asking of me, both lamenting.

–Follow me, I say.

I walk ahead; my parents shuffle behind me. I bring them to the end of a dark alley. I climb the wall and jump down to the now.

I wake with a start. I'm indignant that this ridiculous dream has found its way into my sleep. I have a shower and decide that I'll take Freddie's route to work.

Freddie's not talking to me this morning. He sullenly gives me my rag and I smile at him. He withdraws further. People are divulged from the underground. Swollen crowds go to their workplace. Fighters stride, Progressives swagger, the Lost wander and the Drifters honour their namesake. I hear two women on a street corner talking about the weather.

–It's getting darker, they say.

–Daylight has gone and got thrifty, they whisper.

But I don't care. Let the women talk, let the darkness come, let the daylight seep slowly, let the good men run.

I stir my coffee. I've had a productive morning. Oh, Laurence, my old friend. Let me take thee to lunch!

There is a Fighter of some description handing out leaflets on a street corner. I take one and ram it into my mouth. I grin and chew. He does not smile or find me amusing. Fighters are generally serious people. Also, I wasn't being funny. I was being a smarm. I can't understand why I'm so actively cuntish these days. I'm not concerned, just amused. I think I'm showing off for Laurence. I still feel apathetic but something in me has been aroused. I seem to be asking for a fight.

I go sit in the park. There are children playing on the battered swing sets; guardians of all ages watch on. Some people are there to watch for the wrong reasons and I like to watch them watching and being watched in turn. A black man with greying hair and dimpled skin comes and sits down beside me on the bench. We don't acknowledge each other. We sit in silence. This chews a little time. Then he decides to speak.

–I'm blind, he says, but more than being a blind man, I'm a tailor.

I look at him but I don't show any sign of interest because I have none. Anyway, he can't see my face. He insists on talking to me and I wonder if perhaps Laurence gave him some sort of encouragement, slipped a little something past me. I shudder and rearrange myself in order to cut off all lines of communication he may have found with this man.

–I've worked the same business for over thirty-two years, he's saying, I make good clothes, good suits. But I also mend stuff, take up hemlines, that kind of thing, before everybody started using that Glustick. Anyway, this woman, Nelly Fontaine, used to be a customer of mine. Now in order for you to understand the whole debacle, you'll have to understand how I work. 'Cause I can't see, I have to feel my way round. I can take all the measurements I need with my hands. I know the human form better than most, as I said, I'm a very good tailor. Well, Nelly used to come to me 'bout every month, maybe every two months. She used to always bring a dress that needed altering, a dress that needed to be brought down a size and she wasn't that small to begin with. She told me her sister kept sending her dresses, real expensive dresses, fine material, dresses the sister'd no longer wear. First time she came I really liked her, we did the fitting and I had to measure her with my hands—like I always do. This happened for a couple of months. Nothing out of the ordinary. But then—well, I got good senses, I need them more than most. Anyway, one day, I felt Nelly's body, reacting to my hands. I dismissed it as politely as I could. *Might be medical*, I thought at one stage but then she shuddered and I knew that shudder. I make my wife orgasm all the time. Anyway, I said nothing the first time, didn't want to embarrass her, didn't want to have to say it for myself either. So I let it go but she came back the next month. Same thing happened, right through to her picking up the dress. Me saying nothing, same price, the lot. She came back again the month after, and I said, –Hey Nelly, I think we can do this without you going to the bother of getting measured. I'll just bring it down a size.

And as shy as Nelly was, she insisted I measure her. Her body started to react and I started getting real uncomfortable. Then I stopped the fitting and said, kindly mind, –Nelly, I don't feel too right about this, I'm blind but I can feel what's going on.

And then her body started to shudder all over again. I wasn't touching it now but I felt it next to my face, her blubber shaking, as she sobbed her heart out. She said sorry over and over and over again. I said it was all right over and over again. The two of us there chanting—she holding her face in her hands and me holding a pincushion. She gathered her things together, then herself. I was still on my knees when she left. –I don't have a sister, she said on her way out, I'm an only child. –It's OK, I told her as she walked out the door. Well, the reason I'm telling you all about Nelly is that she came in today for the first time in over two years. Knew her voice the minute she said, –Hello, Jude. Turns out she wants me to make her wedding dress. Lonely Nelly met some guy. I said I'd make her the most beautiful dress she'd ever seen. Way nicer than the ones you get on the Wedding Channel. –I still know your size. –No, you don't, she said and grabbed my hand. Lonely Nelly's gone and lost a fortune of blubber. So I guess I'm telling you all this 'cause I think it should be told, should be passed on—story like that makes us all feel a little better.

He looks at me then for a long time. My eyes are telling him that I'm not the man for carrying stories around. He can't see them but I know he feels them burning into his skin—branding him pathetic. He looks at me long enough to tell me that he's too happy to care and he's got all the energy in the world to tell it again. Laurence rejoices so I leave him there and I get up and walk away. I think about his story knowing that I will never tell it to anybody else and that it will die in my thoughts. I find empathy disturbing. I don't think it's a currency I have ever dealt in. I don't even remember feeling it as a child. I remember need but not empathy. The curious thing is I can sense it. I see it all the time, weaving itself around others' exchanges. I see it and it repulses me. Physically, I have to remove myself from its presence. I think a man should know what suits him. Love does not fit me so I don't wear it. I don't care to change my style. Nelly! Choosing me of all people. He should have told the Doctor. I picture them on the park bench, telling stories, hatching plans ...

I wrench my mind back in and wipe it clean. Savagely scouring away all traces of the Doctor. Forensically forgetting—now forgotten. I breathe deep and push my way back to the office.

I'm always expecting calls but today I'm expecting one in particular. I am ready.

5:2: Telephone Transcript

In Search of Infinite Relief, C.W. Sisle
Contracted to Gleeson Media Group
Subcontracted to Employee 12
Recorded at 4.19 p.m. on 13/04/****

C78 A music outfit left alone on the editor? 9 letters, 'e' as the second last letter so that's the editor. Not much help really. It's Molly.

E12 Ehm—It's not a very good clue, but it's 'abandoned.'

C78 Fuck, I should have got that. Music outfit!

E12 Anyway, tell me things. You always run away too soon.

C78 Ask me a question then.

E12 How's the writing going?

C78 Next question.

E12 No. That question reissued.

C78 Fine then. I just have to get the computer looked at. I'm going to bring it in on my day off. I want to get things set up a certain way first. I'm going to be doing a lot of writing.

E12 You only need a pen and paper to write, Molly.

C78 You sound like Isha. I know what I'm at. I'm getting myself ready.

E12 Fine. How's Isha and the gang?

C78 Isha and I are OK. Anyway, that's not really important. She's got other things on her mind. She told me all about the Boy. Daniel.

E12 I know. You told me.

C78 What?

E12 You were drunk, Molly. You called yesterday morning.

C78 My stomach is turning. What did I say?

E12 You told me all about him, and his mother being a bit of a floater. About him living—or kind of living—with Chivers, about Chivers bringing in all of Daniel's drawings to show Puckie in the bar. You were laughing at that. You told me lots of things. About him being a good runner and Chivers' dogs running after him. Lots.

E12 Did I say anything else?

C78 Like what? What do you think you said?

E12 I don't know. I hate not remembering what I said because I could have said anything. Literally anything. Even things I don't actually believe. It gives me the fear ...

E12 Molly-Mae?

C78 Do you think I sounded jealous?

E12 Are you jealous?

C78 I hope not 'cause that would make me an awful person. I'm a bit too old to be jealous. I should be beyond any of that shit.

E12 You weren't jealous, Molly. Not in a bitchy way. You may have seemed a little hurt though. You said that if you didn't have Isha you wouldn't have anything, or you wouldn't be anything for long because she's the only person who's able for you. You said that it hurt because you thought you'd always been her Molly but maybe that was what you made up in your head and all along she loved Daniel more. He wasn't as much trouble as you are or as you seem to think you are.

(*Caller 78 starts to cry*)

E12 Molly. Molly.

(Caller 78 crying)

E12 OK, so I understated it a bit when I said you seemed a little hurt.

(Caller 78 laughs)

C78 Sorry, sorry. It's just hard to hear you say those things because I thought they'd never find their way out of my head. I told myself that those kind of thoughts were only baby thoughts—not even formed yet. I thought I'd talk my way over them, beyond them. Whatever.

E12 They are fairly sturdy babies. They managed to scramble their way to the top. I think you should think about them.

C78 They're not even worth talking about, Laurence. I know Isha loves me. It's fine. I'm just a little down at the moment and I was drunk. It's my time of the month too, so that never mixes well with drink. I'm all emotional. Forget it. Did I say anything else?

E12 I don't think I should risk it, Molly. I might set you off again.

C78 Go on. I'm half man, remember, and the other half is a fairly tough little lady ... be she menstruating and all.

E12 OK. You said that recently you got the idea into your head that maybe Isha doesn't really like you. You know she loves you, 'cause she has to, you said, 'cause she's your grandmother, but maybe she doesn't really like you. Maybe you seemed to promise so much more as a child. Maybe she's tired and disappointed. Maybe you're not the kind of Molly she wanted, and then you said you're a little embarrassed 'cause you presumed all along that she thought you were wonderful. She always got a great kick out of you, is how you put it. Maybe that was never true. You said that maybe you made that up. You think maybe that's just the truth of it. Maybe everyone knows you're mad except you, maybe they just get a kick out of you. You presume because you think everyone is great that they think you're great. Maybe you're a little delusional. Maybe Molly can't be trusted to make those types of observations, I think is how you put it.

C78 Fuckin' hell. I'm so melodramatic and 'maybe' must have been my word of the day. I don't really think like that. I know what's real and who's real. I do. That was just plain stupidness talking. Did I say anything else?

E12 Yes.

C78 Course I fuckin' did. Go on.

E12 You said that lots of people say really nice things to you. People have said that they get energy from your energy.

C78 Stop. I feel sick that I told you those things. I might as well come clean now and tell you that I've a compliments drawer.

E12 You told me.

C78 It's not a real drawer.

E12 I know. It's a mental drawer. You made that very clear last night.

C78 I'm a mentalist. I actually store away the compliments people give me. How fucking polluted is that? Actually, I may even live off them at times. Dip in and help myself to a compliment that a friend may have given me, or Chivers, or Isha, or even someone drunk at the bar, when we've all been opened up by beer. I keep them in a drawer in my head and take them out for an airing whenever I need one. I even misfile things people have said in the compliments archive. Now that's *really* sad. Someone may say something and it's not even meant as a compliment, like, *I like the way your glasses are stacked to the exact same height*, and I'll say in my head, *Wow, I'm a good glass-stacker*. Into the compliments drawer it goes. I'm so fuckin' needy, it's disgusting.

E12 Can I laugh, Molly? I have to laugh.

C78 Glad you're finding me so hilarious. I'm filing that away as we speak.

E12 What's so bad about having a compliments drawer, Molly? I think it's funny. I want one. I'd prefer Monkey but I'd settle for a drawer.

C78 The point, Laurence, is that I'm a sham. People are paying me compliments I don't deserve. That's why I put the glass-stacking ones in there because when I can't believe some of the 'grander' compliments at least I know that I have a good sense of the symmetric.

E12 I still don't get how you think you're a sham, Molly.

C78 Because … because when I'm up say, or living in my world, I'm full of energy and smiles and laughing and shit. I can allow myself to imagine that this really is Molly and she's good but sometimes I get told that it's all a lie. The lot of it. Sometimes I get the feeling I made it all up because somewhere I know I'm not such a nice person underneath it all. When the Lows come, they tell me what's really in store for me. They tell me I'm fucked, that I'm damaged to the core no matter what other people may think. Life A goes out the window and Life B is full of empty ambitions and dry skin and a constant effort to outrun myself before finally wanting everything to stop. After a bout of the Lows, it's hard to get up and start daydreaming again. Because you think they were right. You think you know too much to ever pretend not to know. And you feel delusional hoping for anything else. You can even get a little embarrassed in front of your own thoughts. And as I get older, even though I'm only a child to you, it gets harder to know what's real.

E12 How do you feel now?

C78 Well, I suppose that's why I'm calling. You might have to do an Isha on it for me. I'm too disgusted and embarrassed to go to her again. Especially now she's sad about Daniel. I think they're just around the corner. They're due. I'm tired and my head is beginning to chatter. That's how I know. And Laurence, it's important you know that I'm not foolishly wanting to be ecstatic every moment of my life. I know there is room for sadness. I've been proper sad but it's wholesome, you know. It purposeful. I'm grieving for someone or something. It's part of the process. I understand that. But the Lows are different because they are riddled with fear. I'm disgusted with myself for not being able to override the fuckers. They empty me so I've nothing to give to people. They make me want to hide. They make me ashamed. And that's when I just want to go to sleep. Does that make sense to you?

E12 What else about the Lows, Molly?

C78 This woman in school made me write things down. You know how they got in those examiners because of the suicide rates? We were the first year of that. I still remember how I wrote it. 'The Lows, by Molly Mae Haebicus'. Take no notice of the writing. This was years ago. The Lows. The Lows are mean and full of cynicism. They're anti-idealistic. They mock your dreams by day and give you nightmares. They make you see things you don't want to see. Everywhere. They follow you round your days, stopping your attention at all the wrongs, all the sorrows, all the indecency, all the unfairness. They open you up to everything and leave you raw. They take away your robustness so that everything hurts. They steal your sense of humour and turn it back in on yourself. They flirt viciously with your happiness and make you distrustful. All the time pulling you away from people, because they're clever—they know you will find an escape route from there. They make you think that nobody could like you if they knew you in this state. But you fight because you remember the taste of happiness, the taste of easy sleep and small joys. And you want to be liked. You want to be good company. But it's exhausting. You're fighting all the time to keep yourself afloat. They manipulate all your thoughts so some days you feel like you've lost it all to them. You lie in bed and try with all your goodwill to coax yourself out of bed. You form all your good thoughts into a spatula and try to scrape yourself free. But you can't form them quick enough and by the time you have freed your head, your legs have re-stuck. Fuck, I can't believe I tried to get away with that egg metaphor.

E12 I was smiling at that. I like it.

C78 The examiner smiled too. Smirked actually. She mustn't have been very good because four people committed suicide the day after she'd been in for the assessment. In a pact. They locked themselves into the trophy cabinets along the main hall and took poison. Everyone saw them the next morning, all pressed against the glass, big cow tongues sweating against their cheeks. Anyway, they're the Lows. I feel better for having talked to you.

E12 Have you talked to Isha about all of this?

C78 Yeah, but I'd say her patience is a little thin. She doesn't get the Lows. She's very even. And she's looked after me

so much in the past. I think I've spent my allowance in that shop already. And she's different these days. She's tired, really tired, as in she's cranky. Sometimes I think she even seems defeated. I'm not blaming her or giving out, I'm just saying I don't want to be hanging off her anymore.

E12 I can imagine she'd want to help any time. I don't think she puts rations on her care.

C78 I know. But I just feel shit about it. I don't know how to help. I thought that when I moved home this time, I'd be better. I wanted her to see me as a young lady even—self-contained and all. There must be a way I can do this on my own.

E12 You and Monkey.

C78 I suppose. Thanks, and sorry I went on there.

E12 You know I don't mind. It's why I'm here in a way. But there are some things I want to say to you before you go. Firstly, I think you're lucky, Molly. I think you're lucky to be so articulate. Some people can't even describe what's going on in their heads. They're left with a head full of powerful feelings they can't even begin to process in any real sense. That's your first weapon, Molly. You are a communicator. You can communicate to yourself and to others. You're lucky too that you have people to communicate with. Good people, good friends. You know that. That's weapon number two. And you're determined. You've still got the will to fight. A lot of people have lost it. And if it's not lost, it's dormant. Anyway, determination is weapon three in our artillery.

C78 Our artillery? Are you taking up the fight with us?

E12 I've already fought for my relief. I'm a contented man, Molly. Can I use a line I stole from yesterday's *Intervention*?

C78 I always end up crying when they agree to go for help. Every fuckin' time.

E12 You'll definitely cry at this then. Listen to the sincerity in my voice.

(Employee 12 clears his throat)

E12 *We've covered a lot of hard ground here today, Molly, and we'll travel further still, together, on another day.*

(Caller 78 laughs)

C78 I'll pack the sandwiches. Thanks, Laurence.

E12 Thank you, Molly.

End of transcript

5:3: Molly

The Village is in uproar. I can't sleep. My nightmares are back except this time something is a little different. I'm fully awake for one, and standing upright in a room that is no longer my own. I'm pissed off because I'm tired and terrified and I want to sleep. There are toxins in me and they have reacted with something to give me this terror. For all the highs of my drinking, this is my return. There is another six hours before daylight and I wonder if I can sit among my fears till then. I'm not sure I can as my heart has been beating too fast, too long, too hard, and I think I might have a heart attack. This becomes a very real concern and overrides the spiders crawling all over walls and the shadowed faces I can see in the mirror. Someway relieved, I walk about the room considering the possibility of a heart attack. I'm sure it wouldn't be fatal. And it would take me out of this room and put me in the care of people who might be able to chase away the two children I can see looking at me through the window.

My stomach drops to know my bedroom is on the second floor.

A heart attack then. Somewhere between the children and me, this becomes a very practical, sturdy idea. It takes me several seconds to register the ridiculousness of it all and I laugh. *Always one for making things twice as complicated as they should be, Molly. Good girl. Maybe you could stop drinking, might be a little easier.*

There are jolting pains coming up from my legs. And I can see the movements of people darting round my peripheral vision. Probably the same people who keep poking me from behind. I try to find a corner of the room where I can keep a watch on everything. But every corner I turn my back to has another corner behind that. So I decide to patrol the room, circling the outskirts. I try to focus on the parts of the wall that remain unspoiled but the imaginings follow my sight so there is no relief. I order the men to clean up the place, tidy my thoughts, wash out the back sheds, but they are unaccountably immobilized. There is no response and I wonder if I can hear their muffled cries for help where barked orders should be found. I leave them to fight their own wars and turn to the now. Sadly, I realise that somebody has even gone to the trouble of etching horror stills to the inside of my eyelids. The unspeakable. Images, all depicting acts of savage cruelty and gleeful violence. I see the face and I know now that the expedition has taken a wrong turn.

I hope with every aching thud that Monkey is not here. He mustn't see this. He mustn't see the mess that I inhabit and exhale. I look out the window again and the children are smiling in at me. My stomach knows why. They are smiling to tell me that they have Monkey. I start to cry because he looks so afraid and I don't know how to tell him how sorry I am. His head is bent and he'll not look up at me. The girl puts her arm around his shoulder and I can see his little body retract and shudder under her fingers. He doesn't like to be touched by strangers. I breathe through hot teeth. I charge towards the window and wrap on it viciously. *Take your hands off him*, I shout through salt-stung tears.

Then I remember that none of it's real except for Isha sleeping

in the room down the hall. I mustn't wake her. She doesn't have to know. Instead, I decide to go into her bed and lie beside her. I have all my hopes running on this. I sneak out onto the landing and into her room, into her feathered eiderdown, into her smell.

–Are you OK? Isha asks.

–Yeah, I say, I'm just having a bad night.

I think Isha has fallen asleep again. I know she has for Isha's sleep is precious—respected, solid, wholesome, deserved. She has full days and full nights. I find comfort in the fact that someday I will find this kind of peace. When I grow up I'm going to sleep like Isha.

I lie beside her quietly until my heartbeat is set off again by the faces I see leering in at me from the darkness. I look over to Isha for comfort. She's propped up on her elbow, staring at me. She does not respond when I whisper her name. She's staring and smirking. I know not to believe this. I know that she's prostrate and asleep. The toxins are just playing up again and I can't believe they have found me here in the safety of Isha's bed. I lose hope. I scramble out of the bed and out into the bright lights of the landing. I try to push through the wall of my chest to hold my heart in my hands. My heartbeat will not stop. Isha appears in the doorway of her bedroom. She's still staring, still smirking. Matron-like. She's wearing my father's hat and my mother's shoes. She holds out a length of cracked and jaded transparent rubber piping. I recognise it as part of her ancient home wine-making kit.

You left this behind in the bed, she says.

I go downstairs and call my friend, Cochlan. She's working overnight at the hospital. She gives me what I want to hear. She gives me a plan and promises to call in an hour. When she does I'm calmer. My heartbeat is back to normal. And all I can see is the faded wallpaper of our living room and the odd darting movement from behind. I close my eyes. The stills have been painted over with a thick layer of relief.

Just as the night winds down I call my friend to say thank you. Then I climb the stairs to my room and lie down. My desk lamp looks ashamed, head hung, turned away from me. I have not the heart to turn it off. So I look at it until my eyes hurt and then think of Isha. I imagine her sleeping in the next room and I want to tell her I understand, that despite all the toxins of myself I can help her. I think about how I can make her hurt less. And then I think about the Boy. I think about finding the Boy but I'm defeated at the first hurdle by my own self-serving vision. So instead I decide to make her a present. A small gesture but something I can do. My past is good for presents.

For-when-my-love-is-all-abrimming-the-paper-I'll-be-trimming-in-a-love-gush-all-aswimming-their-love-I-will-be-winning.

For-when-my-love-is-all-abrimming-the-paper-I'll-be-trimming-in-a-love-gush-all-aswimming-their-love-I-will-be-winning.

The men are chanting. They are trying to keep control. *All the presents in the world*, Matron whispers, but I can't believe her now even if she is right.

Get up, Molly! Get up, they shout. So I do. I get up and I shower—bringing my mind back all the time to the present I will make for her.

For-when-my-love-is-all-abrimming-the-paper-I'll-be-trimming-in-a-love-gush-all-aswimming-theirlove-I-will-be-winning.

Keep your mind on the present, keep your hands on the wheel. Get out into daylight. Throw yourself into the crowds. Walk briskly, inhale. Stop scratching at your hair. Stop twitching. Get out of the shower. Get dresses. No, not dresses, dressed. A flyaway 's' there. Hah! Wear your runners because your jeans are clean. Moisturise because you can, because this time you didn't forget. Good girl. Find the daylight. Leave a note for Isha. Tell her you got up early to go feed the swans. She'll remember the swan story and laugh. Isha will laugh today. Maybe that story is packed away with the perishable goods. I don't need a belt with these jeans. I've put my house keys on the locker. Get them.

I pull my mind in here and won't let it go any further until it has decided to calm down. I call for quiet. I stand in the bright lights of the landing. I refuse to take myself away until my head sees some order. I breathe deeply. Eventually it sees sense and we descend. Several men appear to take up watch. I do not scold them for their gaping absence earlier. Instead, I let them start their day and lock up any stray mad thoughts they find.

I'm up earlier than my appetite so I share the morning with a cigarette instead. I feel better. I take big breaths and set off to find the Paper Maché Man. I wonder if it's too early to call but I think I've understood him correctly as a morning person. The men move in to check my motives but I keep Isha and the present to the forefront.

Ugly motives that want and need.

I clean out my mind, purge the Village of all miscreants that think they know better. I do or the men do. Whichever. The streets are cleaner now.

I pass a set of abandoned sleep cubicles. I remember how Isha tutted when they were introduced by the City Council. There was no more space for hotels, no more space for anything really and most times people just wanted to put their head down for a few hours. So they gave us sleep cubicles. Self-cleaning. Just swipe your card and then crawl in. Thermostat-controlled. So for the small hours of each morning, bedraggled bodies would find themselves crawling into these boxed-off beds and shutting off the City, long enough to take the sting out of their eyes. Most of the cubicles are defunct now, humoured by broken people with bitty lives. I have slept in them once or twice. And then, once, for the wrong reason. I shudder to think of it now. I put my head down to take them out of sight. My skin crawls in recollection and I grow sad that my body has this shitty memory to digest.

I keep walking until I find myself outside his home. There are yesterday's papers left at the door. His is an affordable art but it's not cheap. I've seen his shapes and sculptures. They are truly beautiful. Hours spent smoothing each tiny definition, each curve. But for the doughy paste smeared on his hands, the Paper Maché Man could be working with a material not yet known to this world. I ring his buzzer.

–It's Molly, I tell him when he picks up, I was hoping you could help me make a present for Isha.

–Hey Molly, he says, come up.

–Will I bring up these papers here? I ask.

–If you can manage them, he says, thanks.

I gather them in my arms and mount a staircase that huffs and puffs like an old man with a bad chest. He is waiting for me at the door. I'm nervous that he'll try to kiss me here so I puff myself up like a man-child. He gives me a kiss on the cheek anyway and a small part of me responds, unafraid. He relieves me of the paper and I can see he has a tiny picture of a woman caught in his beard.

–You have a woman hanging out of your beard there, I say. Jocular. Tough. Avuncular even. Defusing the spark that insists on flying.

He walks over to a mirror hung above the fireplace.

–Ah, that's Flambyotti, he says, I've been wondering where she got to. Only cut her out this morning.

I laugh.

–She looks happy enough, I say.

–She does, he says, I might leave her there for a while.

I sit down and take in his home. I've been here before.

Five times—drunk and drinking.

Five times—I have left in the morning.

The room is full of him. I'm relieved by this fact. His home is too cluttered with him for Matron to find her space but Monkey is agile and starts playing up to a sculpture of a donkey. I smile to myself, and then the Paper Maché Man smiles at me.

–I want to make a present for Isha, I say quickly. Declaring my motives, giving us an order of business. He makes me nervous because our chemistry always overpowers everything else. My body talks to his in a frantic language I can't fully understand. There are quieter things I want to tell him but I don't know how to make myself heard over the din of our physical connection. If I like his body, I like him more. He's not afraid of life. But he respects it as he finds it, in every fold of his living.

–Is it her birthday? he asks.

He has never met Isha. I wish he could but I'm not sure what shape I'd have to make in order to bring these points of my life together. I might wrong the shape on its formation—the diagrams are hazy and I was never one for figures. From the corner of my eye, I see a strand of hair sticking out from the side of my head.

–Shush! I say, I'm receiving an order from the high command.

I point to the hair and nod my head in receipt of a transmission.

The Paper Maché Man looks at me funny, and then laughs. I grin and look away a little as he swallows me whole with his eyes. Yes. We are safest when we are laughing.

–I know what it looks like in my head, I say, I could draw it for you. Maybe you could just get me started. I know you've other things to do. But would you mind just …

–Course not, I love presents.

–I know, I say, I remember you telling me before.

We sit down to creating then, he and I. My head slowly unwinds. I tell him about Isha and Daniel, I even tell him a bit about my toxic nightmare.

–You should give up the drink, Molly, he says.

–Maybe, I say.

I don't tell him things he doesn't want to know. Instead, I roll us a joint. I inhale the smoke and savour its taste. My thought-process melts and my mind becomes beautifully fluid. It's the smoke and the creating. Here, in this overlap of relief, I'm happy. I find an open, childish articulacy that helps me make sense of things. And I'm with an open audience. He receives me without complication, without question, without awkwardness. I don't have to watch my words. It's joyous. I send my men out to the frontier, to create and build new thought-structures for me to build on when I next have the time. I tag every structure with a code-name that will serve as a reminder for the days when I can make them whole and give them life on paper.

–I like making things—it's therapeutic, I say, feeling the paste between my fingers.

–Everybody has a creative side, he says. Everybody—across the board, no exceptions.

–Is it just the precious who claim it as their own then? I ask. Thinking of my own claims on writing.

–Yep, people are precious of things that aren't theirs.

He doesn't look for a response because he sees me smiling over at something else in the room. Monkey is up to mischief with one of his sculptures.

–What are you smiling at? he asks.

–Nothing, just thinking about something funny.

–Tell me.

I don't want to tell him about Monkey so I tell him about the Village Lunatic instead.

–He wears nothing but a long coat and big black boots and he plays the fiddle.

–Fuck, Molly, I haven't heard that word used in years.

–I know, Isha still uses it. Every stringed instrument is a fiddle to her. Even a cello.

–I like Isha, he says.

–You've never met her, I say. Almost accusing.

–I like her from all the things you've said about her—remember I did that exclamation rig out for you.

–I remember, I say and I realise that he has always been about somewhere—the Paper Maché Man.

Always I go back to him.

Always I run away again.

–You can meet her whenever you want, I say.

Almost inviting.

–Maybe, he says, tell me more about the Village.

–There's a whole Village up there, I say, tapping my head, and most of the time things are ticking away nicely. We have good fun. I like wandering about up there.

I don't really want to tell him more.

–I'd say beer festivals are a big thing in your parts, he teases.

–Yeah, they are, I say defensively, but we get our work done.

–What happened last night then? Put that in the Village context.

–Never mind that, that was just the drink.

The Paper Maché Man says nothing for a while. Neither do I. We sit creating and humming to ourselves. Nothing is said for an easy eternity.

–Sometimes it's like the bad mad thoughts start rioting in their block and the guards are overrun, I say to the paste, to my hands.

I can feel his eyes roaming my skull, searching out my eyes.

–They get all trampled on and it takes a bit of time for the men to get back up and re-establish order. But they always do.

–The bad thoughts shouldn't be in jail—they should be exiled.

–It's not that easy, I say, they're clever. They'd find their way back. It's better to know where they are.

–You'll figure out something, we all do.

Just no one goes on about it as much as you do, Matron says from the doorway.

And she's right. That's why she's here, to make me bigger, to make me stronger, to fill me with shame so that I will grow out of my notions and into myself. The self that she says she knows. I don't tell him about Matron, because bad-mad women are not attractive to the opposite sex. Beautifully odd women ... maybe.

–Where's Molly in all of this? he asks out of nowhere.

–Well, it's my Village, it's all me. I'm only telling you this because I'm stoned and I feel I can tell you stuff without you thinking I'm mad. Anyway, you're half mad yourself and I'm only ever really a Village when I'm on my own. When I'm with other people I'm in theirs. It's like travelling when I'm in the company of others. Does that make sense? I ask hopefully.

–No, you're scaring me. I think you should go now. I'm going to get my village policeman to escort you to the border. It would be easier if you didn't resist.

I'm laughing. He comes over and playfully pretends to cuff me but I freeze a little because we have no understanding that he can touch me. Not without other people around, not without being drunk. Sober touching makes me nervous and afraid. Maybe not me, but definitely my body. It reacts badly to it. Someday we may wrestle aimlessly but today I don't know him that well. He senses that I'm uncomfortable and lets me go. Playfully. He's not the type of man to be hurt by this. It goes quietly acknowledged as I pick up where we left off and ask him to describe the village in his head.

–To be honest, Molly, I'm not sure too many people could describe their town-planning like you can.

–Yes they could, I say, if they put a bit of thought into it.

He makes me lunch later and I suggest we take out a bottle. The Paper Maché Man thinks I should leave it off for a bit but someone has a plan, although I'm not sure exactly who it is. I'm not sure if it's Molly or the Village Vamp. *Does it matter?* Matron asks. *You're both as bad as each other.*

But the Village Vamp just shakes her petticoats at her and I can afford to laugh. We have two drinks to toast Isha and the circle, two more for health and happiness and then one more for him because I don't feel well.

–Can we go and lie down? I ask. I'm drunk now.

I want him to hold me and let me drift off dreamlessly. Float away from the horrors of last night. My mind is tired now and my body agrees. I want nothing more than to be held. I want to hear his sleeping, the radio crackle and the hum of the afternoon traffic beneath us. But as I'm told afterwards these are the wants of a child and I'm living in the body of a woman.

We go and lie down and I keep laughing gaily to expel the taut urge that is rising quickly between us. The same urge that always finds us when we are together. It crawls under the covers as I do. And it pushes me to him, scrambling over our bodies to make room for the drunken loving. I put us here, in this bed. I did. I know I did. I wanted to be near him, or for him to be near me—I even thought once that he might be the one but I'm cleverer than all that now. None of them are the one and none of them will make everything better. It's stupid and childish and dangerous and hurtful and destructive and desperate and non-productive to think so. We have gone over this one before, the Villagers and I. This is one understanding we have in the bag.

So why are you here? Matron asks from her place in the next room. *You and that Vamp.*

I don't know, I say, *but I don't have to take everything so fucking seriously.*

Well, just so you know that I know, she says.

I can hear her playing with her watch.

So I tell myself what I do know: *He's a good man—he likes me, I like him. This is good.* I hear Matron snort. I turn away from her and call out to the Village Vamp. And somewhere between the hands and the sleep we have sex. The Village Vamp adores it, and her rhythm saturates the afternoon haze in a creamy sweat. When she's finished she skips off and leaves me there on my own and I have to run after her to bring her back. She refuses to come. She's not interested in the holding. *That's your thing, Molly-gal*, she says.

He sleeps and I get up and get dressed. I start to cry for some inexplicable reason and think about sneaking silently away. But someone, somewhere, wants me to stay and I crawl back in beside him and listen to him breathing. I think it was me—Molly. I look around for Monkey but he's not here.

–Why are you dressed? he asks on waking.

–I don't know, I say.

–Come here, he says and reaches over to take me in his arms.

He holds me and makes fun of me. Gently. I'm happy that the holding has arrived. The Village Vamp was right. This is where I find my relief and I reach out drowsily to claim it as my own. I go to sleep, daring to hope that he'll kiss me on the forehead when we wake up, and not on the mouth again. I don't like it when they want my mouth. When we do wake again, he pulls me to him hungrily. I sit on him like I sit on all of them because I'm small and here, perched astride their desires, they can't find my mouth. I look down on him. I don't know if he is greedy and self-serving or a good man, free and living. I don't seem to know much except I liked him when I came here this morning and I like him still. After, I cover my face with my hands and peek out at him through my fingers. He smiles in and finds Molly and she smiles back, unafraid. We have fun then, the Paper Maché Man, the Vamp and I, and it's the nearest I have come to being honest with a man.

The Village Mayor calls for order and I know I have to get up and put myself back into my life.

Don't forget your knickers, Matron says from the end of the bed. She says this to mock me, to make me hurt, to keep me away.

The Village Vamp tells her to leave me alone. *You're just jealous*, she tells her, *because you're old and dry and bitter and our Molly's wet as a tempest.*

Matron says nothing, there's little she can say to a Vamp that will not listen, to a Vamp that's turned her back on her and has started to walk away.

6:1: Mr. ****

There are only three computers between us. The house feels that we would be less productive if we each had one at our desks. They are right although the Doctor's treatise on Trespassing advises regular e-mailing. I go down to the computer room and go online. I find a search engine and type in the Doctor's name. There are several listings: the place where he works, lectures he has given, papers he has published. I print out anything I can find. I'm repulsed he has brought me this far. I take them up to my office and put them in my bottom drawer. I'm not that curious a man. Instead, I rifle through some papers I'd requested from the house archives. There is a lot of groundwork to cover for this stint. Many of my clients have made reference to things that I can't find in the book. I have lost a few of the older clients but this was to be expected. I have recruited new clients who are ours for the future. The house is happy.

I pass the day at work, the calls coming and me, becoming.

Davy comes to my door at the end of day.

–Dennis is working up at the house, he says.

I nod. Davy wants to get to know me. I know this by the way he finds his way to my door. I feel like kicking him, hearing him squeal a little. Instead, I do my best to ignore him, even when he stands before me, wide-eyed and wanting. I decide to give him a look I normally reserve for Freddie. It works and he leaves. I know his type. He'll forget the understanding we've accomplished and he'll stand before me again, eager and puppy-like. When he goes, I get up and leave.

I walk past Kitty's Laundry even though it's out of the way. I look in at her. She looks out at me. Satisfied, I walk on and find myself in front of my house. The Ghost is haunting Cynthia this evening. I go and sit in my chair. The minutes are more full of life than they've ever been. They refuse to die quickly. Instead, they give themselves up to thought and thinking. I don't feel like sitting or going to my restaurant. For some reason, I don't have an appetite for draughts or the Dishwasher. I decide to take a walk and watch people as I go. I will go to work early tomorrow. I look at the disc on the locker beside my bed. I put on my jacket again and leave. I will find a new restaurant for this evening's passing. I walk for an hour then go into the first restaurant I see. A girl accosts me at the door.

–Have you made a reservation, sir? she sugars.

–No.

–There are no free tables at the moment, perhaps you would enjoy a drink at the bar while you're waiting.

I look at the bar. The barman is smiling at me invitingly. There is no one else waiting. He looks like a talker. I grow weary at the mere thought of sidestepping conversation. I turn and walk out. I'm hungry. I decide to go into the bar next door. There is a neon burger sign outside.

–Can I get a burger here? I ask.

–Yeah, the bartender says, take a seat.

He takes out a pen from behind his ear.

–Do you want all the trimmings?

–Yeah, I say, also a glass of water.

He looks at the pen before putting it back behind his ear. It's a gambler's pen. Short, butty, convenient. Everyone gambles on something, I muse as I sidle into a booth. It's dark and no one seems interested. I grow relief.

I watch the barman play an interactive quiz show on the box. He is standing on a stool in order to reach the monitor. I can see the greasy paw-prints his fingers have made. He must have lost the remote. Everything now is interactive. Every surface is home to touch. The Media gave us a voice so we could tell them everything they need to know to subject us.

The barman scores badly and someone from the corner shouts at him to change the channel.

–We're the hecklers paying for the beer!

–I couldn't give a fuck, the barman says over his shoulder to the nine or ten drinkers in the bar. Shout!

He keeps on surfing till someone tells him to stop at CH39. It's porn and the barman sighs and moves on.

–There! shouts another man from the corner of the bar.

It's one of the major news networks. Two presenters sit side by side. They are talking over some footage being played in the background. It shows a man with an unruly beard giving a talk in some university. He is wild-eyed and gesticulating. His whole body speaks of exasperation. I know this man. He is the voice of popular dissent. He is the voice of an angry generation, but here, on this channel, he has no voice. It has been taken by the mocking commentary of the boys in grey wool, sitting proud to the forefront, sniggering, tanned.

–The man is obviously mad, says the suit on the left.

–Look at his hands go, says the one on the right.

These subscribe to only one kind of passion. It's filtered through wealthy conglomerates, flows through the news desk, floods their headsets, flushes out debate. I take my hat off to the Media.

The barman looks around for consent.

–Keep going, someone shouts.

So he does until a lady calls out from the back. He looks around at her and stops.

–Back one, she instructs.

He goes back. It's an old western.

–For fuck sake, another voice calls from the dark, this ain't a museum.

–I like horses, she says.

–I touched a horse once, someone else says, it had scabs.

No one seems too bothered so the barman lets it play. My food appears from the back kitchen. The barman finds some cutlery wrapped in a napkin and motions to the horse-lady in the fur coat to bring it over to me. She slides off her stool and wobbles over to my table.

–Enjoy, she slurs.

She makes a face.

–I ask for a lot of things, four-flusher, but a lot of folk are deaf, she says.

–Can you hear me now? I ask.

–Perhaps if I was listening.

She walks off. The barman is watching so I give him something to watch. I hurl the food at the horse's hind and walk out.

I'm not done with bars yet. I walk for an hour, then walk into an old gin mill I see on the corner.

A wave of laughter hits me by the open door. A man with a dark head and a beard is telling a story. He stands by a table of old men, bent over, all laughing. The dark head laughs too. A high, manic outburst, off beat with the steady howls before him. Nobody notices me come in, nobody except the man with a cloth in his hand. I know his breed. I want to walk out but he is challenging me to stay. I accept and take a stool at the bar. The man with the cloth walks in behind the counter and waits for me to order. I order a whiskey. He chooses on my behalf. He polishes some glasses by steaming them over an old, cracked teapot of boiling water. I know by the way he listens to the dark head telling the story that he has heard it before. He laughs with the others. He waits for the lines that carry all sensibilities to a comic torture. A woman in their midst keeps banging her hand on the table.

–Stop! Stop! Stop! she cries through a laughter that has crippled the room.

I listen to his story. I feel like skewering their hysterical merriment and throwing it on the huge open fire that roars in the corner. I know the man with the cloth is gauging my response but I don't give this one anything to watch. I look at him, expressionless. He wants to come in and get me. He wants me to affirm the good things in this life. He wants to warm me up before sending me out into the City again. I turn away from him. The dark head is talking about some mythical folk hero sitting on the edge of a country, chain-smoking, dipping his feet in the ocean and throwing stones at a man-child king in the country across the water. The barman looks over at the table of bleary-eyed revellers and sighs happily to himself. He asks me if I want another one. I'm about to answer when an old man comes up behind me and puts his hand on my shoulder. Carelessly, as if I was one of them.

–I rode that one senseless, he says. That man has some imagination.

I can feel his hand heavy on my shoulder.

–Here's a new face, he says. He's all gums as he turns to me and grins. I see the barman watching. Something inside me stirs. Tightening, I shake myself free, then get up and walk out, breathing hard, hunted by a look that saw the *something* in me. I clean up, I scour my thoughts, I walk to reclaim myself. I think about calling in to see the Dishwasher but I decide against it. Instead I'm pulled to my chair. I kill half an hour then go to bed.

I find myself in the bar again. I remember the laughing and the smell of the lady's perfume. I remember sitting there, swirling my whiskey and looking at the big barman with the cracked teapot, polishing his glasses. He looks up and catches my eye. He points to the wall behind the bar, just under the box. *What?* I ask, with my eyes. *Look!* he says, with his. He walks over to the wall and viciously punches his elbow through it. When the dust has settled I can see my mother and father looking in at me.

I wake suddenly. I can't believe my sleep has been pillaged again. I get out of bed and run the disc under the tap. I get back into bed. An hour later I get up, put on my shoe and stamp on the disc until it's in pieces and I've broken a sweat. I shower, then get back into bed. I reclaim what is rightfully mine. I sleep.

I will not be bullied. I get up fighting, indignant. I feel like waking the Ghost, playing with her. I open the door of her bedroom. She's sleeping. I listen to her breathing. She looks peaceful, and a resentful anger rises up within me. A bottle of deodorant lies on the floor by her bed. I pick it up and consider spraying her in the face, but I don't want to have to listen to her screaming. So instead I throw it at her as I leave the room. I hear her body rustle as I close the front door.

The streets are awash with people, all breeds, breeding. A man hands me a flyer as I make my way through the Isolation District.

–We can change things, he says, ordinary people like you and me.

I look at him with his soft features and felt hat. The notion that he and I are alike is ridiculous so I tell him so.

–We're all human, he says, unperturbed by my aggression, smiling even.

Repulsed, I keep walking, throwing the flyer into a magazine stand on the corner. I wonder why I stay in this life, surrounded by people I truly despise. But the notion of death seems futile. I stay here in this City to spite life and all that breeds within it. Life is worth tormenting.

Let the people ferment, let me drink them dry.

A woman with a child walks by. She looks at me and I see that she has remembered.

–****! she shouts across the bobbing heads of passing traffic. ****! she cries.

I think about obviously ignoring her. It's what I did for most of the time I knew her anyway.

–****, she says, you haven't changed a bit.

Neither has she, still chubby, still smiling, still trying. She touches my arm, holds me to her.

–This is Gretal, she says, smiling down on the child.

I smile, or maybe Laurence does. The child smiles back. Laurence shuffles about a bit. I shut him down. This is just the type of woman he might respond to. I have nothing to say to her. I never had. But she was always there, skirting along the edge of everything because no one would let her in. She's proud of the child.

She wants me to see that she has come that far, she wants me to see that she's at the epicentre of something.

–What are you doing with yourself these days? she asks.

–I work, I say in a tone that suggests I can't stand her and that I never could.

–That's good. It's always good to work. Gives us something to get up for in the morning. Gives us a routine. Very important.

She stands before me then, smiling, tone deaf, with a weighty silence wedged between us.

–The City's getting bigger, she continues, I never meet anyone I know. Not that I'd be bound to recognise anyone with this mask business. Still, worth it in the long run. My oldest has hers all done up with sequins. Looks quite pretty. Matches her eyes.

I look at her and can't understand why she's still talking.

–Are you married? she asks.

–Yes, I tell her, I have six beautiful children.

I say this hoping my imagined brood has outnumbered her own.

–Good for you, big families are always such fun in the end, as manic as things may get. Ordered chaos, that's what you get with a big family. Your wife is terribly fortunate, what with the statistics in the paper these days.

I put the silence out there again, securing it between us.

–So all is well and happy, that's wonderful. I'm very happy for you. It's good to see one of the old gang getting on.

My stomach heaves to realise that she has filed me in her school memories. That she has plastered my image into some notion of the 'old gang'. I can't understand how she could have done this, how she could be so deluded, but then a certain realisation steps forward to meet me. I was also skirting around the edge of everything; we met so often on the periphery of her perceived notion of popularity. I'm disgusted that she thinks I did not choose this position, royally, for myself. I chose it because I knew more than they ever did. I was never like any of them. I never wanted to be. Everyone was so full of life, in all its desperate forms. They all reeked of a want and a desire to be.

I want to put her straight but she already looks satisfied with the pleasantries exchanged. She's gathering up her limbs to leave and return to the life she's so smitten with.

–Goodbye then, she says, really is nice to know that you've been fortunate enough to become a family man. It's a bad time for family, we need to keep it alive.

She has wrapped us both up in a common-idealed *we*. I feel like slapping her. Instead I take her by the arm. I refuse to look at the child who stands looking up at me. I know I'm hurting her.

–I was never part of the 'old gang', I say calmly, I spent those years laughing at you from my side of the room.

–Well, thank goodness someone spent those years laughing, she says and laughs so hard that her child becomes infected.

–Come on Gretal, she says, wiping the tears from her eyes with the back of her milky hand. Good to meet you again, ****.

She leaves me then. Firing. I have to get to work. I have to get into the office that affords me peace and the quiet knowledge of my genius.

As I push my way through the crowds, I can't get the image of the Doctor out of my head. I can see him before me, talking kindly with the chubby woman as Gretal smiles up at him. Admiring the blind tailor's stitching on Gretal's dress—fresh from Kitty's laundry.

FUCK THEM ALL.

I buy a paper from some random that shoves a wide-one in my face. I have no stomach for Gonzo today.

WAR is promised as usual. They've been stirring up the City for weeks. The Media are rife with stories that suggest it's them or us. Theirs or ours. The truth-mongers have their sources twisted at every turn, but I don't care either way. I *really* don't. That's what keeps me fed while the City starves, malnourished as it is by the vacuous ideals the Media inflates, one burst bubble replaced by the next.

I make for my office. A face I do not recognise stands by the front door, talking with Fathead. He looks at me intently as I pass. I return the favour, unafraid.

–That's him, Fathead says in a voice so fat it spills over into earshot.

I look back and the man by the door is smiling at me. I roar. Anyone but the Doctor.

6:2: Telephone Transcript

In Search of Infinite Relief, C.W. Sisle
Contracted to Gleeson Media Group
Subcontracted to Employee 12
Recorded at 5.43 p.m. on 17/04/****

C78 The note is after a murderous embrace with tea. 7 letters, t/u/g as first, third and fifth.

E12 Hi Molly! It's hard when you just call them out of nowhere. I have to see them written down. Leave it with me though. I'll be thinking about it as you're going on and on about yourself.

(Caller 78 laughs)

C78 OK then. Tell me what you did today. Let's test your lines out.

E12 Got up.

C78 When?

E12 At sunrise.

C78 Course you did. Then what? An hour of exercise on the roof?

E12 No. I read the papers on the roof.

C78 Are you kidding?

E12 No. I like the fresh air.

C78 There's no fresh air in this City.

E12 To pilfer one of your phrases, there is in my world.

C78 Nice one. Go on.

E12 Then I'd breakfast and went down to—

C78 Don't tell me. Dreyton's.

E12 Yes. And had a coffee and talked with whoever was about. Then I went home and worked on my music till lunch.

C78 Come out with anything good?

E12 I think so. Something broke through anyway so I can pick it up there tomorrow.

C78 Wouldn't you just have finished it off when you were there?

E12 It was more of a small breakthrough rather than a rush. They don't come every day. The breakthroughs do though, mostly. I just have to keep working on it.

C78 Are you trying to make a point about my writing?

E12 No. Hey, this is my time, Miss Molly!

(*Caller 78 laughs*)

C78 I'm very bad. Sorry. Go on.

E12 Then after lunch I went down to the centre to work on some details for this concert we're organising, came home and now I have the good fortune to be talking with your good self.

C78 I was going to say that I'd go to the concert but ... Anyway. What are we talking about today?

E12 You tell me. How's Isha and the gang?

C78 OK. I've been working a lot recently. And Isha's been doing her own thing. But she's fine. I'm making her a present. It's impractical but I think she'll like it, or more that she'll appreciate it—appreciate what I'm trying to say.

E12 What are you trying to say?

C78 You know that I'm sorry about everything that happened with Daniel, I'm sorry he's gone and she's sad and Chivers and Puckie are too. It's for all of them really. But it's for her really. She's not too gone on raw emotion. But she has her own way. We have our own way. This is it. There's a lot of things we don't have to say.

E12 What did you make her?

C78 It's kind of like a statue of all of them. It's made out of paper maché. I know this guy who makes these amazing sculptures from it. You wouldn't even know it was paper.

E12 Does he sell them?

C78 Sometimes. He works with computers. That's how he makes his money. He works from home. I don't actually know what he does exactly. He's a good man though. I've known him a couple of years. He made me a fancy dress outfit once. It was funny.

E12 What did you go as?

C78 I slept with him.

E12 OK.

C78 Not just the last day—a couple of times.

E12 This is good?

C78 I don't know.

E12 Does it feel good?

C78 At the time?

E12 No. Do you feel good about it now?

C78 I don't know.

E12 Would you sleep with him again?

C78 I don't know.

(*3 seconds' silence*)

C78 Probably. If I was drunk.

E12 Molly …

C78 You asked, Laurence.

E12 Well then, would you sleep with him sober?

C78 Probably not. I'd like to though. I think.

E12 Drink muddles everything up, Molly. Especially emotions.

C78 Muddles … that's a loopy little word, Laurence. Muddles. I think I'm muddled up.

E12 I'll muddle you up if you don't talk straight with me.

C78 I get nervous when I'm sober.

E12 Like how?

C78 Like my body goes rigid and I yawn all the time. Like I can't get enough air.

E12 That's your body trying to get more oxygen. Have you ever had sober sex, Molly?

C78 Nope.

E12 Do you enjoy sex, Molly? As you've experienced it?

C78 Yeah, I suppose. I think so. It's a feeling other than nothing, you know. It's a very definite something. And I do like a good spooning after.

E12 You don't have to sleep with someone to get spooned, Molly. You do know that, I take it?

C78 Yeah. Yeah. I know. I think …

(*4 seconds' silence*)

E12 Go on, Molly.

C78 I think sex is easier.

E12 Easier than what?

C78 Than kissing. I find that difficult.

E12 Like how?

C78 I find it very … intrusive. And I suspect that's not the way it should be.

E12 Maybe kissing is more intimate than sex … as it's sold today anyway.

C78 Intimate. Intimacy. Yeah. I find that hard. Anyway, that was me yesterday, ridin' away …

E12 Molly! About the whole getting nervous thing. Is it the pleasant butterfly sensation? The whole feeling of sweet anticipation?

C78 No, Laurence. My body just isn't into it.

E12 Maybe your body knows more than your head does so.

C78 Even with good men, Laurence? With men I really like?

E12 Still—maybe your body's trying to tell you that it doesn't really know them. Maybe it would like a bit more time to get comfortable with them. Maybe you shouldn't rush into bed with anyone.

C78 I'm not rushing at everything that moves, Laurence.

E12 I didn't say that.

C78 But if I did wait then they'd become my friends and I could never see them in the other way.

E12 Now that makes no sense to me.

C78 Doesn't it?

E12 I'm archaic, Molly. For me sex, on its own, is part of our animal instinct. Romantic sex, or loving sex, or whatever you want to call it, is an expression of something that transcends our basic animal urges.

C78 Fuck, you are archaic.

E12 I think demoting sex to a purely physical act is naïve. Sex is a very powerful force. That's undeniable. We can't act on it every time we have a chemical reaction with someone. Imagine, we'd be taking each other in the streets, over the desk, on the bus. No. I don't believe we should feed our sexual desires every time we get the urge. We have to treat the exchange with a little more respect than that. When we were monkeys—

C78 If we were monkeys …

E12 Absolutely, Molly. All of this here is just my opinion. Everything I say is open to being stripped down. You know that though. I don't want to have to keep qualifying the status of everything I say.

C78 Whoa. Sore spot! Go on. I believe in evolution too.

E12 What was I saying?

C78 When we were monkeys …

E12 When we were monkeys, even way back then, we picked a life partner. But before that even, when we were still travelling on all fours and living in trees, a male monkey—

C78 Sorry now. Last interruption. Can we go with ape, just 'cause of Monkey and all.

E12 Right. The male ape could come up behind a female, with his urge, and give it to her and she wouldn't bat an eyelid. She'd just wander off, eat a banana.

C78 Smoke a cigarette …

E12 Seriously, Molly. Happened. This all makes perfect sense. So because all evolution is designed to ensure the future of a species, mankind included, the sexual act had to evolve.

C78 Huh?

E12 So she wouldn't bat an eyelid, right, but she'd get pregnant. Even the apes understood that they wouldn't survive if there were unclaimed babies all over the place so we evolved and sex became a more intimate affair. It was in the interest of the species. As we evolved the sexual act evolved too. We developed more erogenous zones, eye contact began to play a more integral role in the exchange, we developed acts of foreplay. In short, it evolved into an emotional as well as a physical act. We, the apes, picked life partners, set up camps, divided out the child-raring duties, in order to establish the most efficient, most reliable means of securing our survival. So all I'm saying is that we should spend a bit more time sniffing about potential mating partners and understand sex as a very profound, very emotional expression of a special relationship. Does that make sense?

C78 I'm speechless. You're priceless. You're fuckin' priceless.

E12 I do love my bit of evolution.

C78 Where does homosexuality fit into the equation?

E12 Personally, I think it's nature's way of curbing birth rates. I think homosexuality has a very special place in the evolution of mankind. I don't think the forces of evolution make mistakes. I think man does. I think it's a mistake to sell sex the way they do today—as a purely physical act with no potential emotional repercussions.

C78 Or the way they use it to sell stuff.

E12 I saw an ad the other day using sex to sell fertilizer.

C78 I saw one the other day using it to sell insulation slates.

E12 Yeah?

C78 Yeah, your house will be so warm you can take your clothes off and romp around the place naked. What was the slant on the fertilizer?

E12 Fields, fertility, virility. Anyway, getting back to you and your ape.

C78 As opposed to me and my Monkey.

E12 Yes. You and this Paper Maché Man.

C78 Maybe we could just paper maché our offspring instead of ever having sex. We could just maché them up with extra layers every year.

E12 They'd have trees for cousins.

(Caller 78 laughs)

E12 Seriously. You should do something constructive with him next time—something that doesn't involve drink. Go to the cinema or something.

C78 What if the film has sex in it?

(Caller 78 laughs)

E12 Go see a cartoon then.

C78 I was kidding. My history teacher told us a man would stick his dick in a keyhole if he could. Her words, not mine.

E12 She's not far wrong. We're simple creatures. But we're not all dick, you know. We've been known to have emotions.

C78 Can't believe you said dick!

E12 Maturity levels.

C78 I know. Staggering. So you reckon sex is a gift from the source eh?

E12 So you have read the book!

C78 Nah, it's just one of the buzzwords I picked up on a flick through.

E12 At least you're flicking through it. Better than using it to make offspring.

C78 It's an instinct, isn't it? Sex?

E12 Yep. Same as love or hate. Like a note on a piano. Neither right nor wrong in itself but can be played at a right or wrong time. Depends on the music.

C78 I got up and cried, Laurence—after the sex when he was asleep. I wept, for want of a better word and in keeping with my taste for the dramatics. If you asked me why, I couldn't tell you. I wanted to be with him.

E12 That'll be the emotional repercussions … and the drink. Maybe it just wasn't the right time for you.

C78 Sometimes I don't think it's Molly who's actually having the sex.

E12 OK …

C78 I mean, obviously it's me but I act like some vamp who, in turn, acts like she thinks she should act but sometimes she lets her guard down and lets Molly in. It's all bullshit really. Sometimes I think the only way to Bedroom Molly is through the drink. It's the only way I seem to be able to let go enough to come up with the desire.

E12 You're not a lesbian, Molly?

C78 No. If it were that simple, I'd just become a lesbian. Bring up the headcount a little.

E12 'Where have all the lesbians gone?' It's like a musical.

(*Caller 78 laughs*)

C78 I feel better for having spoken to you. It's so good to get things out. Otherwise they just play chasing in your head and then start inviting every fuckin' odd thought to join in until you have a mad orgy of stupid fuckin' notions having a laugh at your expense.

(*Employee 12 laughs*)

E12 Yeah. It's good to talk.

C78 Sometimes I wonder about all this self-exploration shit though. There's a lot to be said for just getting on with things.

E12 I don't think it's any wonder you're confused about stuff. You were born into the Media age—everyone is always trying to sell you something, but no one can sell you the things that'll help you find completion. No one can give them to you either. They have to come from you. So it's all bullshit. All the selling, all the products, all the crap they come up with. Hunt down alternative knowledge, Molly. Fill your head and heart with constructive thoughts and follow through.

C78 I was in a hypermarket the other day and they were selling apples—skinned, cored, sliced and vacuum-packed—for some outlandish price.

E12 This is what you're up against.

C78 Bottle of cop-on a day.

E12 That's it, Molly. Nothing like a bottle of cop-on.

C78 Wait till you see—they'll put that on the shelves next.

E12 Wedged between liquid-happiness and friendship-tonic.

C78 Funny man. What do you talk about with all your other 'friends'? I'm using some smart finger work there. Do they all talk about themselves as much as I do?

E12 Sometimes, especially in the beginning.

C78 Then do you talk about that stuff in the book?

E12 Sometimes.

C78 Will you explain it to me? Tell me about the Wanting.

E12 It's man's innate desire to satisfy the wants of 'I'. It leaves us in a constant state of wanting. It can be dangerous. Especially when we start wanting more.

C78 Why, exactly? Surely it's the thing that keeps us all ticking?

E12 Like a time bomb.

C78 Are you saying all wanting is bad? What if I only want good things?

E12 It's the state of wanting. It's hard to be content if you want for something. Malcontent is corrosive.

C78 I think it's healthy to want things. Makes you motivated.

E12 I know. I understand that. I'm talking about wanting on behalf of something else. Lessening the want inspired from the 'I'. If we see everything from one big 'I', we will live in fear and wanting. It's how nature made us. We are always afraid for the 'I', we are always wanting for it.

C78 What?

E12 It takes a while to explain.

C78 I don't mind. Tell me. What if someone wants to be happy? Is that so bad?

E12 Course not. But we have to stop conditioning it for the 'I'. Some people's quest for happiness means they're constantly being chased from behind. Followed by the *if*s and the *when*s. All sorts of measurements and factors condition

their happiness. Most of us spend our entire lives wanting, actively wanting on behalf of the 'I'. But the 'I' by nature is near impossible to satisfy, so we're most likely going to spend all our conscious years in a state of wanting, a state undercut by a feeling that we're never quite satisfied for long. Never quite complete.

C78 I know that feeling.

E12 Everyone does. The question is how do we stop the Wanting?

C78 Tell me. Will it take long?

E12 I will but you have to know it's only what I believe. All I ask is that you listen with the ears of a friend.

C78 OK, you want to tell me now?

E12 I've a lot to say. I'd rather it was said over a string of calls.

C78 That's a good ploy, Laurence. You boys know what you're doing.

E12 Molly, I thought you said you were going to do an Augusta on this. I need you to have a little faith. Not blind faith, that'll come, but not from me.

C78 I'll call you tomorrow?

E12 Whenever you can. Bye, Molly.

C78 Thanks, Laurence.

End of transcript

6:3: Molly

I really want to see Puckie. He's not here but his troupe of regulars are so I sit among them and give myself to a few drinks and a generous wit that finally grows into conversation. These are good men. Always welcomed by Puckie and they, in turn, recklessly extend this welcome to others. They are open and agendaless. They have learned to sit back and take on time. The Dill asks me how I like being young.

–I could only tell you over a lifetime, I say.

–What could you tell me over a drink? My grandson seems to have forgotten how to speak.

–Well, it's like anything, some days I love it, some days I don't. To be honest, sometimes I can't see how things add up fairly. I find it hard to believe that this is it. And that's what people say, they say that this is just the way things are.

–Well that's one philosophy, he says. It's the cynical point of view.

–It's easy to feel stupid then, if you're not a cynic, I say.

–What would you change, if you could change things?

–Fuck, I don't know, Dill, the obvious things. Things can't be

that complicated—people tell you they are, but they can't be. This is just the way things are, people say, but things aren't just at all.

–Man complicates everything—it's in his nature.

–I can understand that all right, I say heavily.

–And women ... he arches his eyebrows playfully in my direction. I laugh.

–You can write that one up, I say.

–I wish I'd known what to fight for when I was your age.

–What did you do when you were my age?

–Drank, he says, danced, cavorted, worked, loved, lived.

–You've had a good life, haven't you?

–Yeah, no, it was grand, he says.

The Dill is silent for a bit, then he tips his ash and says 'grand' with a conviction that belies his demeanour. Then he turns to me almost violently. There's a hunger, an eagerness about him.

–I just can't help wishing I did all that and a little bit more, he says. I wish I'd caused a little bit more trouble instead of just being complacent. I'm angrier now at seventy-two than I was at twenty-seven. I'm an old man in a rage and to be honest I don't know if I'm more angry at the state of things or at myself. I see those politicians working it, Molly, I see them working the system and the rhetoric and the charm and the paperwork and I feel like giving them a run for their money. I feel like causing trouble. I feel like going in there and having absolutely nothing to lose, I feel like going in there with no—and I mean absolutely no—motives, except to get a few things done. I don't want a fucking career, I'm seventy-two. But then I think, maybe the system is as frustrating to work with as it is to watch. Maybe you just have to work the system. I don't know, Molly. There's a lot to be said for stirring things up a little. Bertrich was caught making deals behind the curtain and then we re-elected him again. How the fuck does that happen? It's like the whole City is in an abusive relationship with the political system. We do it to ourselves. We're all too fucking busy looking after ourselves, me included.

–I didn't vote, I say quietly.

–Why not?

–I don't like politics, it's way over my head. I never even read the papers. I mean to, but I ... I suppose I'm just into other stuff.

–I didn't vote either, he whispers.

–Why not?

–I was in here drinking, looking after the thirst. If I'd timed the day right, I could have voted and still have been here for opening. I didn't march either. Too fuckin' complacent.

–I didn't either. Too fuckin' self-obsessed.

–Assholes. The pair of us.

–Next time, I say, we'll both go to vote. I'll meet you here and we'll roll up together.

–OK, Molly. Done deal. But it's this situation with Vileous, it's given me the rage. And the thing is, I'm not too sure a vote makes that much of a difference anymore anyway. We saw the polls. Maybe this is the return on complacency, maybe they took all the power when we weren't looking.

–A friend of mine says they gave us pocket money and sent us out shopping for new lifestyles—he says that's when they swooped in and took our minds, but I don't even know what that means really. Sometimes it takes all the effort to get yourself set up first.

–Well, some people grow up in battle, he says.

–What exactly should I be fighting for?

–Others, the Dill says.

–How?

–You're the one with the imagination, Molly. I don't know. We've never had so much information though. That web ... If I were you, Molly, I'd use all the new technology to foster a global dialogue between peoples.

—Listen to you.

—I know. I've been ranting a lot in my head recently. Giving myself lots of mock interviews. I'm all about the dialogue and the fostering these days. Anyway, I think I'd try and give people without a voice, a voice. I read somewhere that the greatest fear of an abused and abandoned people is not torture or displacement or humiliation or any of that shit. People can adapt and survive the worst conditions. No, apparently the greatest fear they live with is that no one will believe them. There's a name for it. Victim's Gap, I think.

—There's a name for everything.

—We've never had so much language to describe our feelings. Never. This is the age of the self-aware. Everyone is starting their sentences with I.

—The internal.

—I'd head for the external if I were you, Molly. I think I'd fight and give my voice to others instead of screaming to be heard here amidst the clash of the 'MeMeMe'.

—You just started your sentence with I.

—You see, the Dill throws his hands up in exasperation. I'm seventy-two. Far too old to outrun myself. My mind is getting a little crumbly. Get to the young, Molly, that's where the change will happen.

Puckie's head appears at our table and deflects my response.

—Well, he says smiling at his troupe.

—Well, the troupe say. All winking and nodding.

—Do you want to get some food? I ask Puckie.

—Yeah, he says, we're quiet here.

He goes to get his jacket and speak with the barman on duty. He finds ten empty glasses on his way and brings them home. I gather my affairs for the second time that day and promise the Dill I'll fight.

—Good girl, you can put what's left of mine with your own.

We go to walk out.

–She's a good girl, Puckie, the Dill shouts after us.

–Nothing but trouble, I say, hitting Puckie hard on his mammoth shoulder, smiling back at my gummy comrade.

We go to a cheap restaurant that has old comic books in the toilet. Puckie appreciates this small gesture to home comforts. And the food is fair for the price. It has no pretensions. It has no box. I sidle into my seat.

–How are you? I ask. And how was your trip?

–Fine. I was only away for a couple of days. What have you been up to?

–I've never seen you cry before, I say. Sorry I froze.

I mean this but Puckie and I have never been two for uncomfortable sentiment so I quickly reach for a humour that will poke fun at both of us.

–I could give you a hug now if you want, I say. I have one put away especially for you.

Puckie throws his eyes skywards.

–It's got your little name on it, I tease in lollipop tones.

I rise, with budding hug in arms.

–No, you're OK, he says, hold on to it.

–Are you sure? I say, 'cause it's all here ready to go.

I shimmy some, cheese-like.

–Seriously, he says, keep it.

So I sit down and smile at him for the minute that parades before us.

–Where are you coming from anyway? Puckie asks, not to break the silence but in respect for it.

–Did I ever tell you 'bout the Paper Maché Man?

–No. I'd have remembered, he says. Dryly. Wryly.

–He makes these sculptures from stone, I say.

–Then why the fuck is he called—

–I'm taking the piss. He makes these sculptures from ... paper maché. They're incredible, Puckie. You should see them. He spends hours moulding each curve. Days even.

Puckie arches his eyebrows, but I keep talking, trying not to give his cynicism time to breed.

–Anyway they're amazing. One time he was walking home from wherever and he sees this little girl stopped in the middle of the street. She's all wide-eyed and excited because she can see this bird unravelling a homeless man's hat. But the mother just keeps on walking, pulling her along and screaming at her to shut up. So my friend follows them home to find out where she lives, then goes home and makes a huge replica of the bird and the homeless guy. Then he drags it down to the girl's apartment block, rings the bell. This is about two weeks later. He rings the bell and hides just to make sure the girl sees it. He's pretty sure that her parents won't appreciate it cluttering up the place. In fact, he knows that they'll probably just get rid of it but it's important to him that the little girl knows that someone or something remembers or saw or understood. Isn't that an incredible thing to do or even want to do? I ask. Looking to Puckie for his approval.

–He must have very little to be doing with his time, Puckie says. He could have spent those two weeks volunteering at a homeless shelter.

I know that it's not as harsh an observation as it sounds; Puckie's artistry lies in hard work and a near perfect eye for detail. Both men have that much in common.

–What were you doing then? he goes on. Helping him with one of these things?

–No, he was helping me make a present for Isha.

I find a pen amidst the fluff that gathers in the underbelly of my bag. I draw a picture on a coffee-stained napkin that I flatten furiously with my palm. He watches me, and the waitress, until I have finished.

–It's not the best drawing, I say, but that's the Boy, Daniel.

–And what's that?

–That's meant to represent you, Isha, Chivers—the circle that's been broken.

–Where's our other lady?

–What other lady? I ask. Confused.

–What did Isha tell you, Molly? he asks.

–She told me ... oh, you mean his mother, the nurse's outfit.

–No, he says, tell me what Isha told you.

So I tell him. For a second I think back. Is it possible I have forgotten a chunk of the story? My mind could have slipped away for a bit but somehow I can't believe it did.

–There was another lady, Puckie says when I finish, as much a part of this circle as anyone, if it's a circle at all. I hate putting shapes on things.

Then an incredulity puts its hand up and halts the traffic of Puckie's thoughts.

–I can't believe you don't remember her, Molly. You must have met her, maybe even only once because you weren't around as much then.

–Because I'm a self-absorbed nutter, I say, and never managed to make the time.

–Shut up, Molly, he says kindly.

Then stops. I'm searching my memory furiously but it's all fluids that won't stand still long enough for me to remember all that much about anything. It evaporates and reforms. In the end, all my memories are what I have made them. And others are dead weights I'd rather forget.

–You did, Puckie says nodding his head, you did. You met her in Chivers' house. She was there when you and Isha called in to collect a painting for that charity art auction Serge organised. She was wearing a yellow dress.

It comes to me vaguely and I catch a glimpse of this memory before it sidles away.

–Big hair.

–Yes! says Puckie. Happy his frustrations have ended here.

–Everyone remembers the hair—the Dill used to call her the Big Wig.

He stops again. Puckie is swimming in his memories but I don't jump in because he's not drowning, he's taking his time.

–She lived a couple of doors down from my old place, she adored Daniel and he adored her. They had great old banter between them. And she wasn't particularly maternal, not in the normal sense anyway. She never fussed over him like Chivers did. Now he was maternal—he used to wear this little pinny when he was making his dinners. It even had a fucking pocket on it, with a rainbow or something.

Puckie shakes his head, laughing at the memory.

–No, he says, she was his friend. They had some understanding.

–Who? Her and Chivers?

–Yeah, but I meant her and Daniel.

–Was she married? I ask for reasons beyond me.

–No, he says. Surprised at the question, taking a huge bite out of his sandwich.

–I proposed to her though, several times.

He says this with his mouth full. I feel like I've been slapped. I can't believe Puckie proposed to someone. He laughs again but now he is laughing at himself. I feel for him. A sadness that has crawled up into his eyes looks back at me now. I really never thought Puckie would propose to anyone. I don't know why.

–She used to accuse me of trying to save her from herself, said she liked her life the way it was.

I think of Isha.

Puckie stops and I say nothing. I don't know what to say, I don't have a grasp on where this will go and I'm a little afraid.

–Chivers used to say she was more creature than woman, he says, and it kind of made sense. She was out on her own. Did what she wanted but she only ever seemed to want to do ... nice things. I can't believe I just said that. That's Chivers taking over my body again. I'll kill him the next time I see him. He's turning me into a fucking woman. Slowly and surely.

–I'll tell you one thing, Molly, that always struck me. She and Chivers could spend hours talking about all their fancy arty shit and whatever else but I could spend hours just watching her be her.

Puckie stops again and looks over at the waitress. I look over to her and to him.

–She was everything to everyone without being false to herself. She understood everyone. She made people she met happy. That's simply what it boiled down to, but ...

Puckie stops again. His conversation is full of corners and edges. It jumps. He looks helplessly to me for some kind of wordless understanding. I can do nothing but return his look. Unaltered. Helpless still.

–Well ... she was a whore for all intents and purposes, he says.

He spits out the words, then retracts from his own anger. –I'm sorry, he says.

As if to her.

–I'm sorry, he says again, his head lolling shamefully.

–She just ... she just ... she could have chosen a different life. That's what makes me angry. She could have done anything.

–Did she work in the District? I ask although, again, I don't know why I need to know this.

–No ... no ... no ... Puckie says, that wasn't her style. Everything she did was ... even her whoring. She had clients. They came to her house. Roughly the same five men. Decent enough men if you had to put a name on them. She was their escape. Lonely middle-aged men who found themselves in a life or a marriage they didn't want to be in. She probably gave them books to read, talked to them about their kids ... oh, I don't know. I was never there. And never on the weekends, just five evenings a week. Then she'd come round to me and chat over the bar until everyone had gone. She'd help me clean up and we'd sit down for our quiet drink. Just the two of us, and Chivers, if Daniel was at his mother's. We never really talked about it because she knew how I felt. She'd talk to Chivers though. He seemed to accept it or at least understand it. I couldn't. It made me queasy.

–Did she have any one special man? I ask. Like a boyfriend?

–No, Puckie says—tonguing his teeth, she seemed to have no real interest in men outside of it all. I don't think the tidiness of it all excuses anything. In my mind, she sold herself for money and I can't forget that even if she did make them happy and understand them as men or as fathers or whatever it is that Chivers goes on about. It made me angry.

I'm entranced by Puckie's ramblings. I've never seen him so exposed.

–I'm not being possessive of her or anything, he says, pushing his plate away. I just don't think it's right. Especially when you choose to do it. Makes a mockery of all those poor girls who have to do it or think they have to. I don't care what anyone says, it's not an easy life. Not really, not after everything's said and done. And there's a lot done that can never be undone. Your granny didn't like it either.

I realise that this may be Puckie's first time saying any of this aloud to someone that wasn't there. All these feelings must have peppered his existence since. I feel an overwhelming closeness to him. I'm thankful to my world.

–Where is she now? I ask. Knowing that she's gone.

–I don't know, he says, she took off even before Daniel was taken away. Left her house as it was. Just left.

–Taken away? I thought he went missing. I think I thought he ran away.

–No. It's a long story.

I was going to say, *Ain't they always the ones worth telling?* because I'd heard a man at a bar counter say it once. I thought it was a solid prompt. But not now. Puckie looks tired and this is not my drama. This is not the time for tailored one-liners. This is real.

–You can tell me again, I say, it's getting late.

Puckie nods gratefully.

–I have to go finish a story in one of those comics I stashed behind the toilet, he says. Half smiling at me, half at the floor.

I sit and take in the other customers. There are round children with bulldog faces being scolded by parents that have given up listening for the sound of their own voices. Opposite, a group of boys belch bravado to impress a table of giddy girls. Nervous, self-conscious behind the smoky haze of false confidences, I watch their darting eyes, surveying the eyes upon them, fox-like between each exchange.

I realise that I'm tired too. Puckie comes back, having settled the bill. He laughs aside my insistence to pay at least half. He is recklessly generous and sometimes it's decent not to fight him on this score.

We walk back to the bar together. Puckie brings out the man in me and I pump up my chest as I walk beside him. I tell him this and he pushes me off the kerb. I run after him, charging into his mammoth back. I bounce off him and together we take in the City.

We walk and watch the advertisements on the outdoor monitors.

There is an ad for a Regression Clinic. It shows men and women, nappied and talced, playing happily in a sand pit. They are smiling inanely. A compassionate voice coos an invitation to relive our infant years and emotions in a loving and open environment.

–Where the fuck are things going? he says. Sadly.

I decide not to tell him about an article I'd seen the last day where mothers photographed their babies dressed up as various celebrities. There is just something wrong with a thirteen-month-old in a sequined dress and heels. Puckie is too weary tonight. We get to his place. Last drinks are being served within and I imagine the sense of completion his troupe will feel when Puckie returns. I try to say goodbye but Puckie finds his words first.

–Come in, he says, I want to tell you what happened. You can ring Isha from the back room.

–I don't need to know tonight. Don't worry, I won't go upsetting Isha with questions when I get home.

–I know—I want to tell you.

I nod. All puffed up and manly. Understanding.

Then he says with a girly lisp, –We'll make some coco and pretend we're sisters.

I laugh so hard that I lean on the window ledge and cackle into a puddle. I laugh for so long that Puckie leaves me there. Watery-eyed, I grope my way into the bar. I like the way my laugh interrupts everything. I'm glad I've stopped apologising for it. The Dill says you should grab every laugh you can and ride it senseless.

I call Isha and tell her I'm with Puckie. She makes me promise to get a fare home.

I have a last drink with Puckie's troupe, then one more with Puckie himself.

–You know the Barman of the Year competitions we used to have here, he says.

I remember them not because I was ever at one but because I

have watched the discs. They are something else. I brought copies down to the Clap and the others. We watch them after work. The two men doing the commentary are priceless. Puckie had the whole thing worked out. At one time there was serious money to be won. But it was never about the money. It was about the craft.

Puckie thinks good bartending is an art form. He's right. He used to set small traps behind the bar. Tiny things like lipsticked glasses and empty soda bottles. The contestants had to be all-rounders. Even things like their banter and general knowledge was tested. Puckie thinks that all barmen should be intelligent conversationalists. They had to read the papers, watch the news, know odd facts. He chaired a panel that watched each contestant— clipboards, note-taking, the lot.

There was a round called Sunday Afternoon. Locals were roped into acting as customers. One guy specialised as the Asshole. And Puckie and the panel watched as the contestants tried to deal with him. It's very funny to watch, especially listening to the commentary. It was a real night out for the regulars at Puckie's place. They were hustled together and went in as The Crowd for the Saturday Night Round. You can see them on the disc, Puckie keeping them in check until it's time to charge the bar. Puckie would nod at the contestant. He'd nod back. Fearfully sometimes. Then Puckie would give the nod to his boys and they'd all go in shouting orders all over the place. Jostling each other at the counter.

I remember the barman who won it one year. He stood back and ignored them all. He just stood there smiling, surveying the ruddy crowd before him. Then he walked deliberately to a tiny quiet man who'd been pushed to the end of the counter and asked him politely what he wanted. The crowd stopped shouting and the barman took their orders, calmly, methodically, quickly. Puckie loved it but he was a controversial winner. As one of the commentators said, –In a sport that's all about speed and getting the drink out there, this runner is an unlikely champion.

I wonder now if this is the fireman that Puckie called on that night. I ask him this and Puckie smiles.

–You've got to know the people to invest in, he says, I'm not talking about money either. Always work in the currency of people, Molly. It always pays off in the long run.

I love his analogies. I rejoice in the articulacy of others. I get one of my men to prod Scribe, make sure he's awake and taking notes.

–Anyway, says Puckie, we had the competition that night—I asked Chivers to help out. You know Chivers. He never brought Daniel to the bar. He was a good mother. So we agreed that Daniel was to come down here and sleep on the couch upstairs in my place till Chivers could bring him home. Julia was to come round after. It was a Friday night.

Puckie tells me the long story I'd asked for. He revisits it himself and is reminded of all the small things that make up this life, some of them near forgotten, now unearthed and dusted off.

It leaves us both heavy-hearted and sad.

Isha is asleep when I get home. I'm fit for crying, for anger, for want, for fear. All of them have me as they choose. My lamp looks on ashamed. On my pillow, I see Puckie's sad smile.

–In ways, he had said, you remind me of her.

Tonight I'm not scared of spiders or children. I'm scared of myself, of the girl Matron says she knows.

7:1:Mr. ****

The Ghost looks at me funny when I leave the house for work. I'm not sure I've seen this look before. It leaves me uneasy. I see Cynthia watching from her kitchen window. I'm repulsed by people today. Positively repulsed. In this state, I can't pick the lesser of two evils—Freddie or Gonzo. I walk until my feet choose Gonzo's route. He is a worthier adversary and he'll not have his chest hairs exposed by a greasy shirt.

Gonzo sees me before I see him. This upsets me more than I would ever have guessed. Gonzo seems to have been waiting for me. First the Ghost, now Gonzo. I meet him with a silent, violent effrontery. To tell him that I would not wait for him.

–It's getting darker, he says.
–It certainly is, I say. Not to be bullied.

I crease my face and proffer a smile. He seems thoroughly satisfied with our transaction and gives me a paper. I imagine him toasting 'a good life' with the Doctor, and for an instant, I feel afraid. I take my paper and smile once more to tell him I know.

I look down on the headlines as I walk. The divided world is now divided again. Everything is being broken into the fractions and factions I enjoy so much. Wholesomeness is the dream of a shepherd in a dressing gown. The traffic of snide diplomacy and heady insults betrays the progress supposedly being made by the near-desperate GSC. WAR is coming. The placards will rot in the damp outhouse of a dark afternoon.

I'm giddy. I'm aflame. I march to work.

I arrive at the shed early enough to avoid the procession of hollow greetings that parade down these corridors. I think of Davy—panting, waiting to jump all over me in excitement, pissing all over the floor. I go into my office and close the door.

I sit at my desk and think about reading some of the Doctor's work but I'm not given the time. It's devoured by a fat knock on my door and the appearance of an even fatter head in its frame.

–****, glad to have caught you before you start in on your day. I wonder if I could have a quiet word with you in my office.

Fathead smiles bluntly.

–Now? I ask. Eyeing him there in my door.

–Yes, please, he says. Waiting for me to get up.

He leaves me walk behind him, hating him through his rumpled suit.

Davy meets our seething party. He winks at me. –Our man's in trouble!

He hits me playfully on the back. Fathead smiles and so do I. But my eyes are telling Davy to pat himself playfully on the back and push himself down the stairs. The puppy doesn't see my look because his yelps are for his own amusement, not ours. I wonder if he'll ever sour, if life will take him to its den and have its henchmen kick him around the place.

I follow Fathead into his pathetic office in the basement. There is another man waiting for us here. I'm offered a seat before them, the chairs prearranged with a sloppy cunning.

–Ah, ****, Fathead says, heaving himself into his leather swivel, this is Mr. Frank Wontdo. He's from our house uptown.

I nod at him. Bemused. I recognize him as the man I'd seen asking after me on the steps of the shed. They'll not ambush me with their mock leather and silly names.

–We've been listening to some of your recordings, Wontdo says, from your current stint. You're extremely talented, Mr. ****. They are testament to everything I've heard about you up at the house.

–Yes, I say. I don't feel like saying more.

–There is just one point I'd like to make though, Wontdo says.

And I realise then that Fathead is just a facilitator to a meeting between two people.

–It's in relation to your referencing the nature of our industry. You directly referred to the book in question. You talked outside the lines, as they say.

–It was only to one caller, I say. Tightening.

–Yes, he says, I understand that ... Caller 78.

–How many recordings did you listen to? I ask. Pushing it through the tightness, delivering it to the edge.

–Oh, I listened across the board, Mr. ****, he says, I just happened to stumble on this one. She's a real biter ... this Caller 78. She's good for business and you seem to enjoy a real rapport with her.

I don't enjoy anything with my callers, I say to myself.

–However you see it, Mr. Wontdo, I say.

–But in my defence, I continue, I consciously spoke outside the lines because it fitted the context.

Wontdo nods his head sympathetically.

–I understand, he says, it's just something we're keeping an eye out for up at the house. Not just with you but with everybody here in the shed. We're trying to raise the standards a little, we're trying to progress, in a good way. And to be honest, Mr. ****, I brought this contract with me when I joined the house. I guess you could say I have a vested interest in it. I think it's a relevant piece of work.

I realise now that both Fathead and I are facilitators to a meeting of one.

Wontdo nods his head in closure. Fathead does his best to make a graceful exit from his chair. He walks around his desk to fetch me and I realise with horror that he has notions of walking me out the door. My fears are confirmed when I find his swollen hand on my shoulder. I'm queasy. He greedily helps himself to a small slice of the meeting.

–This really is one of your best stints, he says, you really seem to be enjoying it. That's what we like to see, or hear, rather …

I move out of the way of his laugh. I will not have his humour spluttered all over me for the rest of the day. Wontdo's eyes follow me up the stairs as the office door closes in on his vision. Finally, it cuts his off and I breathe a little easier.

I go back to my office, sit at my desk and answer the phone when it rings. I imagine a third party engaged in my morning dialogues. Wontdo. Up at the house. Listening to his vested interest. I consciously try to sound unselfconscious. I don't feel like myself.

Between calls I'm unnerved by the knowledge that something is happening to me. Either something is missing or something else is growing in me. My self is a little ajar. I know exactly what it is. No. I'm lying. I have no idea. I lie again. Not in myself but on my truths. I nestle into them and they grow to fit. I bring round my conclusions, invite them to parade before me. Up and down, with their leggy notions and lipsticked potions. But the one in the corner, the one with the swollen ankles, she knows the score.

Hey Ankles, I yell, scratching my chest. *What's going on?*

Something's happening to you but I'm fucked if I know, she mumbles. Her head lolls on her chest.

And with that she has said what all the other conclusions could not.

What do I do? I ask her.

Fight, she says.

I exhale. I can't concentrate on my work although I'm waiting to work. I think about going to Kitty's but the possibility of the call is keeping me here. It does not come so I take all the other calls instead but none satisfy me. I never hoped they would. I want to wait. Somewhere, I'm writhing in ecstasy. I just don't know where yet.

I finish the day or it finishes me. Whichever way it'll be had. I don't care. On my walk I look to the building on its hill, jutting up and out from our stony flatlands. It reminds me of an old woman. I have often looked at the building on its peak. A monstrosity that will not die. I look at it now, before me, behind me, beside me. It follows me through the City, while they watch from inside—my father's eyes occupying the rafters, his horny toenails scratching on its bell.

I turn up my street. I decide to stay in that evening, to stay in and play chess with myself, to eat what the Ghost will prepare. I see them both through Cynthia's window. The Ghost looks at me. I know that, in this instant, she's expecting and inspecting my mood from a safe distance. I scowl to tell her that I want my chair this evening. I want my peace back. When I get in the door, I notice a present emptiness, an absence. There has been no food prepared here for weeks.

I walk out onto the street and beckon the Ghost. She stands at Cynthia's front door and expects me to shout over my concerns. Here—in the middle of a neighbourhood, with human ears and snake ears and hamster ears all waiting, knotted into streetlights. I motion for her to come with me, to come into the privacy of our selves. She comes and stands before me.

–I want to eat in an hour, I say.

She starts for the kitchen and Cynthia is left shaking her head in the distance, bemoaning the unjust exchange. I get into my chair and immediately my body responds. I can hear the Ghost's awkward fumbling with the pots and pans. I decide to humour her a little by getting out of my chair, carrying it into the kitchen and sitting back down again. From here in the corner, next to the fridge, I murder time, watch the Ghost and think about swapping verbs.

I sit and stare. I can see her inspecting the ingredients on offer —a dowdy collection of old spices and dusty cans. She finds a bag of rice and carefully measures two cupfuls with a cracked ceramic. She leaves the dishevelled bag within my reach. I fall for its bait and lean forward to grab a handful. The Ghost feels my movement and, directed by a nervous curiosity, she sends her eyes to my corner.

I finger the grains of rice before throwing some at her. She has returned to her cooking. I imagine she has always wanted an old-fashioned wedding. Elfin children in her train, confetti fell like summer rain.

Yes, I imagine the Ghost has always wanted an old-fashioned wedding. Perhaps she dreams of one still, I muse, as I crawl further into her fantasies—watching her cook as I hurl rice at odd intervals. She does not react or respond.

Then the doorbell sounds and I'm indignant that Cynthia should interrupt our domestic communion. The Ghost looks at the door— bewildered. She knows I will answer it. I open the door viciously to find the Doctor before me. I freeze, then unfreeze, in seconds. In this time, he unfolds his smile and leaves it there for me to discover when I have composed myself.

—Good evening, Mr. ****, I know—

I do not let him finish.

—Doctor, I don't want to speak to you or ever see you again in my own time.

I close the door. Revelling in my own composure. But haven't I always been composed? Composed, cold, controlled, cunning, conceited, conniving—any of the above will do. Will do. Wontdo. I am what I am. Tonight, I'm composed. Tomorrow, I'll be fighting.

I see the Ghost at the kitchen door.

—Go inside and finish my dinner, I say.

But she waits because she sees the letterbox open before I do. The Doctor's voice invades the hallway.

—You might take a look at this, it says.

A disc is prodded through. The Ghost and I watch it fall. I want to walk away—unaffected, and leave it there, disgraced and abandoned after its wonderful entrance, but I don't trust the Ghost. So instead, I walk on it and trust that she'll pick up the pieces after she has picked the rice grains from her ridiculous hair.

I go and sit in my chair. It's from here that I first notice it properly. Something has awakened in the Ghost. Something, outside my grasp but now inside my house, pacing the floor before me. She has a glint in her eye that I've never seen before. Even her hair has started to shine.

7:2: Telephone Transcript

In Search of Infinite Relief, C.W. Sisle
Contracted to Gleeson Media Group
Subcontracted to Employee 12
Recorded at 4.22 p.m. on 23/04/****

C78 Hey Head!

E12 Molly! How are you?

C78 Grand, yeah.

E12 Have you seen your Paper Maché Man?

C78 Nah. I think I'll leave that lie as is.

E12 And what about Isha and the gang?

C78 The gang! Every time you say that I picture Isha on a huge chopper.

E12 Sorry. What'll I call them then?

C78 I don't know. They're friends. Yeah, all fine. Everybody's fine.

E12 You fine?

C78 Yeah. Let's talk about your shit.

E12 My shit, eh?

C78 The stuff in the book. This Law of Human Nature.

E12 So you did read it?

C78 I had it in my bag last week so I dipped in and out of it.

E12 And?

C78 And I haven't the faintest idea what you're going on about. Saying that, I was a bit tipsy reading it and my concentration span is limited. I imagine it's very well written to those who read very well.

E12 Well, it was written sincerely, if that counts for anything.

C78 Course it does. Go on.

E12 Right. My first question is do you believe in some kind of law of fair play, agreed on by mankind as a race?

C78 I believe in lunatics on telephones. I'm kidding, Laurence. What? I can't believe we're straight into mankind as a race.

E12 It'll stop you thinking about yourself.

C78 Cheap shot, Laurence, but brilliant. I suppose I do. Actually, maybe I don't. I believe in laws of fair play being agreed upon by societies rather than mankind as a whole.

E12 There are variations, of course. But I believe all men are born with some idea of fair play. That's why men quarrel instead of killing each other. In the book I call it the Law of Human Nature. All bodies are governed by physical laws like gravitation, for example, and all organisms are governed by biological laws. I believe man is governed by his own set of laws, the—

C78 Law of Human Nature. But that's just you saying that, right?

E12 Yep. This lunatic on the phone.

C78 OK so. Give me the whole spiel then.

E12 Well, I believe that man can choose to disobey this Law. The animals and organisms don't have any choice. That's the first important thing to note. Also, if you study every civilisation and culture that has existed or exists still, in no civilisation, no matter how foreign or different, has selfishness been admired as an ideal.

C78 And have you?

E12 What?

C78 Studied every civilisation and culture that's—

E12 Well, I made an honest attempt.

C78 Fuck, Laurence. Do you take bookings for table quizzes?

E12 Only if there's biscuits. Now, there have been so many variations as to what exactly men should be unselfish to: war, family, community, friends, art, cities, commerce, politics, leaders. Course, people disagree about it, debate it. That's healthy.

C78 Yeah and these disagreements lead to war, which leads to killing, which leads to—

E12 Yeah but that's my point. We have to declare a supposedly honourable reason to kill. The WAR we're in now was started to defend the rights of others.

C78 If you believe that then—

E12 I'm not saying I do believe it. I'm saying they had to sell it to us like that because most people agree that killing hundreds of thousands of innocent people to further your own motives is wrong. It shits on the rules of fair play.

C78 We should send Treehouse a copy of your book.

E12 I did.

C78 Some intern will probably call you looking for chats.

E12 He did.

C78 Fuck off!

E12 Anyway, I understand the Law to be real, in the way the laws of mathematics are, whatever—

C78 What do you talk about with the intern?

E12 Stuff. This stuff. So this Law is real—whatever the version in play—acknowledged by man in his every action, even unawares.

We all know the Law and yet we all break it every day. And we have our excuses. Oh, I was tired; I was drunk; I didn't mean anything by it; if you knew what she's like you'd understand; I did what any other person would've done. Let me ask you this, Molly. If we didn't believe in decent behaviour, why are we so quick to make excuses for having behaved indecently? We do it all the time. All of us.

C78 Yep. You're probably right there. So this Law then, if I understand the book, is designed to comfort us?

E12 No. People always want to believe in something that will make them feel better, but it's not that simple.

C78 What? Why?

E12 What I mean is that you can't get comfort by just looking for it but if you look for truth you may find comfort in the end.

C78 Laurence, that sounds like a bad riddle from a third-rate movie. I'm sorry but—

E12 Looking simply for comfort won't find you your truths, Molly.

C78 What is the truth then, Maze-Master?

E12 It's this, Molly, for now: human beings are haunted by a very real feeling that they should behave in a certain way. This feeling is based on some understanding of the Law of Human Nature, which we break time and time again. We've got to understand this if we are to contemplate the state of mankind as it finds itself now. Someone once wrote, 'Be kind because everyone you meet is fighting a great battle.'

C78 A battle of the self?

E12 Yeah, I honestly believe that this is the war we'll have to win if mankind is to survive as a species. And on a more short-term level, I think it's the only thing that'll effect social change on any real scale. It's the only way I see of stopping the Want. And it has to be left untouched by man. Nobody can go claiming it for their own and making up silly man-made rules to go with it. The Law resides in all of us from birth—we need to create a world that nurtures it, and leaves it untagged to develop naturally. And it can't be pushed on people but you can remind them why it's there.

C78 What if this thing you call the Law of Human Nature is just part of our herd instinct? 'Cause that's been done. We definitely have the instinct to help each other survive as a species. I saw a programme on it. That is, on instincts in general. Because they do exist—as a definite. You do agree that we've all got instincts?

E12 Absolutely. I believe in all our instincts, Molly—self-presevation, love, hate, sex, fighting. All very real instincts. People have put that to me before, you know, but I always tell them the story of the child in the alleyway. The Law lies outside our instincts.

C78 Go for it.

E12 Right, you're walking home some night—

C78 Falling home. Go on.

E12 And you hear a child being attacked down a dark alley. What do you do?

C78 Well I suppose ...

E12 Hang on, let me break that question in half. What should you do? What would you most likely want to do?

C78 Course I should help but I'd want to walk away.

E12 Which one would be stronger as an instinct? Be honest.

C78 To get the fuck out of there, I suppose. Yeah, although for one split second I'd really want to help. My instinct would be to help, my conscious thought would be to get out of there.

E12 Fair point. So let's say that there are two basic human instincts at heads here: the herd instinct to help and the self-preservation instinct to survive. Now, you tell me that the second is stronger. We have to rouse ourselves, wake our herd instinct and prod it till we go in after the child. Would you agree with me so far?

C78 Yes.

E12 Oh. Good. I always expect you to object.

C78 No. I agree with you. I think I see where you're going. I think I'll agree with you there as well.

E12 OK. So what I was going to ask was: what differentiates between these two instincts? The thing that mediates between the two and encourages us to follow one or the other can't be either of the instincts. Take music. A sheet of music, the thing that tells us which note to play on the piano, can't itself be one of the notes. The Law tells us what tune to play, our instincts are like the keys. If you want to take that metaphor further—

C78 Do. It's better than my fried egg one.

E12 OK. Well, you could say that, the thing which tells you how loud or strong a note should be played at any given time, can't itself be that note. If the Law was indeed one of our instincts, by logic, we should be able to follow one instinct that we always regard as wholly 'good'. A reckoning gauge. Like love of humanity. But out of proper context, every instinct, even those we consider to be wholly good, have the capacity to become offensive or hurtful to others. Take a mother's love—if this is taken to extremes, it can lead to a mother being unjust to someone else's children. A piano is not made up of good and bad notes, or right and wrong notes. Every single note is right at one time, or very wrong at another.

C78 I like the piano metaphor. I like the thought that goodness is a tune that can be played as long as you realise that there's an infinite number of tunes.

E12 Course. With a good ear we might all become better musicians.

C78 And all serial-killing psychopaths are tone deaf.

E12 Now she's firing. So this Law keeps evolving, through discussion and mistakes and love and time's passing, we know more. This is how it should be. The more we know, the more we find out, the easier it will be for us to play that tune. Things will seem much clearer, much simpler. It will be a relief.

C78 You and your crazy shit.

E12 This crazy shit could be your saving grace, Miss I'm-so-Low-I-Could-Just-Lay-Down-and-Die.

C78 I can't believe you said that.

E12 I'm teasing, Molly. Anyway, you should be able to laugh at them. When I'm finished with you, you'll be able to ridicule your Lows from a height and still fall down laughing.

C78 Imagine.

E12 I want to tell you the most bizarre thing about this Law.

C78 Go on. What's so bizarre?

E12 Well our Law, man's Law, outlines not what we will do but what we should do but often don't.

C78 That makes sense. Most scientific laws, like gravity, tell us how something will act according to the law, not how it should act. I get that.

E12 Which means there is something outside the facts. We have the facts, i.e. how men do act, that's what we can observe, and we've got this feeling, this knowledge of how men should act. There's that something else.

C78 What do you say to people, Laurence, who say *Why should I play fair if no one else is?* I've said it. I've definitely thought it.

E12 What can you say to them, Molly? The simple, common-sense answer is that man should be unselfish, especially if we ever want man to be happy. It's that simple in theory. I'm not saying it's easy in practice but the theory is too obvious in its resolution to ever question its end message.

C78 You're right. It's the practical application that gets us.

E12 That's part of our condition, Molly. It's the way it was written. We didn't make it up for ourselves. And yet it's not a fact in the most ordinary sense of the word, although we know it to be very real.

C78 So what then? Where did it come from?

E12 So are we good to go on the knowledge that man's law exists over and beyond the realm of actual facts that may be observed externally or scientifically even?

C78 If you say so ...

E12 OK. I look at a stone drop and I can observe what the law has outlined. The Law of Gravity says it will fall. But with man's Law, we can't observe or make notes as to what it constitutes. Imagine if stones—no, forget the stones—imagine if foreign beings were to observe the human race, they would never guess that a very real law exists over and beyond behavioural facts.

C78 Maybe stones have a consciousness or a law we don't know about. By that reckoning I mean. I don't believe in screaming carrots myself.

E12 As much as I love you, Molly, shut up.

C78 Sorry, I think I just have to hear my own voice every ten seconds or else I feel left out.

E12 Before I go there, tell me how you think we got here?

C78 I know how we got here. Don't we all. It's pretty much a hard fact, a real truth, as you would have it. You're the evolution bunny.

E12 Yeah. I just can't stop wondering why.

C78 Are you saying you can tell me the meaning of life?

E12 No. I can tell you these little tit-bits I've gathered from years of non-scientific research. Science and the art of observation can't answer the 'why' or even the 'where' but all is not lost. We have another way in.

C78 We do?

E12 Yeah. We have inside information. Humankind is the one thing in this universe that we know more about than can be learned from external observation. We are in a prime position to explore the Law of Human Nature and find out where it came from and maybe even why.

C78 Where then? Answer me the where.

E12 Well, personally I think it came from a higher consciousness of sorts, without getting too quacked out about it. I really believe this, and it's a different kind of believing to how I believe in evolution.

C78 Believe what exactly?

E12 I think the Law is designed to help us find our way to happiness.

C78 Shit. I've just realised the time.

E12 What? You have to go?

C78 Yeah. I've got work.

E12 I was just getting warmed up.

C78 I know. So was I.

E12 Are you teasing me?

C78 Yep.

E12 Talk soon so?

C78 I'll call you tomorrow.

E12 Bye, Miss Molly.

C78 Bye, Laurence.

End of transcript

7:3: Molly

I go to work. All the time thinking of the music but the music fades as the night drags her feet. I come home, drunk and knowing that the Lows are coming and that they are tone deaf. I think about calling Laurence but I've never called him this late and I presume that he is home with his wife or lady, in bed and breathing softly.

I lie on my rug. A few of the channels show the marching. *They'll go to WAR anyway.*

I light a cigarette and take off my shoes. The Manots Family comes on. I'm excited because I've never seen it before but my heart sinks because I know too much by the opening credits. I can't believe any of it. It's cheap and crass and obvious and obnoxious; it reeks of moneyed men with sweated pits telling boys wrapped up in clipboards to go with it. Always going, always running, always pushing, always shoving—no care, no craftsmanship, no intelligence, no passion, no love, no understanding.

Maybe you expect too much from a sitcom, Matron says.

Well, I say, *it's the least anyone deserves from anything.*

Lofty ideals have people swinging from lofts, Matron says, *because sometimes it's the best place for them.*

Matron smiles and bends down to stroke my hair. I pull myself away from her and think of Isha sleeping upstairs. She pulls back—rejected.

I look back at the box, at the Manots Family. Wendy's smile looks like it could spoil, the shoddy showmanship of Terence is pained and Palmer's maternal beauty is desperate. I'm angry with 'family' for being so idyllic. It's not fair and should come with a licence. And I'm even angrier at myself that I should care so much, especially after all my talks with Laurence. I'm so angry I roll myself up in my rug and breathe heavily through my teeth till the stinging in my throat has caught fire. I feel. I close my eyes for as long as it takes but something outside of me rouses my senses. I look out my downy tunnel and Isha's slippers accuse me of lunacy. I unroll myself and offer her a monkey smile from the floor.

–The Manots Family are all buffoons, I say. I wouldn't pay that money for a family of ten and a dog, never mind a family of three.

Isha offers me a tired half smile. I go up to the box and pretend to pick Terence's nose during a close-up. This always makes Isha smile. I make silly noises when Palmer alights on the screen. I turn to Isha, laughing, only to see that she's not. And maybe for the first time in my life, I get painfully embarrassed in front of her. It's the most chilling absurdity and I can't understand how we have gotten to this.

–What's wrong? I ask.

–Nothing, she says, I must have heard you come in.

–Do you want tea?

–No, I'm going back to bed.

–How's Chivers and Puckie?

–Fine, Chivers is much the same.

–Do you like me? I ask without my consent.

It comes from a nowhere drowned in drink. I shrink back from every desperate thing that is myself. Isha looks dog-weary. Head hung. She's uncomfortable, rammed thoughtlessly into a corner by a neediness I cannot master. I call it back but it's slow to respond.

–I ... I didn't mean to say that, I say, don't even answer it. I know you do. I know you do.

–You should go up to bed, Molly, she says, you look wrecked.

She turns to leave but stubs her toe on the abandoned torso, commanding a presence from under the couch.

–You should finish this, she says, or bring it up to your room. I'm sick of looking at it ...

I stand up straight and look at her. I don't have a reaction for this. So I find one quickly because my body feels like violence. I take the torso, walk out the front door and put it in the bin. When I come back in Isha is standing halfway up the stairs.

–What did you do with it? she asks.

–I put it in the bin, I say. Harshly. Fighting.

–It'll take up too much room—leave it out beside it, she says and turns her back on me as she goes up the stairs.

I go back outside, take it out of the bin and put it on our front railings, overlooking the street. It looks like a carcass.

I get to my bed as quickly as I can because I can't bear to take in any more of this night. I close the doors and take off my shoes. I get in as I am. I scrunch my eyes tight because I don't have the time or energy or interest to cry. I order myself to sleep; I order my men to stay quiet; I order Matron to leave and I order the Lows to stay away. And then the night shuts down and I give in.

I spend the next day with sleep and wake to find a note from Isha telling me that she has gone to measure carpets with Serge. There are no exclamation marks, just a calm relay. I get up and look out the front window. The torso is still there and I'm not sure if I want to fight or lie down again. So instead I sit at the kitchen table and light a cigarette, forgoing the glass of milk Isha would have wanted for me. With a bitchy satisfaction. Then I feel shit so I drink one and it settles my stomach. I wonder if perhaps I would be happy in the life that Isha wants for me.

Let's not speak of happiness, Matron says, nuzzling up to my ear. *You'll only torment yourself and get yourself all worked up again. I wish you'd stop fighting, Molly, and let me look after you properly.*

I'll tell Isha about you, I say. Threatening her, teary-eyed and hurting.

Molly, she coos, *Molly, I'm only trying to make you better, help you to see that you're not ready for happiness. We've a lot more work to do, you and I. Talk to Isha if you want, but she'll agree with me.*

When will I be ready? I weep.

Happiness is an odd one, Matron says, toying with my hair. *It's not for everyone. Only some people find happiness and maybe you'd be wiser to understand that now rather than later. You might be better off just keeping your head down, keep some modicum of dignity about you. Sometimes your notions embarrass even me and I'm used to you.*

I sit and think about Isha and the embarrassment of a chilling absurdity.

Let me explain about Isha, she says, nestling in closer, *you have to understand, Molly, that she's just found out.*

What? I ask.

You know, she says.

Tell me, I say.

Well it's hard for her, Matron says, *now that Isha's lived with you for a while, now that you can't just ring home with all your big*

stories, now that you can't run off anywhere, she knows. She knows what you're like. She's a smart woman—you know that, Molly. I'm sure she'd like to feel differently. I'm sure we'd all be happier if you and things had been that much different but they're not, you're not. You have to understand how it is for Isha. I'm sure she'd like to like you but, as you said yourself, she has an honest body. People aren't stupid, they'll find the mess you've made eventually.

I sit there and she tells me all the other things I know already. She's right. I know that. But even here, in all the brambles of my knowledge, I can hear the Villagers fighting to free me. *But you can't follow me to a higher consciousness*, I tell her and she laughs so hard that I'm forced to put on music I find at the bottom of my bag.

I light another cigarette but this is the one that tips my belly over. I go and kneel before the toilet, holding on to the sides to steady my aim, my eyes blind and watering. I suddenly realise that it's been a while since I've gotten sick. *Good girl, Molly*, Matron used to always say as she rubbed my back.

Matron liked me on the tiles. I've come a long way from the time when I did this every day. Maybe I've some chance at being happy. The Matron can't know everything for sure. No one can. Laurence said that. I think about going to work and am slightly relieved by the thought. I'm relieved about getting rid of Matron for the night, about getting away from this house before Isha comes home and sees me like this. I want to fill the afternoon with something that might bring Isha back, maybe not today but soon, so I call my friend and ask him if he can help me pick up the computer.

–I'm working late, he says, tomorrow night I promise, we'll get you all fixed up and ready to go.

–OK, I say, talk to you then.

When I hang up the whole day is still before me and Isha is gone to measure carpets with Serge. So I decide to go and see Chivers.

I put on my runners and music and start out through the City. Thoughts come back to me, even before I have escaped the cul-de-sac. They fall from the cavities of the torso, angled wearily towards a greying sky. It's getting darker earlier.

I put my music up louder but it blocks out nothing. Every other day it gives me daydreams but today it's saturated before it can even begin. I think of all the thoughts and abstractions, kicked about my skull by a listless youth, driven through distraction to the all that lies beyond. I challenge him to stop awhile and take his breath. Stop awhile and stop the thoughts. Break them apart and leave me with one word that will make its way over the jumbled sprawl and into sense. *All I'm asking for is one word. I'll give you a cigarette, have one with you if you like. Kick me one word.*

Shush, Molly.

I imagine it coming out my eye, shattering my vision like a greenhouse up in fisticuffs. I picture it getting caught in my jacket, its edge eaten by a loose thread. What word would it be? I wonder. What word would it be? I turn up my music again and keep walking towards the hill that lords over our greying acres.

I go into the foyer. The man with the two matches sees me come in. He comes over and takes my arm. He is eager.

–They says the grass is greener on the other side, he says, and it was, I tells you now, it was. I watches for years. Green and growing, over the back wall, through the hole in our back shed. It was greener, I tells you. Most definitely, categorically greener. I means I could have brought you by the hand, shoved you over the back wall and said, *Which is greener, there or here?* You would have said, *There, for sure.* I swears it.

–Do you want your cigarette? I ask.

–Is it green?

–No.

–I needs a green cigarette.

I smile as I watch him walk away, then I stand at the lift till a nurse comes along and pushes the button. I give her a big smile because she's wearing silly earrings and I like her already. She and I would laugh together if ever I became a nurse—and worked here.

Chivers is reading the newspaper when I come in. I kiss him like I always do. Even Isha kisses Chivers because he always kisses her. Maybe I should just start kissing her. Maybe it'll be good for the pair of us but I like our quiet reserve too much. I like our manly practicalities and tough wallops. I find them easy to digest. I don't tell Chivers about Isha being mad at me because she was his friend first. And I don't even consider telling him that I think she might not like me because then he might be disgusted by me too. Instead we talk about Daniel and Julia. Chivers is good to talk to about people. He gets them, not only on his own level, but on every level.

–We didn't even know why Daniel stopped talking at first, he says. I thought it was because he'd put my marmalade body scrub on his toast. I was even laughing. Teasing him. I brought him up to the hospital. I knew this young doctor there. Gorgeous man, always flicking his hair at people, knew his films. I knew Daniel wasn't in any danger but then all the what i*f*s started making me nervous so I brought him in anyway. I was more embarrassed than anything else. I was this wrinkly old man with marmalade body scrub. Actually, Serge gave it to Isha and Isha gave it to me. This was the morning after the barman's competition. Puckie and I had finished really late, and then I'd woken Daniel up from the couch, brought him home to my house in the middle of the night, early morning really. Puckie gave us a lift. So when I'm up with the young doctor with Daniel the next day, he asks me if I knew what happened to Julia.

He knew us. We'd been up with Daniel before.

Chivers stops. –Puckie told you all this, he says.

–I think so, I say.

–He told you about how she was raped.

I nod.

–So you know then that she'd been in to get her hands bandaged. And you know all about her taking off and coming back that evening. She didn't know we'd been at the hospital with Daniel. She thought he'd told us what happened—he saw everything. Molly, I couldn't believe it when she said it. I knew then why Daniel had been silent all day. And he wasn't just silent, he was closed up. You'd know what I mean if you'd seen him. Puckie was so mad, mad at everything. He wanted to go after the guy. He still had friends from his old neighbourhood. I don't know why I say that because he would have done it on his own. With a hammer or something dreadful. I felt so guilty for not bringing Daniel home earlier. I never let him into that pub. He'd wandered up to her house because he couldn't sleep with the noise downstairs. It's always a really hectic night. Everything was so deeply off kilter. Julia felt responsible for being raped. She said she'd taken a child's voice away. Puckie said we all did and that we shouldn't have been playing mummies and daddies with a real child in the first place. –A child's not putty for void-filling, he'd said. And I thought he was right. Then. Not now. We did our best for that child. And even if we weren't the ideal family, that child was happy. I know he was, Molly. It's taken me over two years to forgive myself and come to believe that. I think Puckie's still angry with Julia for 'doing what she did', not that night, that wasn't her fault, but every other night. He thinks her lifestyle invited in that demon, and I can understand that, but I don't think it's true. Plus he was hopelessly in love with her, so it was never going to be simple—or as simple as Puckie would like everything to be, or thinks everything should be. Isha thought along similar lines. Nobody said it aloud, but it was there, after it happened—Julia's lifestyle, a raw abscess that had finally come to surface. Isha could never let her in. You know how Isha can react to people. She tries her best to override it but she's too honest for her own good. That's the way she was with Julia. She reacted badly to her, but Isha's as noble a creature as you'll find. She never said anything to me. She knew she didn't have to. And she did her best to be as fair to Julia as she could. And Julia never gave up trying to make her way into Isha. I think Julia really wanted Isha's approval. Julia once told me that she would have picked Isha as a mother if she'd ever a choice. I told this to Isha, which I shouldn't have done.

–Why not? I ask.

–Because Isha felt under pressure, Chivers says, to take to someone who her heart just didn't take to. Not naturally. You're like Isha that way. You react to people.

–Puckie says I remind him of Julia, I say, do you think that's true?

–Yeah, I know what he's saying, I see it in the way you get on with people. You have to find some real connection whenever you meet somebody. I see you doing it. It's in your nature I think. It's a need. A need to connect to people.

–Is that a bad thing? I ask. I'm eager to know whether I can put it in my compliments drawer or whether I have to run further away from myself. Coming from Chivers, it would be invaluable. One I could challenge the Matron with.

–No, he says, I think it's a wonderful thing.

I exhale and smile at him, sitting a little further onto the bed. Chivers shakes his limbs out a bit.

–Remind me to go for a walk later, he says.

–I'll go with you now, I can have a cigarette outside.

We gather our things and make our way outside.

–It's so dark, Chivers says before I light up a cigarette.

–Tell me more about Julia then, tell me about Daniel.

–Well, we didn't know what to do, he says, steadying his step with my arm. He didn't talk the next day. Isha and I brought him to a counsellor friend of hers but he didn't open his mouth. He didn't speak that night, or the next day. Imagine, Molly. Imagine knowing this wonderfully boisterous child—you saw him in the video. He was full of life, every mother says that about a child that's gone, but Daniel—Daniel was extraordinary. Everyone said so. He had this liveliness in his eyes, this energy about him. He literally brought joy with him. He was the happiest little fellow I'd ever met. Lots of people said so. Imagine him just closing down, his eyes, everything. I couldn't get through to him. We thought if Julia explained things to him, showed him she was all right, but nothing. She just came out of the room, looked at myself, Puckie and Isha, then locked herself in her house. We knew we had to bring him to see somebody, and we knew they'd take him away from us. We looked dreadful on paper, if anyone was to ask around. People knew what Julia did. And despite the state of things there's still some semblance of child welfare. People are very quick to judge. It's good for children that they do check on these things. But that's exactly what happened. We brought him to see somebody and everything came out, including how ill-suited a group of individuals we were to be guardian of a child, now a child with special needs. Isha applied for guardianship. She looked good, with all the work she does—and Old Fler from your school gave her a reference—but they said she was too old. So they took him away and said it would be better for his recovery if he didn't have contact with us again. I believed them at the time. I thought they were right. But not now. It's taken me all this time to realise that it wasn't my fault. It wasn't really anybody's fault. The Doctor's helped me understand that. But we each in our own way blamed ourselves—and Julia maybe. We mightn't have said as much but I think we did, even if we didn't want to. We were heartbroken for her, everything she'd been through. We tried to get her help, to see someone, file papers at the station, but she wouldn't. She just left instead. We haven't seen either of them since. It was an awful time, Molly. We didn't even want to be around each other. The three of us kind of crawled into ourselves. Took us a while to crawl out.

–Where ... what about the mother in all of this? I ask.

–She wasn't there. She was there but she was elsewhere, if you know what I mean. She never did drugs and she could hold perfectly engaging conversations but she wasn't there. It's the best way to describe her. She was like a vacant shell. Isha called her a floater. She didn't seem to have any real opinion as to what should be done for Daniel. It was very frustrating to watch. I'd to keep Puckie away from her a lot, especially after all this happened. He was near to shaking her like a rag doll to get some emotion out of her.

As I wander home that evening I wonder if Julia ever thought that she was bad, if she got sad, if she went mad.

Bad-mad-sad.

Sad-mad-bad.

Mad-bad-sad.

It's all the same whichever-which way.

Finally! Matron says. *I thought I might have to spell it out for you.*

I walk through the tangled images of man and modernity advertised on every monitor. I turn my music up and light another cigarette. Sold to this life. Isha-less, this day.

8:1: Mr. ****

I'm happy to report that WAR is everywhere. The soldiers scuttle for cover there and the channels haggle for coverage here. WAR is piped into the City, the Media accommodates its passage and plays hungry host to a million images of mortar and rubble and blood and dust and flames and crying children.

But I let it pass. I watch it go. I see it when it finds me. I don't sit by the box. I have my own war to fight.

I get up and go to work. I choose Gonzo this morning against my will. He finds me, standing there with his dirty hands. He holds out his ritual offering. I take the paper, pay him and turn to walk away. But it's too late—I've seen the look in his eyes. The quiet wondering, amusement even. I push myself as far into his face as I can, just to tell him I saw, to tell him to keep looking if he dares. Something stirs so I headbutt him—find his skull with mine. I step back and tell him again to keep looking if he dares. To keep wondering. He will because Gonzo knows what he is. He always has.

This time *I* am satisfied by our morning's exchange. Later I will go to Kitty's.

Yes, I am aflame.

I decide to loiter a little. I find a good spot near a schoolyard.

Children make me itch but I watch them anyway—this motley collection of morons and cretins and idiots with their tiny crusted eyes and half-smiles that dribble and drip. The schoolyard is full of their guttural charms, their under-formed, malnourished words, understood only by parents and high-coloured teachers called Rose. I drink my coffee and watch them play. They are running and hopping, jumping and skipping, limp-armed, heads hanging, some just sit and stare. Suddenly, I wonder where I am. Why have I never seen these children before? An awful feeling overtakes me. For one moment I suspect that I may have been brought here, and sudden as its birth, I kill the feeling. My peace is given back. I sigh, relieved. Then as quickly as it comes it's taken again, in this, the dire tug-of-war that has become my existence of late.

I have grown tides.

My attention is drawn to a boy, sitting on the ground, pulling at his chewing gum. He looks up. He looks directly at me. Everything in me changes as Laurence attempts to smile at him. I have to turn and walk away.

The prospect of work allures and yet deters me—I go there as fast as I can. I know now I'm fighting for me. But I don't know who I'm fighting. They say it's better to know what you're fighting for rather than who you're fighting against. *Who says? Who?* Maybe Ankles knows. With her head bent, she bites the skin at the corner of her lip and refuses to answer my questions.

I see Wontdo outside my workplace. He is standing on the steps, talking to a small girl. I decide I need to get into my office more than I need to avoid him. So I stride with roaring flame of heart, up the street, up the steps and past him, only to be recalled by a hand on my shoulder and his balmy voice in my ear.

–Laurence, he says, this is Molly.

I turn to look at her. She's awaiting my eyes. Hers are wide, expectant and full of something else. Something my tailor and I never discuss.

She's tiny but throws herself up and out to bring me in.

–Hi, she says and laughs so hard that she throws all her hair to the wind.

–I'm sorry, she says through all her laughing. Tell me you're not scared.

–I'm scared as hell, Laurence says, laughing, reaching for his bag. I suspected it would come to this. In fact, I prearranged a cautionary restraining order. It's right here.

Molly laughs so hard Wontdo's excuse and departure go unnoticed. I suspect he is smiling too and I feel grimy.

–I'm not normally one for hugs, she says, but since you're here ... and I'm just getting good at them ...

She lurches for Laurence again and again Laurence reciprocates.

–You're not as old as I thought you'd be, she says. Drawing back and falling down into her own height.

–I'm ancient, Laurence says, but ridiculously handsome.

–You're all right I suppose, she says smiling, you just go on about an awful lot of rubbish. In fact, that's why I'm here. I came to ask you to stop calling me. My ears are burnt to pieces. I appreciate the thought and all, but to be honest you just never stop going on about yourself. Laurence, Laurence, Laurence. It's got to stop.

She laughs again and Laurence laughs with her.

–I know, he says sincerely, but you're such a good listener.

You're the only one that really understands me. I think you're the wisest person I know.

–OK, the mileage's ran out if that one. How are you anyway?

–I'm good, Laurence says. How are you?

–I'm good too, Laurence. An eager sincerity overrides her giddiness. Nervousness.

–I'm sorry for coming down, she says, I know you're working and maybe I should have asked first but I only thought of it this morning and it's my day off so … I kind of wanted to see you.

–Course it's OK, Molly, Laurence says. Did you want to see me about anything in particular?

–No, I don't mean it that way, she says, I literally just wanted to see you.

She looks at Laurence sadly and I squirm.

–Pretty standard psychopathic behaviour I'd say, Laurence says.

–Yep, pretty standard, she says, but wait till you see what I've done to your house. That—I have to say—is something a little special. I surpassed myself.

Laurence laughs and waits for her to open up. I start to itch somewhere on the inside.

–Well, I'd better go, Molly says. Reacting to me and the skirmishes beneath my skin.

–How's Isha? Laurence asks. Pushing me aside.

–She's OK, I didn't really mean what I said about her not liking me. I was just drunk.

–I know, says Laurence softly, and there's nothing wrong with the people that like you.

–I know, she says defensively, I never said there was.

–And there's nothing wrong with the men that like you either, Laurence says.

–I know, she says laughing, embarrassed, uncomfortable, squirming. Itching under her own skin now.

My self smiles quietly but Laurence is angry—with me, not with her. With her he is tender and will not leave her here sad.

–Well then, he says, so you know there'd be nothing wrong with you if you started to like yourself.

–I have to go, and anyway I do like myself.

–You should, Laurence says, you're beautiful, Molly, inside and out. Ask Monkey, he'll tell you.

Laurence engulfs her in a smile so warm that I have to follow my fears and run away.

I breathe. Then Laurence pushes me aside and reaches out for her. But Molly turns away, walled in by the tears that have started to seep out of her dismay.

–I've to go, she says, I've to go.

She stands there, turned away.

–Thanks, Laurence, she says, looking back at him. You're a good man ... outside any of this crap.

And somewhere I stop to listen.

She smiles at Laurence through all her frustrations and leaves me standing there.

I want to know who sent her. I want them to choke on my defiance. Instead, I go to work. After, I take on the City. I ask it for a bar to get drunk in, a wall to write my name on and a life to take. It provides me with all three, no questions asked. Everyone's stopped asking the right questions, even the City.

I walk slowly, dripping in thoughts and feelings I do not want. My peace has been disturbed; my apathy is verging on empathy. There is an open crack. Am I to be opened like all these despicable cretins that insist on feeling? I have to get drunk.

I walk into the first bar I see. The waitress is gaunt and hairy.

She smiles at me and I notice they're all smiling here amidst the shiny interior and chic leather couches. I order.

–Would you like your monitor switched on, sir? she asks.

I look down at the monitor embedded in my table and nod. As she fetches my drink, my monitor lights up and all its images disembark on my table. I press a button and they start marching before me.

There is an old movie playing, made topical again by the darkness that has descended on the City. It was hunted out of the archives to play on the public's fear. I smile in appreciation but I don't let the images stop marching until they find me. *Dr. Dressman's Table*—he makes a joke about the darkness. It's not funny but the audience laughs anyway. They always do as he chatters inanely, his scalpel splicing the cadaver's chest. There are endless theories about the what*s*, and the why*s*, hanging over the City. *Let them all talk,* I think. *I've drinking to do.* I finish my drink and leave.

This time I know where I'm going. I'm going to the Depot. It is always full of life. I have been there twice before, and twice before the City has kept its promise.

I'm stopped at the security gates by the guards, greasy-palmed and slavering. Most pedestrians pay willingly to be left alone and unchecked. The drivers and loaders have passes and cards and gates. I have my work identity card. I produce it for the guard on duty. He is young and doesn't seem to get it. He raises his eyebrows as the prelude to a question. Economic with his time, I answer him.

–I'm working a stint, I say. Pointing to the name of my mother house.

–A man has to make a living, he says. Smiling seedily.

–A man has to understand, I say.

He does and waves me through.

I hear my own footfalls on the tunnel floor before it spits me out to the chaos that meets here in the City's Depot. It's a complex mass of loading bays, docking areas, parking spaces, administrative blocks, station ports and bars. Bars, hotels, restaurants and more bars. There is even a cinema where drivers go to sleep.

Behind the neu-plastik façade of its modernity, there is a world that has always been here. A world where few will have noticed the sky's new shadow, this onslaught of darkness that has kept the streetlights awake for days—and the days to come if the scientists are right. Here, in this world, are the drivers and loaders that never sleep beside a loved one. Their love is tailored to fit none other than themselves.

I sit at the bar. I nod for a whiskey and I look around. The men are rowdy, mean, half-spent on a raw emptiness that foreshadows their collapse into sleep. There are half women here, scrawny and restless, lipsticked and vacant, biting hard on their nails or sitting white-thighed on their knawed hands. There is a thing in the corner. A tiny figure eaten alive by leather trousers and ratty hair. Her rodent face is bespeckled, cupped in enormous mannish hands. But someone soon will have her too.

I watch a man play on the slot machines. His movements are fluid and they entrance me. Psycho Cash Beast Machine Club. The music from the machine is full of the hunt and the hunted. It's vulgar and menacing, the flyaway chase running through the hushed murmurs of the bar. I nod my head for another drink and scan the monitor on my table. The old film is still playing. The heroine's shrill cry winds itself up the stairs of a lighthouse. I will write my name on the bathroom wall tonight. The man playing the Psycho Cash Beast wins and everybody turns to watch as it hurls its load.

There is a talk show to the right of the finished film. There are

thousands of broadcasts strung together and hammered mercilessly into the black hours. The camera spans the audience and despite make-up and wardrobe, I can see that the clappers have been recruited from the streets. The more coherent will be asked to ask questions, cued on the light-box above. Others have been warned to stay quiet but generous with their smiles and applause. *Heap on the applause*, they'll say, over their clipboards, into their mics.

It takes me a while to deflect from the audience and concentrate on the debate. The host is holding up a brightly coloured box. I have no idea what it contains but I can read the large red lettering on the front. TORTURE!

–So what exactly is your objection to Nacler's new product, Prof. Fenguy? the host asks the woman on his right.

–I think that should be pretty obvious. The game makes fun of torture, it encourages kids to inflict pain on each other and also to devise new means of hurting each other. Have you tried out any of the instruments yourself, Vessi?

–No, but I believe my research team went to town on each other. Literally. There's a spiked saddle included, folks!

The audience laughs on cue.

–Would you like your kids playing with it, Vessi?

–If it meant involving their little 'friends' from next door, sure! Never did forgive them for that cock-up with the clothesline. Love thy neighbours, folks! Ain't always easy.

The audience laughs on cue.

–Are you listening to yourself, Vessi? Do you actually ever listen to yourself or do you just pay people to listen for you?

The audience hisses on cue.

–Tom, what do you make of it? Kids' toy or threat to the future of all humanity?

The audience laughs on cue.

–I think Prof. Fenguy and her brood of hysterical followers would ban fun if they could. Kids are always gonna play rough. Vessi, we all devised ways of torturing each other when we were kids. We all played around with our pain thresholds. Sure, we didn't have all this bright plastic gear in a box set but we had hammers and bicycle chains and wet towels. Banning TORTURE! ain't gonna stop kids being kids. They might even grow up that bit tougher eh? TORTURE doesn't have to be a bad word, Professor. They're gonna learn about it when they're older.

–But why do they need to know about all that so young? the professor asks. They should—

–All that, hisses Tom, all that! You can't even bring yourself to say the word. It's torture. Are you hearing me? he asks her, TORTURE, let's not be afraid to use it. TORTURE, TORTURE.

–I'm not afraid to use it, says the professor.

She tries to protest, she shouts over an audience aroused by her opposing panellist.

The host sits back and sinks into his orange wrinkles, smiling.

TORTURE, TORTURE, TORTURE, the audience chants.

TORTURE, TORTURE, TORTURE, the light-box flashes.

TORTURE, TORTURE, TORTURE, the host urges, waving the box set in the air.

I switch it off.

There is an atmosphere here that excites me. I scan the room looking for its source. I'm led to it by a smiling driver, striding in from the front door, his clogs heavy on the stained wooden floor as he makes his way back to his gaggle of cohorts. There is laughing and back-slapping and something else I have missed of late. I watch them sink a round of shots, then watch as a small weedy man gets up bravely, lifted by his playmates' roar. He walks out and I follow him. One of the larger men checks my interest but my eyes speak of our understanding. I follow the weedy man into the lot. I see him hike himself up into a truck, parked in the bowels of the darkness. I can see his foggy breath. I take a last glance at the neon sky hanging over

the front wheel. I go back inside and order another drink, down it, then go and write my name on the bathroom wall.

I walk back into the night air. The Depot hums, clanks and gargles before me. I see the weedy man climbing back out of the truck. I stand and wait for him to scurry past me, his chest rabid as he makes his way back into the den. I approach the truck. Her face is lit by the neon light. She looks panicked and hopeful, pleading and desperate. Through the window I can see her mouthing the words 'please' and 'help' over and over again. I like watching her and I keep turning to look at her as I walk away.

The City has come up trumps again. It gave me a life—two even, if you include the bundle she holds in her arms.

8:2: Telephone Transcript

In Search of Infinite Relief, C.W. Sisle
Contracted to Gleeson Media Group
Subcontracted to Employee 12
Recorded at 3.41 p.m. on 25/04/****

C78 Is this the Centre for Non-Scientific Research into Modern Man?

E12 Yes. How can I help?

C78 I want to speak to the director, please.

E12 Hold the line.

(*Employee 12 hums*)

E12 Director speaking. How can I help?

C78 This is General Blaut speaking on behalf of the Treehouse Administration.

E12 How can I help, General?

C78 I'm calling with instructions regarding the Law of Human Nature. I believe you are its main proponent.

E12 I'm somewhat familiar with it, yes.

C78 So we're informed. I presume you are aware of the procedure accompanying any call that comes directly from the Administration?

E12 No, General, I'm not.

C78 The content of this call will be monitored for security reasons. Also, you are legally obliged not to discuss the following conversation with anyone. I mean that in the most traditional sense. I'm sure you understand.

E12 Yes, General. But I would like to take this opportunity to—

C78 This phone call affords you no opportunities, Director. Please refrain from talking. Now. The Treehouse Administration would like to make some legislative amendments to the Law as we understand it. We claim legitimate power to amend the sections dealing with war, murder, genocide, power mongering, deception and greed. These will constitute what we like to call the Initial Surge of Reform. A Second Surge will follow when our recognized legal team have had time enough to evaluate and interpret fully the Law of Human Nature and its long-term effects on national interests. We have been warned to treat the Law and the alleged power behind it with suspicion. Is that understood, Director?

E12 I'm afraid that man does not have power to make any such amendments, General. It's outside our sphere of influence.

C78 I don't think you quite understand, Director. This order comes directly from Treehouse.

E12 Be that as it may, General, the Law can't be tampered with by man. It's definitive. There can be no changes made.

C78 If the Law can't be changed then we'll have to have it abolished. Let it be understood that your uncooperative attitude will be reported to the appropriate committee. Good day, Director!

E12 General!

(Caller 78 laughs)

C78 I like the way you can pick up a story, Laurence. You've got a good imagination.

E12 Thank you, Miss Molly. Good to see you the last day.

C78 I hope you didn't mind. I just wanted to see what you looked like.

E12 Why?

C78 I just wanted to get a feel for you in person.

E12 Look who sounds like a pervert now …

C78 Shush! I've a very honest body. Like Isha. It doesn't lie. And I'm happy to report you're in the clear. There were no bad reactions anyway.

E12 I'd a huge body stocking on.

C78 What?

E12 I've actually no idea why I said that. It doesn't even make sense. Could it be struck from the record, General?

C78 Struck.

E12 So have you been thinking about the music since we last talked?

C78 Yeah but it's this Law business that's making me think. Do you know what's weird, Laurence? This Law shit makes you very self-aware of your actions, your motives and your intentions. The works. And Laurence, to be frank, I don't think I like it. It feels restrictive.

E12 We've got to keep our heads about us. Let's not go martyring ourselves to the music. It doesn't work. It's bullshit and it's conceited. We just end up feeling hard done by. Or people take on too much because they're trying to be bigger than they are, and they end up in little pieces.

C78 So do you follow the Law?

E12 I try but that's about as much as we can do. I nearly drove myself mad before. I probably was mad by all accounts. I became really conscious of all my intentions. Tried to chase down every 'I should'. I was riddled with fears that I wasn't good enough. I used to get these waves of shame. I'm talking about, sheer, unadulterated shame. Thick stuff. You talk about your stomach. My stomach used to literally heave with the shame I'd feel in seeing myself as I really was. Without any of the 'nice' wrapping I'd put on myself. At some point, I thought I was evil, Molly. Actually evil. Imagine the vanity of presuming I could be something as huge as evil. But then I remember going to an old piano teacher of mine. I broke down in tears and told him the way my head was working. How I kept thinking that nothing I did came from the right source. How desperate I was to escape myself. He told me that I was making a balls of the whole thing and the first thing I should be doing was not trying to be any better than I was. It was a waste of time that could be spent in healthier pursuits. –Stop thinking about goodness, he said. He told me there's a land where they don't even call it goodness, where they don't even think about it because they're all too busy laughing and basking in its source.

C78 I like that idea.

E12 –If man, he said, can open himself up to the source, all our decent actions, previously claimed by ourselves, can now correctly be attributed to this source, or this music I keep talking about. We lose the burden of ourselves. We become freer. He says that we give up our selves to become our real selves.

C78 How do you mean give our selves up exactly?

E12 There's a lot in it. It's not as scary as it sounds. In fact, it's an aspiration to lose the self to something better. The self, as we know it, is not all that great. Not as great as we'd have ourselves believe. When we give it up, we want for less and less. Because left to our devices, we'd never be satisfied. At the end of the day, we're only human.

C78 I like humans. I'm feeling quite defensive of us. In fact, I think we're wonderful.

E12 So do I, Molly. That's why I think we deserve every chance at richer lives. Being human restricts the human spirit—we're tied up by natures we can't change. These are things we can't escape.

C78 Why should we want to escape? We are what we are. You said yourself we shouldn't try and be more.

E12 We shouldn't try to be more than human, but we have to understand fully what it means to be human. As I said, we are restricted by our very nature. If we open this nature up to a higher source, we can safely free it from the restrictions of the self and still maintain our essential understanding and acceptance of human nature. Our spirits can soar.

C78 It's sounding funnier and funnier, Laurence. And not ha-ha funny either. What do you mean by soar?

E12 It's a state of being, Molly—a thrust, a feeling, an escape from everything that keeps us frustrated. Also, if we have risen to a position of some influence or power, it ensures that we will not fall to our lesser natures or stumble to abuse. It allows us to rise in good faith, understanding the music that got us there in the first place because we are all vulnerable to being devoured by greed or power or conceit or selfishness. None of us are immune. None of us. There is no man better than the next. A man's actions may be deemed worthier but there is no man actually better than the next. There's the capacity to destroy in all of us. Your contract is no longer between you and fellow men—it's between you and this something else. Once you get a taste of it, Molly, you stop caring what other people think, things become infinitely simpler if a little more ridiculous. The music tells you to go and live the life that's in you. Does that make any sense? I feel like hugging you right now.

C78 You do?

E12 Yeah. I'm excited for you too. I'm excited for your future, even if you're not.

C78 Thanks. It's a lot, you know. Especially to fresh ears. I don't think you can even understand how it sounds to me.

E12 I can imagine, Molly. Let's leave it there for today. Let's talk of other things.

C78 Too late to pretend you're normal, Laurence. Casual banter won't save you now.

E12 How are you then? I know you won't be able to resist the temptation of talking about yourself.

C78 I'm no longer my own. I've given myself away to the most wonderful music!

E12 One day you'll be able to say that sincerely.

C78 I don't know if I want to, Laurence. No offence. It's all a little up and out there.

E12 Where do you think the horizon is?

C78 I'd forgotten about our quest for the horizon. Anyway, I have to go. Talk to you soon, right?

E12 OK. Be good.

End of transcript

8:3: Molly

Here, our night begins, heavy as it is with every possibility. To be everything, just large enough to imagine fully, and better yet, to live.

And more beautiful than this arrival is the throbbing knowledge that this feeling, this potent concoction of head and heart, has many friends here. This warmth of belonging, as shy and as self-conscious as it is, has met its own, these feelings have been brought out late at night when the revellers are gone and our tongues are dripping with wild notions and banter and dreams and belonging. Knowing each other as everything we are and that which we would like to become, someday, when we get ourselves together enough to leave a place that has baptised all our heroics in beer.

We work—the hours descrambled by the countless orders, processed and wiped clean for the next.

And after, when the crowds have thinned to the bleary-eyed cluster by the door, comes a sweet and heartfelt weariness that leaves us silent and working. It collapses in on all our giggles and lets them out to scramble over the sweating glasses that sparkle anew.

It's here behind the stained wood and walls that giddiness takes us for herself. Greedily, she claims us all and we find laughs rolled up in dirtied beer labels under the old dishwasher. We find them every place and throw them back for more. Later, quietly, by the stacked glasses that sit tall as towers, comes the understanding, wordless and rich, that tells of friendships, launched and carried, by the high seasons of dirty work. And sometimes, very softly, it finds a voice, in the small hours, by the cigarette machine. It speaks of all the small things that want to be heard.

I take my thoughts away from the counter and out onto the roof. I carry them up the back stairs and share them with you.

You are here waiting for us all to gather, in your place, up on the roof. You said we should toast our new lives from a height. So we did, our friends, you and I, gathered to talk of all that is possible in a heart that still believes, gathered in your place with its quiet shelter, perched on the City's lip. You were drunk but had plans for a new sobriety. That's what you said, Augusta, up there on the roof. You said, tomorrow, bottle eighteen, and the day after, a bottle less. Descending numerically, you said, but you, ultimately ascending. And all your friends drank to the drink you would not drink. And you made us barter for all your bottles. I promised you a page for every bottle that stayed on the shelf, and you promised me my words would take their place. Lou said that they didn't sell novels in the off licence, and you said in your world they did, then laughed and fell.

After you're done sleeping, Augusta, we'll keep our promises and toast the City again from your place on the roof. The sober and the scribe, reintroducing ourselves to the City and each other.

I read it again and decide that I'll bring it in to Augusta tomorrow. The nurses say that reading things aloud may bring her round. It's been two weeks now. That's what days do, they change things. They take Augusta from the rooftop and put her in hospital.

Everyone says she's lucky to be alive and I smile at them because I've nothing to say, especially to those who never took the time to know her. Especially to those who knew I loved her and still never bothered to ask after her. Especially to those people who suddenly take themselves away from the me without getting properly mad at me first, especially those people who hide away into themselves and close the door behind them, especially those people who don't believe in me the way Augusta does and she doesn't even have to. Especially to those people who probably think it's her own fault for being drunk up on a roof and talking about silly things like toasting life from a height. Those people who probably think she should have toasted it from a table like every other normal person. Not like us, the drunk and hopelessly romantic. And even though I don't want to talk to Isha, my body craves her. I want her to come and hug me so I can push her away. I want her to push back, push herself in to find me, because I want to collapse. So she can pick me up. I want to tell her everything.

I take deep breaths. I can hear her downstairs and my stomach responds to every noise she makes. I'm afraid to go to her because I don't know what will happen. She was never one for a scene and I don't want her to go further away. I don't want to make a mess. I take a shower and get it all out there. Then I go downstairs, promising myself that the fuss-free days we used to have were mine again for the taking—just so long as I didn't mess it up again by being sad-bad-mad Molly.

Isha and Baby Mac are in the kitchen.

I feel a lifetime has passed between us since we last ate together. I smile at her shyly. Isha smiles back. She's brisk and airy but resolute as I am to reclaim every small joy we once had.

–Do you want a cup of tea? I ask as an entrance into something.

–I have one here—there's some eggs hardboiled in the fridge if you want them.

–No thanks, I say, panicking a little because nothing else comes to the ready.

I find Baby Mac instead and play with him.

–He doesn't take his morning naps so much, I say.

–He's getting bigger, she says, he doesn't need as much sleep.

I look at him. He *is* getting bigger and I wonder how long it is since everything's been right. I'm ashamed that I have not kept in touch with him as I should, ashamed that I'm lost to myself, wrapped up and choking on the 'I', as it stands to the forefront, poisoned with need. I'm ambushed by a forceful understanding that Matron did not administer this particular dosage of shame. I think of Laurence, raw and unwrapped, opened to the music.

–Chivers is in good form, I say.

–He's glad to have met the Doctor.

–Are you sure you don't want tea?

–No thanks, I have one here.

I bring my cup over to the table. I try to laugh at Baby Mac's antics, the world he governs under our chairs. Isha doesn't join me in this distraction, as she would have done in a script written for two awkward people, wordless and wanting. Isha is bulwarked, walled up safely within herself. Surviving. I take Baby Mac up on my lap and play with him whilst Isha washes up. Nothing is said then except for the great unsaid. I pretend to look at the crossword. Isha finishes the dishes, dries her hands on her apron and goes over to the counter.

–Here, look at these, Isha says.

She is standing over me with a set of photographs. She lifts Baby Mac from my arms so I can have a good look. I know what she's doing. She's reaching out as only Isha does. Never with sentimental words, but with small gestures she knows to be her way. I love Isha in this moment but I'm still angry somewhere and it's coming out to meet me. I take the packet from her. They are old photographs. And some of my memories are aroused and position themselves sleepily where I can find them.

It was Isha's birthday party. I'd organised a fancy dress despite Isha's anaemic protests. Chivers is dressed up as somebody nobody knew. An old writer, I think, or a character from some book. He looks regal and I know that he wore the like in his prime, on his dandier days that have shied away with age. Puckie is dressed up as himself. I remember him acquiring a lorgnette—I can see him in the background of one of the photographs, new toy in hand. I remember watching him that night, rosy and drunk, looking through it and smiling to himself. Pleased. I remember catching Chivers' eyes and the two of us laughing like fond and knowing parents.

I dressed up as an exclamation mark because Isha hates them so much. She refuses to use them unless it's in some serious context, like a written order left on my bedside table telling me to *Put on a wash!*

If someone can't tell I'm joking, she always says, *unless I've gone and put an exclamation mark on it, then I've no business writing to them in the first place.* That is why her notes and letters are so funny to those who know her and so scary to those who don't.

I remember catching the dot in the small electric fire and spending most of the night as a mutant exclamation mark. As a solitary I. Matron winks at me when I register this but I turn away. I'm in Isha's world now. She'll have to wait till I get back, till I'm on my own. I can hear her sometimes, chewing on her own remarks, smiling knowingly at me and waiting. I shake her off and return to Isha.

–It was a good night, I say.

Isha smiles.

–I just found them this morning, she says, it was a great night.

I look at them again. –How come Julia didn't come?

I know the second I've asked it that it's not a question but an accusation; it's a slap from me to her on behalf of Julia and

Augusta and all the other women she has judged with her honest body. It's a slap from me to her and I can see Matron grinning in the corner. *Bad Molly*, she mouths, almost salivating. *Bad Molly*.

But the anger keeps coming and knocks down my apology as it tries to find its feet.

–It was a weeknight, Isha says. Tight-lipped.

–Chivers said you didn't like her, I say in a voice that is unrecognisable as my own.

–It's not that I didn't like her, Molly, she says in a voice I do recognise as hers and I'm utterly relieved that she's stronger than my poison.

–What then? I ask. Hungrily.

–I just couldn't be the friend she wanted me to be, Isha says wearily.

–Chivers said she wanted you to be more of a mother figure.

–I can't just make that happen, Molly, you don't just switch on maternal feelings if they're not there. But I did like her, I did.

I wonder if she's trying to convince herself still.

Isha tuts in frustration then. A heavy tut. A tired tut.

–She ... she just got to me, and I know she never meant to. I suppose I've been a little angry with her since I met her. Sometimes, I thought it was jealously. Plain, simple jealousy even though I was twice her age and ... but I wasn't so much jealous of her, just the way she seemed to drift so effortlessly through life. It all seemed a bit unreal. Maybe I wanted a bit of that. She used to make me feel that I was taking life far too seriously but I don't know any other way to take it. I'm a serious person, I suppose.

I don't know what to say to this.

–No, you're not, I say. Trying to protect her from herself.

–It's not a bad thing, Molly. I'm glad I do. I don't think I'd make a very good frivolous.

–And you think she did?

–No, frivolous is the wrong word. She was sincere. I just seemed to react badly to her, like physically react badly to her company. I couldn't help it. I tried. I used to try and talk myself round, try and conjure up some warmth for her, try and give her a really decent smile, but sometimes I'd just end up grimacing politely.

–Did she notice?

–Course she did, she was sensitive to people, that's why she was so good with them. It was like she was always trying to find a moment for us to have ours. Always looking for that chance to bond with me but I think she probably made me worse then. I felt like I was being ...

I don't give her a word. My anger wants to hear what she comes up with. I want to blame her. I want to know why she can't like me.

–The poor girl was just trying to be friends with me, but I knew that we could never really be friends. No matter how hard I tried. It just wasn't there on my side. Sometimes it just isn't. It's like she presumed we could be, like she took away the choice. It's hard to explain, Molly.

–You're doing all right, I say, for an old woman with limited intelligence.

And Isha smiles then because I have stepped out to tease her. I smile because it took me, and the Matron, by surprise.

There is nice silence then between us. A slow silence that helps us digest.

I want to tell Isha that I can taste the Lows in my mouth. That they are on their way back and this time they'll be worse than the last. That Matron is enough without the Lows conspiring to make her stronger. I say nothing, hoping that she has more to say.

Matron waits as she always does.

–I've been thinking about it though, Isha says, not just since seeing the disc but even before ... before Daniel left. I shouldn't have blamed her for what happened. I knew that but I was so angry at her. I hated what she did with men, Molly. I saw all the tears your mother spent over men, all the time and effort she went to to find what it is that every woman wants. And you. 'Cause it's in our nature, Molly. I'll tell you that for nothing. It's in our nature to find a partner and have a family. As complex as everyone now is making it, it really is that simple. It's natural but she ... she had her weekday men and all the proposals you'd want. Puckie's! Saying no to a man like Puckie!

Isha is not tight-lipped now. She is open and shouting.

–Everyone wanting to make her happy, she cries, and look after her and give her a life. But she was stubborn and took what she wanted. I think I resented her for only wanting the good life as she saw it because it all comes as a package. The good and the bad, Molly. We can't go picking at it and making our own rules. It doesn't work like that, we just have to say yes to life as it is.

The room changes. Isha's eyes start to swell and her mouth twists and trembles until finally it collapses and falls open in tears. I understand that this has lived alone in Isha's head and heart for years. I would've found it easily enough had I taken the time to look. If I'd bothered to open my own two eyes.

Her words are unrelenting and they won't give her a minute to breathe.

–I think about how she must have felt, how much she must have hurt, and I don't want to be angry at her anymore. I want to tell her that I'm sorry, that it wasn't her fault. I'd like to make her tea and leave it on her bedside table as she's sleeping. I'd like to look in at her every now and again. I still don't want to be her best friend, but I want to tell her I'm sorry for everything that's happened.

Isha is crying and shaking so much that she lets me hold her hand, or she doesn't notice that mine has crept into hers. We sit like that for a fleeting eternity. Isha gathers herself then and smiles at me with her red eyes. In this moment I'm pained by the weight of my love for her. It's greater than me and it hurts. I want to keep her safe forever but the world does not allow for such moments—it's wardened instead by life, and life, like everything it maintains, is struggling with itself and its other. There are no forevers here.

–How's Augusta? she asks, trying to scramble away from her own tears.

–She's still the same. I wrote her something so that I could read it to her. Do you want to hear it? I ask. Hopeful. Eager. Challenging her.

Isha looks uncomfortable.

–Leave it there, she says. I'll read it myself later.

–I can't, I'm going to the hospital now. The anger throws itself at both of us, but it's fighting for me. I want it to stop, I want it to leave her alone, but it's bigger than Molly and shrugs me aside, grunting.

I'm not angry at her because she doesn't love Augusta like I do. I'm not angry at her because she disapproves of my lifestyle. I'm not angry at her because she's stopped believing I'll write. I'm angry at her because the hurting won't stop and she's left me alone with the Matron. I'm angry at her because I can't blame her. I'm angry that bad-sad-mad Molly needs somebody to blame.

Blame yourself then, the Matron shrieks. Unnerved. Impatient. *It's so bloody simple,* she screams, *you're the one that's sick and you're making me sick watching.*

The Matron stops and exhales. She smoothes down her pinafore with her shaking hands. She moves closer to me and holds my arms down by my sides. She looks me calmly in the eye. *The sooner you accept it, Molly, the easier it will be for me to do my job. I'm the only one who truly knows you. You can't listen to the people out there, no matter how much you want to believe what they're saying. They don't know you like I do. You can fool a giddy*

pie man, she says, *but you will never fool the Matron.*

She takes me to her and holds me tight. I look over her shoulder. The box is blaring in the sitting room.

–Although the WAR may go on a little longer than expected, it's sure to bring a new age of peace.

He's lying. WAR begets WAR as hurt begets hurt. Sometimes the circle has to be broken and opened so a new order can find its way in.

9:1: Mr. ****

I feel good when I wake. I'm glad I've remembered the girl's face—animated by fear, illuminated by neon.

I get up, shower, and listen for the Ghost. I hear nothing but something tells me she's not sleeping. She's not breathing, here, in this house. I leave for work wondering where she could have gone at such an hour but the where is overtaken by the why. I have never known the Ghost to leave earlier than me. We had our order. It aggrieves me that she has taken the liberty of upsetting it.

I'm angry before I even meet Freddie but the mere sight of him makes me want to spit. So I do. There, on his papers. I keep the one in my hand and walk away. Clearing the shards of phlegm from my throat. I can hear Freddie shouting after me, protesting. I'm too much my own to care.

As I pump through the crowded City, I cry silently for all to hear. I'm strong, I'm willing, I can't be defeated. Life has finally found me. I have met my self. We rejoice in each other. But something is dragging me down from behind. I roll and scuffle in cheap leather before I recognise Freddie's bad breath. He doesn't shout at me. Instead his anger spits and sizzles. He is red-faced and squat-necked with frustration and injustice. People don't stop. I get on top of him and hold his itching fists by his flabby wrists. I'm surprised he chased me this far. Impressed even, if I wasn't the sort to snigger. Freddie is foaming. I smile and bring his fist to his head, then the other. Freddie's boxing himself in the head. Repeatedly, he won't stop. I tell him to stop, to go easy on himself, to give himself a break. But he doesn't listen or can't hear too well, what with the howling he's doing and all the laughing that's coming from the gambling boys on the curb. They seem to make him worse. Poor Freddie. I finally get bored and give him back his hands.

I leave him there and go on to the shed. I look over the rag salvaged from my round with Freddie. The front page is taken up by a full colour photograph of a hostage.

His left eye is a purple and crimson shadow that falls over his sagging flesh. His mouth holds none of the shape it once had. The numbers in the corner of the image are blurred. The counter makes its record. This is the new still life. The City is incensed. The Flanade Convention has been broken and people seem surprised. Morons! There are no rules for war between desperate men. They do what they will and their will will be done, by men who're willing and killing for fun. The unwilling are killing and being undone, by men who'll shoot them for willing to run.

My will, your will, we all will, to kill will. Willdo. Wontdo!

I've been away from my self for too long. *I'm home*, I roar for all and sundry to hear.

Ankles looks up and starts to giggle. She wants me but I want me more.

I have taken three calls when Fathead comes in to see me.

–Mr. Wontdo wants a quick word in my office, he says.

I'm able for both of them.

I follow Fathead down the stairs. I watch his asses hobble after him, chasing his every heave-ho.

Mr. Wontdo rises slightly as I close the door behind me.

–Hello again, he says and smiles.

–And again, I say. My eyes atwinkle.

I'm brave. I'm home.

–I only need a quick word, he says, I appreciate it's mid-morning and the phones are busy. Well, you're busy …

I nod but I say nothing from the seat *I* have positioned to his right.

–It's in reference to your current stint, we want to use it to pioneer an idea I've had for some time.

I nod again, giving him an open floor, enclosed by my obvious disdain.

–Well, I'd like for this house to start calling people back, investing in the more long-term engagements. I'm not suggesting we return each call but on occasions to make our clients feel that they're valued, even up the exchange a little, make it all seem that little bit more sincere, I suppose—in fact, not to make it *seem* more sincere, let's be more sincere. Make people feel wanted, which they are, of course, in the best possible sense. All monies aside, we want to give real value to our clients. Does that make sense to you, Mr. ****?

I nod. He waits for me to say more, so I nod again, my eyes firing with an edgy enthusiasm. Perhaps they think I'm high. Perhaps I am or, perhaps, exquisitely low. My silence continues unabashed.

–I'd like you to make the first return call, to Caller 78. It's her birthday in a couple of days. For now, the calls will be returned on birthdays only.

–We have her contact number in her file, Fathead says, that's also how we know her date of birth, they give us certain information when subscribing. We keep building on it.

Fathead says this with enormous pride. I wonder if he realises that everybody has got everybody else's stats. I wonder how stupid he really is. Fathomless.

–We are also considering bringing in psychologists, Wontdo says, to help evaluate the more frequent callers, help us to help you understand them more, understand their needs, grow with them, form a real friendship almost.

I smile now.

–How did you get into the business, Mr. Wontdo? I ask. You start this side of the shed or the other?

–I understand both sides, Mr. ****, he says. Controlled.

–As a business or as a pleasure?

–As both, he says. Ending this conversation here.

–I must let you back to your work, Wontdo continues, you'll be given the contact details on the day in question. I hope you both enjoy the exchange.

I don't know why he added the last sentence. I don't understand how it was offered, how I should accept it. It reeks of a goodwill that belies our prior sparring. So I take it as it is, a fact I already know.

I go back to my desk and absorb all that has happened of late. I think about her, and the possibility of her calling again. I think about everything that's been said, the urge that came from nowhere, telling of more than it should. I shudder in recollection and roar.

A colleague comes into my office. He hands me a package.

–This was left for you downstairs, he says.

I take it from him, knowing already that it's from the Doctor. The man waits for me to open it but I stare back at him until I reach the hind of his retreat. I get up from my desk and close the door properly. I put a chair up against it. There is a memory knocking on my skull to get out. I don't want any of the men in these corridors to see it.

I sit down again and hold the package in my hands. I can see through its brown paper wrapping to the grey-haired man beneath. I put my head down on the desk and close my eyes.

He is only ten years old and small for his age. I see his cracked brown leather sandals and his white goosy legs hung from his shorts. I hear his frustrated breaths. He jumps up and up, over and over again. His breath hits the old linoleum floor before he does. Every time, a smack and dull thud. The ball stays where it is, stubbornly perched out of reach. He jumps over and over again, each jump dampened by his tears. I can see my father then, coming in to us. He sees the baby jumping and the tall boy sitting down, staring at the baby jumping. It's too late and I know he's seen my smile. He takes down the ball and gives it to the baby, gulping now, not jumping. And my father looks at me, trying with every moment in him to muster up the truth. That was always the thing with my father. Even though I never killed my brother, he knew that someday I could have.

The phone rings and I answer it.

I finish work and make my way home. I pass the schoolyard with all the crusty-eyed children scattered in its embrace. I think I see the Ghost. I call out but the woman does not respond. I've nothing to say to her but I want to make sure she's mine. I see the Boy I saw before. The one with the look more coherent than the others, squatting by a doorframe, scraping it clean with an old knife. I move on before he can look up. I hurry home so I can hurry out again. I need to see the Dishwasher.

Cynthia is standing by her front gate. She's not wearing her leotard. Today she's wrapped up in an enormous jacket with a suede collar.

–I'm heading up north to see my sister, she volunteers.

I stop and give her a smile I find at the bottom of my trouser pocket. One of Laurence's, left over from the day's stint. I blow the fluff off it and leave it room to breathe.

–You seem in good form, she says, but you can't be as excited as she is.

I smile some more to invite her to continue, to have her put me in the know, unknowingly. Perhaps the Ghost hasn't told her of our domestic life. Of our silences and poison.

–He's gorgeous, and imagine all this time he's been in my Tuesday morning class. He's a mute, even though that doesn't take from him one bit. Maybe the City's finally getting a little smaller, Cynthia says. Smiling at me.

I ask her some questions which she doesn't recognise as such. She'll probably tell her sister that it was the first time we really spoke. *He's not at all as severe as you'd imagine him to be from the way he carries on*, she'll say. *He's really quite warm when he trusts you enough to open up.*

I tend to open people up, she'll say, *especially with the work I do in my classes.*

Her sister will smile and pour her another glass of wine.

My head is spinning as I enter the house. The Ghost is not there and this disturbs me more than it should, considering my roaring strength of recent nights. I sit in my chair for an hour, then I put on my coat and make my way to see the Dishwasher. I want to see Anna and the twins—I want to show her my new resolve.

The restaurant is quiet when I get there and Anna is gone. I sit down and make do with a spindly girl who looks stupidly afraid. *What does she think I'll do here?* I muse.

Meet you in the Depot, I say silently to her, *let us talk of our future plans there.*

I think of the girl in the truck—and the bundle. But it's not working, I'm not roaring as I should and I wonder if Laurence had been there too. Somewhere.

I eat my dinner and drink my coffee. Fragments of conversation come back to me, whole sentences are remembered and nest uneasily in my mouth. I feel a little queasy and push my desert away. I want my sleep earlier than usual tonight. I don't want the other voice to come find me. That honeyed balm she keeps coming back for—that they all keep coming back for. They all believe him and worse still, some of them speak of love. Had he not spoke of it? That and hugs. I get up and run to the toilet. I vomit into the sink. The Dishwasher comes out of the cubicle. He is my relief.

–Come back later on, he says, we'll play.

I wipe my mouth and nod, leaving to find my table again. I order my third coffee.

Later, the fat owner comes in and the greasy takings are brought to his fingers. My cup is refilled in his presence and I make my way out back.

The Dishwasher has the board set up. In fact, he even looks impatient. I sit down on an upturned crate. We begin to play.

–It looks like you're losing the fight, he says, you better tell me from the beginning.

So I tell him everything. He looks at me for a long time, then says, –Come back tomorrow night, I'll have more to say then.

I leave with my head down.

I hear a drumbeat on the corner of the Iron District. Irregular. Angry. My feet encounter a small crowd that I'm forced to walk around. I look up from under my hat to see who's making all the noise. There is a tall black man, in tribal dress, banging on a drum and talking to a small crowd.

–Nobody is starving to death in the City, he cries, I mean physically starving to death. People may be hungry but they're not dying from it.

BANG

BANG

BANG

–What I'm here drumming for is the truly hungry. I speak of lands that have gone belly up. Places with no food BANG no waste BANG no addicts BANG no thing BANG but starvation.

BANG –This is a man-made famine.

BANG –Made by one man with a hundred heads, milling around the dreams that are dead.

BANG –Picking at flesh they take for their own,

BANG –Turning their backs on their fellow bones.

He comes in closer to the crowd and says in a generous whisper, –They say if you lie with your ear to the ground, bodies sound, falling down, the earth's hide is a drum skin and the beat that breaks us, comes in rounds. Nature's gone and made a drum skin from the earth's hide. Whose nature we be asking? Man's nature. Keep banging, tummies panging—not here, not yet. Keep our heads down, fight our own wars. We don't much like the news.

I don't care to hear more. The Doctor's people are everywhere. I do as he predicts, I keep my head down until I reach my street. Cynthia's house is in darkness and I wonder if the Ghost has left me. I step into the hall and sniff out her bedroom. I can see a sleeping body in her bed. I think about waking her, letting her know I know but I don't. Instead I go to my bedroom as quick as I can, avoiding my chair and the package on my bedside locker, inscribed again with the Doctor's hand. I get into bed and sleep.

When I follow the line of my body downwards, I see a small boy standing over me. He is looking for Laurence but instead he finds me. I smell his hair and a plan forms in my mind. I think of a way to reclaim myself. In one small second everything seems obvious again.

9:2: Telephone Transcript

In Search of Infinite Relief, C.W. Sisle
Contracted to Gleeson Media Group
Subcontracted to Employee 12
Recorded at 6.31 p.m. on 15/05/****

E12 Hello?

C78 Hi, Laurence.

E12 How are you? I thought you'd abandoned me again.

C78 Thought you'd scared me off with all your mad shit.

E12 Yeah. Where have you been?

C78 Augusta's sick. She's unconscious. I probably called drunk and told you the works.

E12 No, you didn't. You sound closed, Molly.

C78 Maybe. I'm just not feeling all that much one way or another but I'm fine. How are you?

C78 Good. Tell me what happened.

E12 We were on the roof of the bar—we go up there a bit, especially Augusta and me. It doesn't really matter. She fell. That's the bottom line. She's in a coma now. Her body is in relatively good order considering. I have this spiel I rattle off if people ask after her. I won't give it to you. I've said it so often to well-wishers asking after her in the bar. She's loved, a lot of people are asking.

E12 What are the doctors saying?

C78 Time, talking to her. The usual route that's taken.

E12 How's everything else?

C78 Fine. Grand. How are you?

E12 Good.

C78 Let's talk about your stuff again. I've been thinking about it. I must get you to tell Augusta when she wakes up. She'll give you a proper run for your money. I'm inclined to believe most things I can twist to make me feel better. Although I have to say I have a few questions concerning your beliefs and my well-being.

E12 Ask as many questions as you want. It works well against an argument.

C78 OK, well I'm still finding the Law of Human Nature hard to swallow. Not swallow exactly, that's the problem, maybe—it's convincing. I know the feeling you're talking about. The 'should' feeling. But I resent it. I keep thinking I should do this, I should do that, I should do more constructive things with my time, maybe start living in the real world a bit more. There's so much that's wrong. And then I start thinking, you know, should we have been on the roof of a bar at five in the morning? Like you said, they follow you round. And like you said, you have to keep some perspective on it. Common sense. My head's not exactly overrun with common sense—that's why I used to always ask Isha what I should do. But I'm too old to have to keep dragging off her like that.

E12 I know, Molly. But that's why we—

C78 Puckie. Now there's a man who drinks a bottle of cop-on a day. But I'm not like Puckie as much as I might want to be. Anyway, I find this notion of a Law hard. It makes me uneasy. On a very basic level.

E12 We should be uneasy, Molly. Man should be uneasy. Look at the state of things.

C78 It's no worse than at any other time. People always say we're fucking everything up.

E12 Maybe we always are.

C78 I'm not. I'm not killing anyone or trying to take something that's not mine. And I think you're very hard on mankind; most people I know are good. I don't really know anyone who's a complete cunt—excuse the language but sometimes it's perfectly apt.

E12 Molly, it's because I love mankind that I think like this.

C78 Nothing can be perfect. You know that.

E12 I know. But maybe we could tip the balance a little more in our favour. That's why it helps to give ourselves up to something. It's the only vantage point from where we might see some progress.

C78 I don't know, Laurence. I don't even understand how I'm meant to give myself up. I don't even know what you're saying, really, if I'm being brutally honest with you.

E12 In some ways it means being able to see yourself exactly as you are and to understand and accept all that that entails—your place in the world, your relentless desire to satisfy the 'I' and the restrictions placed upon you by your very nature.

C78 Why? Sorry to be so basic but why the fuck should I?

E12 No. Perfect question, Molly. Well, I think the Law exists for the good of mankind. As I said, it's like a bulwark against negative forces like greed, or conceit, or, worst of all, pride. It's hard when you first consider this Law, because it gets in the way of what we consciously want for ourselves.

C78 I take things too far.

E12 So do I, but it's a comfort to know, that with a humble understanding, we can go all the way in the right direction. Here's the thing, Molly. Almost everything we do, the good and the bad, is self-serving. But there's a difference between doing a decent thing and being a decent man. Same as a musician can play one song well but this doesn't make him a good musician. If that musician keeps playing for the music, eventually he'll honestly be a good musician. Same way as if someone keeps on doing decent things, he'll eventually become a decent man.

C78 So he does things for the sake of decency even if he doesn't really want to? It's almost like he has to practice his decency. It's that practical application thing again.

E12 But that's my point, Molly. A right action done for the wrong reasons doesn't help the internal quality or character develop. We forget that it's the source of the right action that really counts in the end.

C78 Do something good because you want to and not because you should?

E12 We can build up this internal quality so that doing the right thing becomes near second nature. It stops being so conscious an effort. We become so familiar with the music, the dance steps we laboured over become a true joy. We start to celebrate life in the everydays. Imagine, Molly!

C78 You're getting closer to a sale, that's for sure. But I'm still having problems with the pack of 'I should's sniffing around at my ankles. I suppose I'm looking for an easier way.

E12 That's the vantage point from the 'I'. It can only see what it can't have. The Law is tough. We should follow it no matter how difficult or dangerous or annoying it is. At first, when we're reminded of it, it seems to be all about rules and duties and worse but it leads us to a place beyond all that. A place that my old piano teacher told me about—where the

Law is not even spoken about, they're too busy basking in its source.

C78 It sounds incredible. Literally.

E12 Why shouldn't it be? Anyway, it's something you find credible in a different way.

C78 You said 'worst of all, pride'. I thought selfishness was the worst thing.

E12 There's no worst thing, Molly. There isn't a list but pride's a little scary. It's the anti-state of the mindset we can hope to get to. It's the most corrosive force in man's nature.

C78 Like how? Explain it to me.

E12 Pride is competitive. It doesn't really care about having any one thing—it cares about having more than anyone else. It has such an appetite. And it doesn't really *care* for the things it has. If that makes sense.

C78 Like it doesn't take care of them?

E12 Yeah.

C78 Go on so. The music.

E12 Yeah. To love anything outside our selves is a step in the right direction. Although, to love anything, even someone, more than you love the music, is a step back.

C78 You see that gets my back up. Where does it say I have to love it more than I love Isha? Do you know what I mean? I know what you mean by the 'I should' feeling, I know I should do this or that, but I don't know about loving anything more than I love her, even if we're not having a heyday of it at the moment. It's a more certain knowledge than most things floating around in my head.

E12 Course you love her, Molly. But she's only human too. She's fallible like everyone else. It's not fair to her to set her up on a place of worship. You're not being a friend to her. Knowing what I know of Isha, I don't think she'd want you to love her beyond anything else. With all of your heart will do.

C78 I always go too far. Sorry. Go back to your pride thing.

E12 Molly, arguing these points is good. We have to ask questions. But pride—it's power that pride really enjoys. A proud man looks down on others, that's why he can't see the amazing power around him. That's why I can't stand people who profess themselves to be 'good' men. Some smart finger work there as you'd say, Molly.

C78 I know those people. Maybe I'm one.

E12 We all are in some sense. I'm talking about people who think goodness itself is something they own. They think they are better people than those they judge to be 'bad' men. No one in this City has the right to judge.

C78 Fuck, Laurence. This is scary stuff. I'm almost afraid to feel anything in case I'm being proud.

E12 Let's make sure we understand it, Molly.

C78 That tactical 'we' again. Nice one. Tell me.

E12 For one, pleasure in being praised is not pride, not the pride I'm talking about. Say if Isha praises you, the pleasure's derived, not from what she says you are, but from pleasing someone you rightly wanted to please. The danger comes when you start to delight more in yourself than in the actual praise. But needing adoration from others, always trying to extract praise from people, it's a vanity but it's reassuringly human. It's childlike. It's shows you're not content with your own admiration, you still value people enough to want to please them. The real poison comes when you look down on people so much so that you don't care for their opinion.

C78 But that's contrary to what you said before, about not needing the opinion of others. I can't remember exactly what you said but it didn't sound like that.

E12 I know what you're saying. Asking people you respect for an opinion is not the same as being paralysed by fear of what people may think. You just have to read the music.

C78 Is it safe to keep my compliments drawer then?

E12 As long as you understand them for what they are. You shouldn't need it, but I don't think you should throw away the memories of pleasing others either.

(*Caller 78 exhales heavily*)

C78 There's a lot of places you can fall trying to get to this source … A lot of places.

E12 Course there is. Where's the fun if you don't get to fall? All you can do is get up and try again. We shouldn't be afraid of making mistakes. We should have a cartoon bravery that helps us laugh at ourselves. Ideally, on our quest for the new horizon we should be able to travel alone if that's how things fall. Everyone needs so much from each other. They tie themselves up in knots and pollute every small joy with need. Molly, I can't tell you how destructive need can be when it's misplaced or forced into the dynamics of a relationship. Need poisons.

C78 Everybody needs, Laurence.

E12 I understand that, Molly. I need too, but I'm talking about a different need.

C78 OK. I'm going to have to stop you there, Laurence. I've to go. But

I won't leave it so long before I call again. I promise. I just ...

E12 Only call if you want, Molly. And we don't have to talk about any of this if you don't want to. We can talk about other stuff or I could just listen.

C78 No. I enjoy it. In a sick way. I'm kidding. I've to go. Bye, Laurence.

E12 Bye, Miss Molly Mae.

End of transcript

9:3: Molly

I don't feel like playing with Monkey, instead I put my head down and push myself out of the crowds I find on every corner. The WAR is being waged on every monitor, there is blood all over the camera lens.

I turn away. I can't digest any more of it. I feel sick. I feel the hospital's shadow on the back of my neck. I think of Augusta. I think of Isha and the last time we actually talked. Isha stands as a huge 'I should' before me. Perhaps she's everything I should be but can't be, my nature having had its way with all possibility of change. I think of Julia and Isha's tears. I think of my mother. I think about Augusta, humming and ducking, and I wonder if she only takes what she wants from this life. She doesn't take much if she does and I love her more in this moment for all the things she's never had. I love her for all the times she never judged, for all the times she smiled instead. I imagine her playing marbles with the street kids, bringing out the little bit of child that the City saw fit to leave them, doling out her own recklessly—always enough Augusta to go round. I want to tell her about Laurence and all the things he told me about the music. I need to know what she would have said. It's important to me that I know. *You can't live in your own world all the time*, Isha says, but Augusta says there's no other way to live. I wonder what my mother would have said. She might have giggled and typed up a memo, telling me that the only way to judge a man is by his shoes. I can hear Matron hustling her weight behind me so I try and pull my thoughts in a little. I don't want her breathing all over them.

I go into a coffee outlet to grab something warm. If this day is cold, it's also heavy—its back broken by the darkness that squirms overhead. I recognise the girl wiping down the trays at the station. We were at school together. She was in the bottom class, I was in the top one. A wave of resentment sparks in my gut for a school that helped create the difference. We were in art class together. It was the only place the two classes ever seemed to overlap. I smile shyly at her. She smiles back. I drink my coffee and bring my tray up to the station, trying to tell her that we are both the same. *Why not invite her round to your soup kitchen, give her some broth?* Matron snarls. The girl comes up behind me with a tray. She wipes it into the bin, ten milk jiggers lost to its pink plastic folds.

–How much milk do people think they need? I ask.

–People just grab as many as they can, they don't think.

–I suppose you can just put them back, but you shouldn't really have to.

–I can't, she says, we're not allowed.

–Why not?

–In case people syringe them, she says wearily.

–With what?

–Bleach, she says. Deadpan.

–Why? I ask again.

–I don't know, because some people are really fucked up? Anyway, we've got to throw everything out that's been out on the floor.

–That's unreal, I say.

–I saw that girl from your class on *Sisterhood*, did you see it?

–What girl? What's *Sisterhood*?

–Some reality show except with all girls, it's stupid really but I just thought you might have seen her. You might be friends with her.

–What was her name?

–Radiana something, she says, looking over at her boss.

–That would make sense, Radiana always wanted to be on the box.

–That's twelve people from our year that have been on the box for one thing or another. My friend Dresnith keeps track. She's a bit obsessed. She's been on twice. She's had her skin dyed. You wouldn't even recognise her now.

–Dresnith had the big eyes.

–Yeah, she says, she still has those at least. She works up in the Commerce District. Collects stats.

–What's here like?

I survey the coffee dock. It's cheap, plastic, music-less.

She half smiles. –Well, I was hardly destined for bigger and better things. My exams weren't shouting for me.

–Fuck it, I say because I don't know what she wants to hear.

I tell her where I work and to call in sometime.

I go back out into the streets. I don't remember what I was like at school. I hope I was nice. I want her to see that I'm getting nicer. That I'm trying. Matron snorts. She was there, in the coffee dock, breathing over everything I said.

You are trying, she says, *I know. And you could spend the rest of your life in that repulsive state but people'll sniff it out, Molly. It's a sickening smell. It reeks. You know that yourself. You can try all you want but what's done is done. People will find out what you are—they'll be tipped off by the sweat on your brow. They'll just have to push aside all your smiles, all your 'I love you's and what-*

ever else you come up with, and then they'll see the poison that I see. They'll see the sickness that's humping the rot.

Maybe I was just trying to make a connection like Chivers said, I cry, *that's not a bad thing.*

Don't mind Chivers, we've gone over all of this before.

But why do people say they like me? I ask simply. Confused.

She scowls when I say this and I wonder if she's a little afraid of the people that live outside my head.

And the Villagers, I say, feeding off her scowl. *They like me too.*

She smiles when I say this because she's not afraid of the Villagers. *They don't know any better than you, you're all as bad as each other. They're off living in their happy-little-land,* she sneers, the same way she sneers at me when I'm happy. *You'll believe me when they eventually get wise and chase you away screaming. You'll come back to me then, Molly. You don't belong out there, you belong in here with me,* she says and wipes my brow. She stoops to kiss my forehead. It's nice to be kissed, even by lips as thin as hers.

Then out of nowhere I hear a fiddle and the Village Lunatic knocks her aside from behind. He looks at me and we both begin to laugh. I'm stunned. *She'll be gone, Miss Molly,* he says with eyes wide as a headlight gaze, *one of these days she'll be gone and we'll all be free to be as happy as we want. And she liked you, that girl there from schooling, she liked you. She just thought you were a little mad.*

Bad-mad? I ask.

No, Miss Molly, not bad mad, just mad and laughing like me.

He plays a ditty on the fiddle and runs away again.

I stop in the street and throw back my head in laughter. Loud. Cackling. Manic. Unapologetic.

When eventually I stop, Matron is clamouring to her feet so I push her back down and make a dash for the hospital. I have too many friends there. She'll have to wait by the door. I think about her calling in the Lows, about them waiting for me when I come out. I'm not sure if the Lows will get past the security of friendship. I'm not sure of all that much these days. I realise that I have started to float a little. Even my yesterdays are a little blurry.

The foyer is the same as ever. It hurts. These greying throngs have not the time to begin again.

I crawl onto the end of Chiver's bed.

–How's your friend? he asks.

–Still the same, I say, I'm going to go over to her after. I've something to read to her.

An old man in a wheelchair is pushed past Chivers' door. We both look at him and listen to the creaking wheels that feel their way across the floor.

–Old people always make me cry, I say.

–I'm an old people, he says.

–No, you're not, not really. You don't make me cry anyway.

–Sorry, Chivers says wryly.

–No, it's OK. Don't feel inadequate. You're just not cute enough yet. You don't even have liver stains. Your eyes don't water.

–Why do the others make you cry then?

–Not all of them, Chivers, I don't cry every single time I see an old person. That'd be some kind of condition. Sometimes they fill me up in a really good way. It's just—take the last day. I saw this old man walking down the street, downtown. He was taking these tiny steps. Now I mean tiny. I'd say it would take him the whole morning to get from, say here, to the end of the hall. He had his shopping in an old laundry cart and there he was, pushing it along, probably happy out. But the minute I saw him, I started bawling crying. I mean, my heart literally broke so I said to myself,

Molly, have a cigarette and then go over to see if he wants a hand. So I have a cigarette, I could have had twenty and he still would have been right in front of me, that's how slow he was. Anyway, puffing, puffing, finish the cigarette. I take a deep breath and then go up to ask him if he needs any help and then he's asking me if I'm OK, if there's something wrong, can he help in any way? I just can't stop crying so I make up some story about a boyfriend I'd just broken up with. Some story so he doesn't know I'm crying for him. So he tells me all about his first twenty girlfriends as we walk home. He was a right ladies' man. I think he could even have been chancing his arm with me.

The bed is shaking from Chivers' laugh. I laugh too, in full recollection of the absurdity that was—gone unseen till now. I feel ridiculous and it's a relief. I think of Laurence and try to remember to tell him this. Chivers looks at me thoughtfully before opening his mouth.

–People are resilient, Molly, given the right encouragement. But we definitely idolise youth now, that's for sure.

–Did you tell Puckie that one? he asks then.

–I forgot about it, I only thought of it now because of the old people thing.

–I'll have to, he says. Claiming it for himself.

–I don't know where we got you from, he says as he wipes away a tear from the corner of his eye.

–So you see why I'm a wreck, I'm emotionally drained from hanging out with all you old people, You, Isha, Shuffles there the last day. I've got to join a youth group or something.

–Jump in the hammock, he says, I need to stretch my legs out a bit.

Chivers has the longest, thinnest, funniest legs I've ever seen in real life. Maybe even funnier than Monkey's. His knees are like two little peanuts. He pulls the covers back and flashes me. His legs make me laugh every time, especially when he makes his feet dance.

I lie in the hammock while Chivers fights the sheets for his own space. I think of the one-man wrestling show he always did with a blanket or duvet. Every now and again you'd see his head emerge, smiling, before being pulled back down into the brawl by some invisible opponent. His back is too bad to do this anymore so I don't remind him of it, although I'm sure he remembers.

–I suppose it's because they're vulnerable and maybe lonely, I say, and some of them must know too much to re-imagine the life that's behind them. I think people lose their powers of imagination as they get older so they can't escape this life too easily. Maybe that's why—

–What are you talking about, Molly?

–I don't know—loneliness, old people, the *Eggaminer*.

–What time is it?

–It's now, I say, looking around for the remote but Chivers already has it in his hands.

He finds the *Eggaminer* on the same channel we find it every week. This really is the lowest of the box but we watch it anyway—faithfully. We comment on all the donators, on their looks, their hobbies, their interviews, their jewellery, everything, and then we decide who we'd buy our eggs from if we wanted to have children. Thirty per cent of the City's women are infertile. There's even talk of impregnating men but it's all hysterics, all hype. The only people taking it seriously are the comedians and the scientists.

Tonight, Chivers and I pick the same woman. We nearly always do. They're always the most well-read. Chivers and I are intellectual snobs. That's what Puckie usually says but tonight he says, –Turn that shit off, as he appears in the doorway.

He comes to rest his huge frame in a sweated chair by Chivers' bed.

–How are you feeling? he asks his neighbour.

–Great, says Chivers, and your good self?

–Fuck off, Puckie says and smiles.

–Chivers and I have decided to buy eggs from one Bonnie Pricewater of Papier Avenue, the Print District, I tell him, she's a 34-year-old Caucasian who loves reading in bed and playing with her two dogs.

Puckie shakes his head at me and exhales wearily.

–You may feel a little hostile to our Bonnie now, I say, but when we're married and the time is right, you'll be thankful for this investment.

Puckie nods his head at Chivers. –I thought you were going to marry Legs 11 here.

–I was until I heard you were throwing away marriage proposals, I say. Unthinking. Now horrified. Puckie looks at me funny then and I know it's time for me to run away from myself again.

–I'm sorry, Puck, I say, I didn't mean that the way it came out.

I'm unbelievably thankful that Puckie's generosity of spirit's bigger than the both of us. Half smiling, he gets up from his wrinkled trouser crotch and walks over to me. He upturns the hammock and sits back down.

–Ouch, they're tiles, Puckie! I shout from the tangled chorus of my laughter.

A figure appears at the door and then another follows on his coat tails.

Chivers smiles broadly. They are introduced as the Doctor and Mr. Nomoré. I wonder if Chivers fancies the Doctor but a Village Farmer shakes his head and throws me a scolding eyeful. *Molly*, he tuts. *You're right*, I say and give my attention back to the room.

–Old people make Molly cry, Chivers says, so try not to look too vulnerable or lonely.

He doesn't make eye contact with me because he has turned to Puckie.

–Remind me to tell you that one, Chivers says to him.

I smile at the two newcomers but hunt down Chivers with a look of playful indignation.

The Doctor is fresh-faced but creased in all the right places and I could give time to each line, as the stories unfold, seated in a smile that is kindly and bold. *Remember that, Scribe*, I tell myself but it's too late and I know that I have already forgotten it. I think about going back in after it but the present company takes me away. And I wonder if I miss Isha at all. I dare myself to think that I don't, I dare myself to feel nothing for her gaping absence. I have all the courage in the world but my heart just won't take it on. The heart is nobody's fool even when it's flailing in anger.

Mr. Nomoré has wild eyes that are taking me in without consulting me first. I smile at him but I'm closed, defensive. He is tall and thin—a cascade of wrinkles. His eyes shine, swimming in excitement. He shakes my hand vigorously, unrelenting. The Doctor tells him to give the girl her hand back.

–You'll only make her cry, he says. Teasing.

This time my look hits Chivers right between the eyes. The Doctor, Puckie and Chivers talk among themselves. Puckie looks particularly serious. I think I hear him cursing under his breath. I can hear Chivers asking the Doctor if this is the best way to handle things. Mr. Nomoré sits and looks at me, his energy bounds back and forth between us. He seems eager for human contact, for interaction. I give up trying to listen to the other three and turn my attention to the man before me. We talk about the hospital for a bit then he asks me to sing a song. I don't want to and I turn to the others for help. The Doctor seems to understand. I know somewhere that he has been listening carefully to our conversation. He seems conscious that his visit is intruding on mine.

–Why not show Molly your studio? Chivers suggests.

I feel like a ten-year-old but Mr. Nomoré is too excited at the prospect for me to even consider making my excuses. I think of Augusta and I grow anger. I smile in feigned compliance and Mr. Nomoré grabs me by the hand. I look at the ground because I can't honestly look at Chivers. I don't have to—he knows that I don't really want to go. I know I should go. I know I should want to go. It's a simple request that'll make an old man very happy. I think of Laurence and the pathway to the source. I think of Laurence and put on my mask. Smiling, I allow Mr. Nomoré to take me by the hand, through a skinny door, up a winding stairs to a room overlooking the City.

–I do the hospital radio from here, he says. I do requests.

With my smiling mask in place, I pretend I want him to play a request for Augusta.

–Tell me about her first, he says.

So I do. I tell him more then I mean to. I can't help myself. I want so much for her to come back.

–She sounds wonderful, he says. Gathering me in with his huge smile.

–I never really took to perfectly rounded individuals, he says then—more to himself, but with a natural generosity that allows me to overhear.

–I think because I wanted to be one, he says, once upon a time. Spherical. Completely even on every front, completely in control. I've met people like that since and they always seem a little unreal. I find it hard to get into their core. I want their loves to stand out, shouting. I want to get a grasp on their passions. I want them to be shaped like no other I've ever met. I want to be able to find a way in through their wounds. I want them to be themselves, thoroughly and utterly.

He waits for a song to finish, then says softly into the microphone –This song is for Augusta, who is taking a little snooze for herself. He winks at me.

The song plays then and it's beautiful. A soundscaped melody full of soft brass that calls for hope's attention. I close my eyes and exhale.

–I've to get going, I say when it ends.

–I hear it's your birthday soon, he says. Come up and visit me again. I'll have a present for you. And I'll play a request for you.

He smiles at me.

–How did you know it was my birthday?

–I watch out for these things, he says and smiles, a wordless mischief in his eyes. I make him a promise that I don't want to keep. I'm already tired thinking about all the smiling I'll have to do to keep an old man away from my ratty self.

I go sit with Augusta and wish she and I could go drinking again. I want to ravage the beer—drink and inhale till I forget. No one else, just the two of us, drinking and swallowing till I collapse on her floor—speechless, thoughtless, closed, quiet, gone until she carries me to bed. Have her come in and get me, feed me water and clean towels. Tell me the day ahead can't be wasted by little people with big appetites. Have her put me on the street again, fighting, resolved to victory.

I put the radio on. It gushes softly by her ear.

All I can hear is the music but it's faint and coming to an end.

10:1: Mr. ****

I get up early the next morning and lick the image of the Boy from my teeth. The Ghost has left the house before me again but her things assure me she'll be back. I have started this day to see the Dishwasher. So I put down the hours at work, come home and go as fast as I can to the restaurant.

WAR is raging. The body count is flashed up on the monitor outside the restaurant. *We've done good,* they tell us. *A clean WAR. A quick WAR. A just WAR.* I ignore as much as I can and make my way to my table. The evening drags out, nearly snapping itself in two but at 11.00 something small gives and I make my way out back. I sit down with the Dishwasher and tell him my plan. He gives me a broad smile and a card.

–There is more than one way of killing a child, he says. I've met men like the Doctor before. They're everywhere, but so are we.

I sleep fitfully that night and wake early. Roaring. Excited. I call work and tell them that I will not be in today and no calls are to be directed to my mobile. Fathead agrees because he has to. I go to the Government District and find the Department of Broadcasting.

I ask directions for the Licensing Department. A woman with painted nails points to a corridor overwhelmed by pot plants and pictures.

–Down there, she says, then take the first door on your right.

I look at her. Relatively innocent, I imagine. Naïve even, with a mother she sees every Thursday night and an aerobics class every Monday. I imagine her to be sincere about what little responsibility they give her. I imagine her to be hard-working and fuelled by an honest endeavour. I stop imagining then because I lose interest. She's like so many others here. They are not the type of people that can help me now. I need the other kind, those that can help me reclaim my self irrevocably. The Government District is rich in my type of men, most of them fooled by their own conceit into thinking they are my opposite. I'm wise to them all. I'm wise because I have no pretences. I know what I am. So did my father.

I pass through the jungle of receptionists, telephones, computers and suits. I show someone my card and they take me into a back office.

–Wait there, they say, he's in the middle of something.

The office looks like it has no real function, like it serves no one save the stranglers that are left here to wait. The computer hums in the corner and the filing cabinet says nothing. The calendar features characters from some moronic show and my mind races forward to the box I will purchase after I finish up here.

I imagine the Ghost's face as I position it in the living room. I imagine the smile I'll give her, the one I've stolen from Laurence, the one I used on Cynthia the last day. I'm thinking about the size of the monitor I'll get when a man enters the room.

–Sorry to have kept you, he says, I didn't expect any visitors today. It's not the best time. We have a presentation due. But that's not your concern—tell me, what can I do for you?

I tell him who sent me and his face shows a small sign of

unease. Not a lot but enough to know he can't leave this business unfinished.

–He's a friend of yours? he asks.

–Yes, he told me you might be able to help with a special interest I have.

The man pulls at his tie and looks at the door.

–I really am a busy man, today at least. Can you come back later?

–How much later?

–Tonight, he says, but don't come back here. Leave me your number. I'll call you and tell you where to meet us. Leave me your work number too and I need your FGT number as well. You understand that this really is a very special interest—we don't do business with people we don't know.

–I understand, I say. Have you a piece of paper to write on?

–There's any amount of paper here.

He smiles and reaches over to take something off the desk. He skims over it, then hands it to me.

–You can write on the back of that, that project's dead.

I take a quick glance at it. A proposal by the ANTI-WAR Movement to televise a discussion between their spokespeople and various government bodies. I fold it in half and write down my name in numbers. He walks me out to the door. He is friendly but not overly so.

I throw myself back into City streets. I keep my head down. I don't want to look up and find the eyes of a Searcher clinging to my gaze. I don't want to see anyone except the man who will sell me my first box. The Dishwasher has given me the name of a shop. –Ask for Tynan, he'd said. So I do. Tynan looks at me with a relish that makes me uncomfortable. He makes me feel edible. I put up my fronts and ask him sharply for the best box in the place. He licks his lips and tells me that I don't want anything there.

–Come in to the stores, he says, we got something out back that I think you'll want.

I follow him at a distance because he smells of sweet cocoa oil, which is making my stomach turn. Also, I'm afraid he'll try to touch me in some way. Any way would be enough to warrant the mileage between us.

–I should have it out in the front by now, he says, but me and boys are getting used to it back here. He throws his hand out to show me a box, propped up on an old wooden table. There is a tattered couch and a coffee table positioned at its knees. The box is huge and thin.

–Flat screen, he says. It's virtually indestructible. These are the ones they have in the prisons, in the mess halls. The boys can't do nothin' to them during a riot. Some new metal alloy that the folks out east have come up with. Same as they make missiles with. Go on, sit down. Let's try her out.

The armrests are shiny and I shake my head.

–Give her a whacking then, he says, punch the screen.

I look at him and wonder how foul his mouth must smell. I stare into the purpled-grey hollows of absent teeth. I want to get the box and get out.

–I'll take it, I say.

–OK, we can order you in one. My boys will be mad to lose this here baby.

–I need one by tomorrow, I say, I was told you would have something in store.

–Who told you that then?

I give him the Dishwasher's name again.

–Ah, he says as if an understanding has been reached, OK then. I can wrap this one up for you and my boys can wait on the next. After all, we do have more than one box in the place.

He laughs then and I leave him to it. I don't want to do business out back in the stores. He follows me to the front and takes my details.

I tell him what time I want it delivered.

–I need that box tomorrow, I say with a look that Laurence would never master—a look that speaks of an assured ill-intent. He receives it with relative dignity and nods his head.

I imagine all the names he'll call me later, safely couched up with his boys, watching some grimy show about grimy people like himself.

It's not yet lunch. I go to the park and sit down. I think about the blind tailor and his nimble hands and then I think about my tailor and our understanding. I wonder if I should go into the shed and open my lines for business. And I wonder then if it's really a matter for the 'I should's. Somewhere I want to. I can't fathom what's so wrong with a man wanting to work until I'm told in no uncertain terms that I want to be Laurence for the afternoon. *Work has nothing to do with it*, Ankles says, laughing at me.

I curse her. Angrily, I throw myself into me and try to find the roar I have tasted as my own. *Go home*, I'm told, so I do. I'm hoping to find the Ghost, find the whats of her daytime existence. Now that Cynthia has gone away, I wonder where she'll spend her waking hours. I think about the school and the Boy. Maybe they are together now. The Ghost is not there but my chair is so I sit in it. It eats two hours and I'm grateful. I look in the Ghost's room. I smell her things and look for the muzzy smell of Boy. There is a trace of him here and a trace of him in the dreams that he left by the foot of my bed. My phone rings and I'm filled with a foreign, hopeful excitement. The grizzled voice on the other end knocks it from me.

–I can't deliver tomorrow, he says, can we drop it off this afternoon instead?

I tell them I'll wait for them and hang up. It makes more sense this way, having it all set up for tomorrow, the afternoon free. I wonder what I was thinking earlier. I smile at the thought of the Dishwasher watching over me, keeping everything in check.

I get back into my chair and wait. It eats the in-between and leaves me free to answer the door fifty minutes later.

Two men I don't bother to look at carry in the box and set it up by the power outlet. One of them moves the Ghost's cushion gently.

–You can just throw that anywhere, I say. Biting.

One of the men hands me the remote as he leaves.

–I'm sure you know how to work everything, he says, if you have any problems, call the shop. Do you want me to reprogramme the VR function?

I stand there and look at him.

–You can choose your own words. My girlfriend did ours. Lilac to turn it on, because it's her favourite colour.

He smiles shyly. –Whatever you want, he says, it's your box.

I think about it. I tell him what I want to use. He smiles.

–Right so, he says, handing me the remote. When you're ready, press that button there and speak into the microphone.

–Can't you do it?

–Not unless you want me calling round every evening to turn your box on, he says. Laughing.

–I'll do it later, I say. Wanting him to leave.

–Fair enough.

I think of the disc lying on my bedside table and the Doctor's wanting.

–Does it take discs? I ask.

–Yeah, most kinds, what kind are you talking about?

–Wait here, I tell him and I return with the package.

–You'll have to take the paper off or else it won't fit in, the man says.

And from out back Laurence steps forward and responds. I get rid of him and tell the man to put the disc on. The man is patient but I'm sick.

He gets down on his knees. –You just put it in here, and then you press play here on the remote. It'll play on any channel. If you want to control it from the actual box itself, you'll have bring across this dial on the remote.

I nod at him because my mind has been taken away by the image on the screen. It's the Doctor. The man gets up and looks at me, looking.

–Those two there are your volume control, he says. He turns it up and the Doctor's voice invades my room. The man hands me the remote again and leaves.

I stand in front of the box. The Doctor is talking to me, telling me the date, the time, the patient name and number. I can see my father shuffling into a chair behind him. Then the camera finds my father's face, surrounded as it is by the Doctor's questions. His face is grey but his eyes are as I remember them. The Doctor asks him about his early life, his first job, his marriage. My father is excited, articulate, gentle, coherent. He smiles back to the memory of my mother, telling the Doctor that she always used to tease him from the bath.

–We both loved music, he says. I would have liked her to see me up in the radio station. She would have laughed at me but she would have been proud. We could have done a good show together. All the men would have wanted her. You would have liked her, Doctor. She had an enormous laugh.

–I'm sure I would have. Tell me about your children—the two boys.

–One boy and a tin soldier, my father says calmly, but his guard is up. He begins to twitch.

–What exactly do you mean by that? the Doctor asks.

–We've talked about this before, Doctor, you know what I mean.

–You've called your son a changeling before. What changed him, do you think?

–I don't know, maybe he was born that way. Do you think that's possible, Doctor?

–I don't know.

–They say you can only give what you receive, my father says, but he got lots of love from both of us, from all three of us.

The camera catches his hands gripping the arms of the chair. His jaw locks in anger.

–I know and I know you don't like talking about it but—

–It's not that I don't like talking about it, Doctor, but every time I do I'm given medication to calm down. Can't a father be angry?

–Absolutely, but I need you to tell me exactly why you're angry, who you're angry with. I want you to say it to the camera.

–I'm angry because we were given a changeling son.

–And you think this changeling son, this tin soldier, killed Rajem?

–No, I don't, my father half shouts, and you know that, but I think he could have if things had been different. You know that too. He's fighting the flesh all the time. He won't accept any. He wants to keep his tin.

–Who's that? a voice from behind me asks.

The Ghost is standing there, looking at the screen. I scramble to find the remote, I can hear my father shouting that he had never given up on the tin soldier, that the tin soldier had given him up instead because he was afraid of the flesh. I can hear the Doctor's soothing voice trying to calm him down. I can hear my father throwing back the chair and demanding the Doctor to make sense of why things happen like they do.

The Ghost stands still. I find the remote and press something, anything, until it stops.

–Is that the disc the Doctor gave you? she asks.

–Take it out, I shout, take it out!

I give her the remote. She finds the right button and I can see the disc slide out into view. I grab it and stamp on it.

–Don't bother breaking it, she says, I've no interest in it.

Her words sting; her tone cools the sweat on my brow. She walks past me then and into her room. I stand there, listening to my own breath, trying to get away from my father.

She stays in her room. I don't go in after her. Instead, I sit in my chair and wait for the call. It comes and I go out. My directions take me to a man's apartment. It's not the same man I met in the office.

–He'll come later, the man informs me. But I won't be there. All I want are the codes to the broadcasts. He makes me stay for a drink, shows off his swanky goblets.

–I was talking to your friend today, I say, he told me a little something of your interests.

He parades around the room and tells me about a little something he has, a little something he made himself, some time ago, in a small house with two lamps on the bedside lockers.

–I burnt my own hands a little, he says, showing me his fingers, but the whore got the worst of it. It was very symbolic. It looks good. I have it here on disc, along with some other stuff you might like. Codes can be messy.

He goes over to a shelf and leafs through some discs. –I've them named and dated, he says. Proud. He finds what he is looking for and brings it over to me.

–This is one of my best pieces, you wouldn't believe some of the people who've got copies of that, but I don't tell tales. Not yet anyway, he laughs. Threatening me.

I look at the disc.

–What's this? I ask. Pointing.

–Her name, he says. Throwing out his hands in affected exasperation.

I can't quite believe it and I smile up at the Dishwasher as I imagine him now. The City does seem to be getting smaller.

I go home and look in on the Ghost—the sleeping body in a bed. I imagine the smell of the Boy's hair, the musky smell of a child's scalp, Rajem's head before me on the pillow, his soft breathing as he sleeps and my father's shadow falling in the doorway.

10:2: Telephone Transcript

In Search of Infinite Relief, C.W. Sisle
Contracted to Gleeson Media Group
Subcontracted to Employee 12
Recorded at 7.28 p.m. on 18/05/****

E12 Hello?

C78 Hi there. It's Molly.

E12 How are you? How's Augusta?

C78 The same. Both of us. I've come up with a little something on pride. I'm quite proud of it, in fact.

(Employee 12 laughs)

E12 Let's hear it.

C78 Well, if you think you're not proud, then you're very proud indeed. Please note the casual usage of the word 'indeed'.

E12 Noted. I'm proud of you.

C78 I shall now delight, not in myself, but in the pleasure I have given you.

E12 Wonderful!

C78 Tell me more stuff.

E12 Ask me questions.

C78 I've lots. Here's one. Say if we do as we should, and we've given ourselves up completely to this source or whatever you want to call it, is there anywhere left where we can make our own plans for self? Am I allowed keep any of my self for myself? Do you know what I mean?

E12 Yeah. I asked the same question with the same desperation, but you have to stop thinking in terms of being allowed or not.

C78 I'm not desperate.

E12 I was. I used to try and believe that there was some quota on what I'd to do before I could safely go back to my poor natural self and give it some chance to do what it liked. It doesn't work. I've tried it. It's because we are still taking ourselves as the starting point.

C78 I don't know, Laurence.

E12 It's harder the other way. It's harder to keep the self and be good and happy.

C78 Why does it have to be though? Why can't we live decently and be happy?

E12 Because the 'I', by its very nature interferes with contentment and happiness, as the Law interferes with the wants of the 'I'. We are letting our heads and hearts chase down all the things that we figure will make us happy, and hoping at the same time to remain good people.

C78 But that seems possible to me. I don't see what's wrong with that. Can you understand *my* point of view?

E12 Of course I can. I've been where you are. I've argued and tried every which way in order to avoid giving myself, and my desires, up.

C78 Did you reach the brink or something? What did you do in the end?

E12 I couldn't argue against it anymore. I stopped fighting, I suppose. I gave in. And I could see it in other people. They had an air about them.

C78 I just can't imagine getting there.

E12 You've got to open up communication, listen out for the music.

Every morning I wake up, in that first conscious moment, all my wants come to claim me. I have to stop a second, shove them aside and try to hear the music. And every morning, it comes to me and fills me up, and it's beautiful. It eats up all fears, it makes me calm. And in the beginning, it only lasts a moment or two, but it gives you a sense of what may come. You start to recognise it more and more in your everydays. And I think it's even good to pretend, to wear a mask. Every time you do, it becomes less and less of a pretence. Like the smile. Because it can be hard, Molly, when the taste has left us.

C78 What does it taste like?

E12 It's funny you talk of how the Lows taste. Because forgetting yourself to the music has a taste too. One day it just comes and everything becomes clear, you become overwhelmed. You heave this huge 'Sigh of Infinite Relief' and then you feel the self-conscious weight of this life evaporate into an exquisite sense of completion. One day, everything that's ever passed as your existence will make complete and perfect sense, and in that instance, you'll feel wholly safe yet wholly childlike, wholly unknowing yet wholly open, wholly excited yet wholly rooted, wholly fearless yet wholly real, wholly peaceful yet wholly aware, wholly yourself, utterly loved and freer than you could ever have imagined.

C78 So you feel like a colander?

(Employee 12 laughs)

C78 Sorry. It just all sounds a bit cheesy.

E12 You're right—sometimes words just don't cut it.

C78 I was being smart. Go on. Please.

E12 Right. Well, in this instance you get stronger and giddier and you throw off all the petty thoughts and small worries that have laboured to be heard under the guise of pressing significance. You redirect your anger, turning it away from yourself—you redirect it away fom the people that have caused you hurt because from the height of this moment, you realise that most men hurt others without really seeing the other at the end. Most men just hurt.

C78 Yep. Your sales pitch is getting better, Laurence.

E12 But all this you'll find out on your own.

C78 Do you think the Lows could find me if I ever got to this place? Seriously.

E12 No. I honestly believe they wouldn't. Not the way they find you now.

C78 I'd really like to believe that.

E12 Maybe someday you will.

C78 Maybe. I'm going to go.

E12 OK. Be good.

C78 I will.

End of transcript

10:3: Molly

I can't get through to Laurence. The engaged tone makes excuses for him. I can't get through to Augusta and I can't get through to Isha. I can't tell her how the Lows are coming again because Matron tells me she'll be disgusted by a grown woman, all messed up in her own dirt. *I know*, I say, *I know*. My teeth get caught up in this bitter clash. They hurt. *Let's keep all your troubles wrapped up here with me*, Matron says.

I can hear the sound of the building site across the street—the banging, the clatter, the wind-swept shouts of the workers. I'm not quite sure where I am so I keep walking, hoping to recognise something soon.

I tuck my nose into my jumper to smell myself. I can't remember when I last showered, although it can't have been too long ago because my face still looks clean. Isha hates it when my mascara has a history older than daylight. Isha says I could be beautiful if I looked after myself more. I don't want to be beautiful. Being beautiful brings trouble on yourself, puts people further away. But I can't say this to Isha because she'll tell me I'm being ridiculous, melodramatic, ludicrous. This is one of the things that Matron has always understood.

I can be beautiful when I grow up though. I'm going to be. I'm not going to let my underwear go grey or my skin flake. I'm going to spank of health. People will say, *That girl there, she looks the very picture of health*. Matron will have to leave. When I grow up, she'll have to go. That's what me and the Villagers have decided on. When I grow up, everything will be different. And even if the Lows come visit me, they won't be able to stay for long because I'll scatter them with a fisty laugh. Chase them away. I won't have the time to entertain them. I'll be too busy writing and romancing this life here, the one that I know except everything will be different. The Village Vamp laughs girlishly when I think like this but she'll have no appetite then for drunken men. Me and her will love one man, like the man with the handkerchief, a man that milks contentment from the small everydays, a man to catch my flyaway thrills.

I feel a presence. I look up to see Matron beside me. She gives me a look that leaves me embarrassed. She tosses her head, indicating the presence of someone else. I turn around to find that the Lows have heard everything and they are laughing harder than the Matron ever has. My stomach drops as they scuttle up around me. They pounce hungrily on my hopes and leave the skeleton of a hollow future. I think about sleeping. I think of Isha away and the empty house. *I'll be off, Molly*, Matron says as she fixes her cape. She's going to leave me with the Lows now. Shift work. *I have other things to do, other people to attend to. You didn't imagine you were my only patient, Molly?* she says. *But of course you did. You really have gone and gorged on yourself. It's no wonder you're sick. I left your medicine where I always do*.

I look around for the Village Lunatic but he doesn't come. She leaves, telling me she'll be back, and I make my way through the streets of the City. I'm going home to sleep. I think of my medicine. I call work and tell them I can't come in tonight. I retract further into myself. No one will find me here. I walk the shell home, coaxing it with thoughts of sleep from within. I look at everybody's feet moving, and eventually I find the rhythm that will take me home the quickest.

–Molly! A voice sounds.

I pretend I never heard it. I mightn't have heard it. I didn't hear it. My heart is racing.

–Molly!

I force myself to look up. I see the Doctor waving from across the street. He is standing with a small newspaper vendor and an enormous woman with even bigger glasses. I panic—deep in the pit of myself, I panic. He is signalling for me to come over. I know that if I go over, I'll have to crawl out to the edge and in doing so, spill open the tears I have put away for my pillow and the long sleep after. I don't want to cry in front of the Doctor and the two strangers. I don't want to be introduced to anybody. I don't want to be mean either. I don't want Chivers to think I was rude to his friend. I don't want them to know me as I am. I don't want for anyone to come in and get me. I don't want to be awake for this moment. I don't want to be me. I don't know what to do so I go over and stand before them, ordering myself to find the last of my smiles and squeeze it out quickly.

–How are you, Molly? the Doctor asks.

There is a soft smell of laundry, reminding me how dirty I am. I smile at all three of them, my face locked in a desperate grimace as the tears slide down my cheeks and into the neck of my jacket. I don't mean to embarrass anyone but someone in the Village insists I let them in. The Doctor reaches out for me but I turn and run away. I keep running till my throat catches fire, then I walk, gulping at the damp air for some relief. I play the still of all three in my head. I see the stack of newspapers by the vendor's leg and

I think of the Paper Maché Man. I feel nothing and I don't care. He could pin me against the wall now and I wouldn't care. He could take me in an alley, push me against an iron gate, press my hands against the lamps on the bedside lockers and I wouldn't fight. I don't care because there is no point to anything. The Village is pillaged by what I now know to be real. I see a child's shoe outside a derelict building. A drummer bangs on about spindle people with bellies like bombs that blow up and blow out. I step over an addict defeated by his craving, but I can't find the anger to care. I have misplaced my fury.

I think of the tablets and think of home. I look up quickly in case anyone has seen my thoughts. I see a man standing outside a nearby hotel and something in me responds.

He is small, ruddied and seemingly weathered by seasons of goodwill. His belly pays homage to a charismatic appetite that attracts only the best foods. I imagine him feasting on the perfect steak. Sinking back afterwards, fondling gently the mound of good fortune that has ransacked his pelvis, keeping it quiet and out of sight. This man with the bulbous belly, he smiles at me. *That's good, Molly*, says Scribe. Out of nowhere. I look to find him lying in the rubble of What-Once-Was. I go to pick him out and dust him down. He makes me promise to describe the man with the belly on paper when I get home. Maybe write a little story about him. A romantic history in case he hasn't got one. *Don't go to bed, Molly*, he says, *we've work to do. You promised.*

I say nothing. I have nothing to say to Scribe. He is on his own now.

The Lows are pushing me from behind so I make a mental note, knowing well that it will gather dust with all the other notes of a mind's passing. I look again at his wonderful belly, at the warm eyes waltzing over his mask. *He probably has a cyst*, a Low shouts out from within. *He's probably greedy as fuck*, shouts another.

He probably comfort-eats because his wife is dead and he's been left loveless, shouts another. *He's probably a dirty pervert. Imagine that belly all over you, Molly*, screams another.

–You've a wonderful belly, I shout. To spite them all. To make one last effort to trample on them before I give in to sleep.

–Thank you, he mouths shyly. I always had a belly, even as a baby.

I'm not sure if he is being playfully clever or simply ridiculous.

–All babies have bellies, I say, big bellies.

–That they do, he says, that they do, my dear.

He turns away and smiles.

Then my stomach drops. I think maybe I've embarrassed him with my silly observation begot from spite. I shy away from him and from me. And I wonder how it is that I spend a lifetime retreating away from myself, from my very nature. *Keep on walking*, the Lows murmur. Fingering me from behind. And I do until his voice catches up with me.

–I like cheese, he says, I eat an awful lot of cheese.

I turn to find him smiling at me with his eyes and I feel safe.

–I like cheese too.

–We've lots in common then, he says.

Swaying gently from side to side.

–And sleeping, I say, I really like sleeping.

–Sleeping or snoozing?

His eyes wild with interest. They throw light on the fallen bodies that pockmark my streets. Some of the men sit up and listen.

–What's the difference? I ask. Wondering. Honest. Thankful. Glad. Awake.

–A world. I'm a snooze man myself. I've spent an entire lifetime chasing after the perfect snooze.

–Did you ever ... have it? I ask.

–5.26–6.03 p.m., near perfect. I remember it well, it was the day Maria came home from hospital the second time. Bliss!

He closes his eyes. Savouring. Remembering. Then his eyes shoot open, and get me.

–I could smell Maria's hair and the radio played. She took me to the place.

–Come inside for a bit, he says then, it's cold out here and I want to show you something.

I hesitate because I don't know him and this is the City. Even if I have seen his eyes. The Lows charge into my hesitancy and fuel it with some theories of their own. I look to the man for help. I think he can see the Lows pulling on my coat.

–We can stay out here, if you'd rather, he says.

–I hope it's warm in there.

Shaking off my resolve to sleep this day, moving nearer to him.

–You have no idea, he says, warm is the place.

We navigate the twirling glass and find ourselves in the foyer. The hotel interior is a dark mahogany that has leaned heavily on its years. A grand stairs opens herself to the floor's charms. I'm seduced by the coupling. I can't imagine who stays here but I want to and I will, later, when I find my time. Scribe and I. For now, I take in the brass railings on either side of the stair. I follow their ascent with my gaze. The blazing brass holds me. It's pure, untouched, lasting. My throat begins to burn.

–I've worked here for seventeen years, he says. Head porter, my dear—the only porter, we're a very small establishment. Only eleven rooms.

–It's incredible, I say, the brass is …

I can't find a word. Scribe stands before it, his mouth agape. He, staggered, and I, enraptured.

The man with the belly smiles in collusion.

–That'd be the gloves, dear.

–The what?

–The gloves, he says again. Extracting a blackened pair from his waistcoat pocket. He puts them on.

–Maria made them for me, from a special cloth.

He starts up the stair, rubbing the brass on either side. He looks back at me over his shoulder and smiles.

–You can just spit on them for a quick one two, or you can go for the hard stuff.

He stops and bends down, whistling. He pulls back a loose board on the stairs and takes out a bottle.

–I keep it in there, dear, because it fits. I won't use it now because I want to show you something else.

He comes back down the stairs and brings me to her flank. He opens a small door and disappears.

–Come in, come in, wait till you see.

I find myself in a small but perfectly formed space. It's cushioned and warm and vulvic. It's the soft folds of woman and love.

–This is the place, as best as I can recreate it. This is the place where Maria used to take me when we snoozed.

–Sit down, he says and turns on the radio.

Something beautiful is playing. Something extraordinary and I'm opened. Tears start to fall but my body is not yet crying.

–What station is this? I ask. The voice is not singing nor is it human.

He gives me an enormous smile.

–It's a well-kept secret, he winks, it's the hospital radio.

–Which hospital?

–The Assumptia, you should listen to it when you can. Or even just when you go for a snooze.

I exhale. I tell him of Mr. Nomoré.

–That must have been an honour, he says.

I offer to introduce him and he says that maybe, one day, we will go visit him together. We are quiet then, the pair of us. Each to our own, wrapped in the warmth of the place. I can hear him breathing gently.

–Sometimes I sleep for all the wrong reasons, I say.

My eyes drip with a weariness I now realise I've been fighting for days, maybe even weeks.

–You keep in there, the small joys will return.

–When? I ask. Demanding. Desperate.

–Is this it? Is this life? I ask. Crying now.

–Any life is just made of days. Take it one day at a time, Molly. Start every day afresh. Every day. Sleep is the tonic.

–And snoozing.

–Absolutely! Get those snoozes in where you can. And know that you're the master of your own thoughts.

–I don't know.

–Every thought must go through you, Molly. Remember that. Every morning, when you wake up, call your first conscious thought back. It'll want to rush out into your head, roaring and shouting and gallivanting, but it's your thought so call it back and have it stand, open-eyed, before you. Then go over your game plan for the day. Talk simple and straight. Don't go into details of the day—the who*s*, the what*s*, the where*s*, the when*s*—you can do that over breakfast in your own time. No, that's all housekeeping for later. In that moment, tell your first conscious thought of the day that every thought formed thereafter will be positive, constructive, compassionate, considered and open.

–What if it doesn't come back when I call it?

–It's your thought, Molly. Essentially, it has to do what you tell it to do. Unless, of course, you're mentally ill. Are you mentally ill?

–No. Not mentally, mentally ill.

–No, I don't think you are. You could be a bit of a drunk, though.

–How do you know what I am? I ask. Not angry, just tired.

–You reek of stale alcohol and you're a bit grey looking.

I turn my tears inwards. They water the pain in my chest until it blossoms.

–And I've seen you stumbling past here a good few mornings. Now maybe it's just your lifestyle or maybe you've a bit of a problem. One honest look at yourself and you'll know either way. But I'll tell you this, an addict that's feeding an addiction, no matter how contained or functional they may seem, has no real control over the choices they make, especially not that first choice of the day.

–First thought of the day or first choice? I ask.

–Every thought is a choice.

We talk, him and I, and after a time, I get up to leave.

–Where do you live? I ask.

–Here, I sleep here now since Maria died.

–When did she die?

–Four years ago.

I smile because I'm too young to have any words of comfort for a man who may have just given me back this day. I make a quiet resolution to come see him again and bring him a small present. I will go to the Village and bring him back something beautiful, handcrafted, something from the market stalls.

–Thank you for today, I say.

–Thank you, he says, and go easy on yourself, Molly.

I leave with the music playing in my head.

I go home and bring the duvet down to the couch. I will snooze today but sleep tonight. I think about tomorrow but the mere thought of it exhausts my new insights so I turn my phone off and put the box on low as the presenter gets high on WAR. I bury myself in the couch and wait for Isha.

All life is made up of days and every day is equal.

11:1: Mr. ****

I wake with a certain knowledge that the day is mine. I set off for work, finding Gonzo before he finds me. I buy my paper, and give him a huge smile to tell him that he has lost our war. I roar silently into his eyes, letting him into the pit. He looks at me sadly. He looks as tired as Kitty does when I leave her by the door.

Davy passes me on the stairs and I smile at him too. He smiles back—panting, unknowing, trusting and wanting. I find a memo on my desk and smile. I think of Fathead, rammed into his faux-leather swivel, thinking of ways to impress Mr. Wontdo. I call the Doctor; his receptionist answers.

–Can I take a message? she asks.

–Tell him the tin soldier is marching on, I say.

I hang up. It was an empty phone call and I don't know how I'm to survive this day at my desk without introducing my good self to someone who cares.

But the morning weaves its course and I sit on it till lunch-time lets me off. I don't feel like eating so instead I wander round the City, getting closer and closer to Kitty's. I see all my sections and subsections recklessly throwing their frailty to this life. I roar silently at them all. I take off my mask and smile at those who will have me. I even try out some Laurence specials—they fit surprisingly well in daylight.

Roar for the children. WAR for the children.

I throw my head back and laugh. Everything seems so perfectly in place and I wonder where the fight had survived for so long. I don't dare to go back in and find out. I'm too comfortable where I stand.

I keep walking. Three men in orange masks spray the leaves on the plastic trees on the Scraggy Walk. Another pointless morning put down like a crippled dog. I look down at my paper. The last city has fallen. The WAR is nearly over. The headlines tell us that this is a great day in history. I admire them for keeping a straight face.

I can smell the Boy's scalp from here but I have to bide my time. Laurence called the school board yesterday. They were very helpful with regard to the time of his release. They would say nothing to my partner—surprise parties were always such fun. My appetite catches up with me. I go into the nearest restaurant I can find.

No, I don't want my monitor switched on. No, I don't want to engage in polite conversation. No, I don't want any additional sauces with my sandwich. No, I wouldn't stop to think twice if you were mouthing words at me from the front of a truck.

I eat and think about going to my restaurant after it's all over. Savour the evening's entertainment with the Dishwasher. Play a game of draughts with my old friend. I smile to myself. I can't wait to banish the Ghost. I so much want for her to see my roar, especially after her cool disinterest of yesterday.

After eating, I walk over to Kitty's. I look in the window. She's sitting by a machine, filling out some kind of questionnaire in a magazine. She has a small dash of ink on her cheek. I walk in. She looks up and puts the magazine down.

–Hello Kitty, I say.

She doesn't say anything because she can see what I already know.

I put my hands on my hips and strut up and down the shop, showing off my new roar.

–It would be better if we had a little music, I say.

But Kitty says nothing because there's no point. She gets up and goes over to the second machine. She starts to take out a wash.

–Be a sport, Kitty, I say, come dance with me.

Kitty starts over for me. I can't see her hands, lost as they are to the folds of her huge skirt. It's too late and she has poured washing powder over my head. It's a ridiculous act. It's beneath Kitty. I smile to tell her so.

–You'll need more than a little powder to clean me up.

She turns away from me and goes into the back room. I can hear her lock the door. I wait for a while but boredom begs to be my playmate. I knock it aside and leave. I wait across the road to see will Kitty put her sign up. Closed. For good. But she doesn't and boredom manages to find its way to my feet, big-eyed and desperate—Davy-like. I kick it away. I think about finding Freddie but he's not a worthy opponent. He would probably run and I'm too full of roar to give chase.

Chasing is for girls and it's time for me to go back to work.

An almond-eyed youth gives me a pamphlet. *The Cloud that Ate a City*. It speaks of the government's environmental policy or lack thereof. The growing darkness is the result of a smog cloud gathering over the City. The pamphlet promises acid rain. They list the names of shelters open to the public and the number to call if 'you would like to volunteer your residency'.

I fold it up and put it into a beggar's hat. I throw a Laurence smile for good measure and I taste his glimmer of hope and the bitter aftertaste of disappointment.

Mr. Wontdo is talking to one of my colleagues in the corridor. He looks up at me.
 –You got that memo? he asks.
 I nod and tell him I'm looking forward to it.
 –This could be the future, he says and I wonder if he's for real.
 I go into my office and sit down at my desk. I look through old files and throw a lot of them in the bin. You need less paperwork when you know who you are.
 I roar.
 The calls come and I take them, one by one. I let Laurence do all the talking. I'm glad she doesn't call. I don't want to speak to her yet. I leave early because it's time. I walk home with intent. Ailing and alive.
 The Ghost is not there so I take my position in my chair. I let it eat time as the darkness outside devours the edges of our cityscape. My blood rushes as I hear her key in the door. It's the first time I've noticed that the Ghost has her own key. I've never wondered. I presumed she came in through the walls and windows. I can hear the rustle of her coat as it falls to the floor. I can hear her put her bag on the small table in the hallway. She comes in and stops.
 Her look is that of horror and a conscious effort to regain herself.
 –Hello, she says but I'm not looking to her. I'm looking at the little Boy, twisted in her skirt pleats.
 –Hello, I say. Smiling at him.
 –This is Daniel, he's the Boy I told you about.

—You never told me about any boy, I say. Smiling.

—Yes, I did, she says, the Boy in the poem. Smiling.

—What poem?

—In the toilets of Eddie's.

—Ahh, I remember.

More smiles.

—I'm taking him home today.

—So I see—you've packed your own things as well.

—Yes, I'm going to give you back your room. I've had it long enough.

She's visibly nervous. The Ghost can see my roar. I'd never really been a threat till now. She must have thought me a ghost too, taking a room in her world. I'm glad that I can overstep her expectations a little. I decide this is as good a time as any to introduce her to Laurence. I bring him forward and he smiles at her.

—We'll just get our things, she says.

The Ghost takes the Boy by the hand and leads him into her room. I follow them and stand in the doorway. I play with the handle a little, toy with the key she has left in the lock.

—You don't have to leave straight away, Laurence says. Hopefully.

She doesn't know what to say because she doesn't know who I am or what I've become. She looks actively uncertain.

—Where are you going to go? he asks.

—We're going to find some old friends, they'll be delighted to see Daniel. They've missed him.

—Are you excited about seeing your friends, Daniel? Laurence asks, leaning down a little to smell his hair.

Daniel says nothing. He smiles at Laurence. Laurence smiles at Daniel.

—Daniel doesn't talk, she says, he's saving his voice for a special occasion.

The Ghost smiles at him and rubs her hand gently across his cheek.

–It seems a pity you should leave so quickly on your last night, Laurence says, maybe you could cook one of your meals before you go.

Again the Ghost does not know what to say. I can see her struggling for a way out. She doesn't trust herself to make the right choice. I'm standing in her way. She's afraid of me, uncertain of Laurence.

–I feel bad about the other day, about making you turn off the disc. It just took me by surprise, that's all. I want you to see it before you go. It's a recording of my father.

The Boy wanders past me then, into the living room, and suddenly everything seems so much easier.

–Have a go in my chair.

The Boy climbs up into it happily. I look at his little legs, too short to accommodate the bend in its ergonomics, his feet hanging over the edge. I smile again, and roar within. I turn to the Ghost. She's pulling a large bag onto her shoulder.

–We really have to get going, she says, thank you for everything. I ...

She does not get a chance to finish her sentence because I'm already closing the door in her face. She runs for it but it has her run into it instead. I turn the key. The Ghost starts shouting, banging violently on the door. She calls out for Daniel. He sits there and says nothing. He does not move or flinch and I wonder if I'm being a little dramatic—tying him to the chair.

The Ghost threatens to call the police but I've already found her phone in her bag.

She was the one who picked the back bedroom, window-less as it had been then and window-less as it is now.

In all the day's excitement, I'd forgotten about the memo on my desk. I remember it now and smile. It's too noisy in here—what with the Ghost manifesting herself in the most undignified manner. Her shouts are raw to the throat and even rawer on the ears. I wink at the Boy, inhaling his hair, and step outside to make a call.

11:2: Telephone Transcript

In Search of Infinite Relief, C.W. Sisle
Contracted to Gleeson Media Group
Subcontracted to Employee 12
Recorded at 7.53 p.m. on 23/05/****

E12 Molly?

C78 Laurence?

E12 Happy birthday, Little Miss Molly Mae.

C78 Wow. Thank you. I didn't expect you to call. Weird.

E12 What are you up to?

C78 I'm going to go to the hospital, see Augusta and Chivers. And an old man I met there. He asked me to call up for my birthday. He says he has a present for me. Says I laugh like his wife, which is why I think he's taken a shine to me. And he's probably lonely. He works in the radio station but I think he's actually a patient. No, he is—now that I think of it. Then I'm going go to the bar for a late one. Everyone's expecting me but it's different since Augusta fell. We're all just waiting.

E12 Have you an hour to spare?

C78 Yeah, why?

E12 I have something I want to show you. Like a birthday present.

C78 I met this porter yesterday, Laurence. I have to tell you about him. You two would have a lot to talk about. He seems to understand this music business too. I have to say though, he put it a simpler. We might have to work on your presentation.

E12 I always over-complicate things.

C78 Me and you both. What district are you in? Will I call to the office?

E12 No, I'm at home. There's someone here I'd like you to meet.

C78 Em ... OK. This is a bit weird though. But in the faith of everything else that's gone before ... We can break open a bottle of friendship tonic and get shit-faced. Kidding.

E12 Thanks, Molly.

C78 Am I meeting Laurence?

E12 I'm going to pretend I didn't hear that, Molly.

C78 What's the address then?

E12 19 Bellatone Avenue, Block C. Get a fare. I'll treat you for your birthday.

C78 OK. See you in a bit.

End of transcript

11:3: Molly

I hang up. I try to call Isha but all I get is her answering machine.

–Hi Isha, it's Molly. Thanks for the card and the money. I got them this morning. I went and treated myself to a day at the cinema—the small one with the dome roof. A friend has just called there. I'm going over to him for an hour or so but I'll see you at the hospital later. Tell Chivers and Puckie they better have a cake. And tell Chivers to wrap his legs up in ribbons so I can have a good laugh when I get there. I hope I'm not giving that poor man a complex. Anyway, thanks again for the money. Sorry I didn't get to see you this morning. You're too early for me. See you later.

I put out my hand and flag down a fare. A small man in a loud shirt pulls over.

–Get in, he says, and we'll fly to the moon.

I tell him we have to stop off at Bellatone Avenue first.

–I'll bring you home some moon sprouts, he says.

–You'll get them cheap, they're just going out of season.

–Well sorrrreee, Little Missy, he says and we both smile at each other.

–What's in Bellatone Avenue then that stops you from flying to the moon with me? he asks.

–A friend—he's got a birthday present for me.

–Happy birthday, he says, tell me how old.

–Twenty-one.

–You don't look a day over sixteen.

–I don't feel a day over ten.

–Listen to this, he says, just got it today so it can be your birthday song. Listen.

He turns up the music before dissolving into it. I watch him fizzle. I smile, then quietly close my eyes. I take my first proper walk through the Village since the yesterdays took over. I walk and listen to the music and I salvage what I can.

He drops me off outside the house. I give him the money. –The extra there is for those moon sprouts.

–Right you are, I'll get us a good deal. Happy birthday, Little Lady!

He beeps his horn as he takes off into the distance. I walk up to the front door and ring the bell. Laurence answers the door and gives me a huge smile.

–Happy birthday, he says and brings me up in a hug.

–Thanks.

–Come in, come in, I've some friends I want you to meet, Molly.

A cry sounds from within. I follow him in—then stop. My whole system goes into reverse. Everything falls. I look out through watery eyes and see a young Boy tied to a chair, facing an enormous screen. It's crawling with images of flesh and blood and violence and sex. I take my eyes away from it. The room sounds with the battlecries of torture. I can hear a woman screaming louder than the rest, closer, and it's a second before I realise it's coming from behind the closed door that sinks onto the living room. I can see it shuddering beneath the dull thud of her efforts.

–Don't look, Daniel! someone is screaming. Don't look!

Laurence smiles at me. But I know now that there has never been a Laurence.

–The door's open—you can run away if you want. But I know you'll remember our story about the child's cry from the alleyway.

I'm frozen. Isha can't lose another.

I try to go to the Boy but Laurence steps in front of me.

–Not yet, he says, there's something I want to show you first.

–This one's for you too, he shouts across the room as he drags me to the bedroom door with one hand and begins to pound on it with his other. His face heaves under the strain. It doesn't take him long to crack the wood and tear out a piece with his reddened fingers. A woman's face appears in the splintered wound.

–Turn it off! she shouts at me. Turn it off!

I go to the box but it's silver and smooth and I can't find the dials. I hit it but nothing happens except for Laurence's laugh and her cries.

–Don't look, Daniel! Don't look!

I turn to see the Boy's eyes blinking in these—the flickering images of the unspeakable.

I stand in front of the screen but Laurence comes to tear me away. I fight and wrestle and bite and pull but I know by the strength of his grip that there's no point.

–This one's for you, Julia, he says to the box.

The screen stops sweating for a moment but the images rebound. I can hear the woman shriek in recognition.

–Close your eyes, Daniel, she pleads.

The Boy sits there, lifeless. Any expression he once had has been drained from his face. He keeps staring at the screen. Blankly. The image hunts me down, pulling my eyes to the silhouette of a woman being raped from behind.

From a memory's recollection I know that it's Julia. I see her hands stretched to the corners of the screen, her fingertips red and translucent, palms held down over the exposed bulbs on either side of the bed. Ten rays of light shoot from between her fingers, stretching dramatically to the top corners of the frame. Dust particles dance in the blue bands of light

–That fateful night, he sniggers, but this is the best bit here.

He drags me across to the box with him. He holds me and points quickly to the corner of the screen.

–Here's little Daniel's screen debut, I love this bit.

Julia cries out as a silhouette appears on the carpet, boxed in by the light of an open door. Daniel's tiny body outlined by his shadow. It stands still for what seems like forever, still amidst the humping violence above it, then silently moves away. Julia is broken. She has fallen out of view. I can hear her sobbing—jagged and arresting.

–The rest isn't so good, Laurence says, definitely nothing worth staying in for.

He leaves me go. I turn to look at him. I go for him, breathing heavily through my clenched teeth, spit falling to my chin. I go for him with every ounce of fight I have in this life. I claw him and thump him but he holds me at arm's length.

–Molly is a Cyclops, Molly is a Cyclops, Molly is a Cyclops, he sings. Laughing.

I want to slap him, scrape his eye out. He knows this and stands before me smugly. I turn my back on him and go to the Boy. I look Daniel in the eye and try to tell him that there will be safety again, in another place, a short time from here. I untie him and take him by the hand to the bedroom door. Silence hits the room as the images are killed. I look around to see Laurence sitting in the chair, smiling to himself. He looks at us and throws me the key. I know now that we can leave, that he has done everything we came here for him to do. He looks calm and satisfied.

–Get him out of here, Julia keeps saying through the door.

I turn the key and she gets up from her knees. She looks for Daniel and I follow her gaze.

–Daniel! she screams.

But it's too late. Daniel is walking back over to Laurence. Laurence is looking off elsewhere, over the horizon to a land that doesn't think about badness at all, a land where they're all too busy laughing and basking in its source.

He jumps when he feels Daniel's small hand on his knee. He looks at the Boy, carried back by his touch to a land that is now. Daniel looks at Laurence, then wraps himself around Laurence's legs. Nobody moves until the silence is eased by the sound of the chair shaking. Laurence is crying. Daniel squeezes harder and the weeping man above him puts his hand out and touches his hair.

Julia pulls a bag over her shoulder and goes over to the Boy. She touches him gently on the shoulder and he slowly gets up and takes her hand.

We leave him there, weeping uncontrollably. The chair shaking and cracking.

–You're Isha's child, Julia says when we're standing outside.

And I suppose I am, more than anything else I know to be true.

She takes a card from her bag and calls a number. She talks very briefly on the phone.

–Should we start walking? I ask when she hangs up.

–He'll be here soon, she says.

We say nothing else. There's nothing to be said. Julia holds Daniel before her, rubbing his chest, his shoulders, his hair. I soak in the two of them and she smiles at me when she looks up. I can hear her sigh when a set of headlights comes into view. The Doctor pulls up before us. He gets out and comes around. He gives Julia a huge hug.

–It's your time to begin again, he says softly into her ear. She starts to cry and he holds her to him for a long while. He lets her go and bends down to Daniel. Neither of them say anything yet something very important passes between them.

He nods at me. –Molly.

–Doctor, I say, nodding quietly. Not needing more.

–Everyone's up at the hospital, he says.

We climb into the car. The Doctor turns on the radio. We let the music come.

12:1: Mr. ****

I sit there weeping for every empty moment I've begot. My roar subsides into a howl. I can smell his hair on my fingertips, as I smelt Rajem's, tousled on the pillow before me. Everything I've claimed as my truths are nothing now before the new knowledge that uncurls deep within my self. Everything is changed and I wonder how the fight survived this long.

Something, not in this room nor of this City wants for me—not for the man it hopes I'll become or the man I could have once been—it wants for me now, in all my wretchedness, for the man it knows me to be. It has travelled through the quiet touch of a child, it has come to take me back. I go willingly, despite myself.

I hear a car pull up in front of the house. I'm ready to go where it takes me but the door stays ajar. I sit and weep, emptying myself of everything that has gone before. I sit and weep until the tears are dried by the hours' passing.

I get up and go back to my City. I take on the streets and leave myself open for the Searchers to find me. I look into the eyes of everyone I can see.

A woman with no teeth asks me for money.

It hurts. I hurt. She hurts. The City hurts.

The Dishwasher is a coward.

–Let me take you for a coffee, I say as Laurence would have said had he been me—now—in this city, on this street.

–I don't want coffee, she says, I want money.

I don't give her any. Instead I tell her she has beautiful skin, because she did have once and could again.

–Fuck you, she says. Her tongue collapsing on the spittle-ridden gummy ledge.

I look into her eyes, trying to drill through the years of hopelessness. I think I've hit something when she spits on me and walks away.

I continue on, not knowing exactly where my feet will take me. I look up at all the monitors, throwing their lights over the City, selling life by the second, taking it back in the next. On the screen the fighting has stopped, the looting has started—the hungry will strip the city of everything needed for it to begin again. A looter runs by the camera with an incubator that has been wrenched from its rightful place. In it nestles the want of 'I'. Mindless, wanting, fearful.

I grow heavy but hope puts her shoulder to it. I throw my eyes over the throttled crowds on the huge monitors. Man will not stop for the bigger life—he'll choose to live his own instead.

–My husband used to say that, she says.

I turn around to see the toothless woman looking up at me.

–My husband used to say I'd skin like a creamery bride.

–Where is he now? I ask.

–I don't know, maybe he got clean, maybe he got dead. I don't know, I don't care.

–Yes, you do care.

–No, I don't.

–Yes, you do.

–No, I fuckin' don't, she says. Pushing me.

–Yes, you fuckin' do, everybody cares. We just try not to.

–I must be really good at it then, 'cause I really fucking don't.

–You get good at it if you put in the hours, same as anything.

–Shows it ain't natural if you've got to work at it, she says, and before you say anything, with your big jacket there, I'm very smart. Always had a way with arguments. Always preferred the arguing too, more than the thing I'd be arguing for.

I start to introduce myself.

–Don't smile at me unless you're going to give me money.

–I'm not giving you any money, I say.

–Give me some money.

–No.

–What, she shrieks, I've got to pretend to care before you give me any money?

–I still won't give you money, I say, hearing Laurence in my ear. I'm just daring you to care.

I laugh at myself then. Molly would never have let me away with that.

–Fuck you, she says, go play dares with the track divers.

She spits on me, then pushes me away. So I spit on her and walk away. She shuffles after me, grabbing me from behind.

–Don't you spit at me, she shouts.

–You spat on me, I say.

–Dare to care, she sneers, dare to care.

She starts to dance under the streetlight. She sings,

> *I'm so light on my pretty little feet,*
> *I've got flowers in my hair,*
> *My life's so full of roses,*
> *I just got to dare to care.*
> *I'm so light in my pretty little kitchen,*
> *I've got a big hubby bear,*
> *My life's so full of roses,*
> *I just got to dare to care.*

I turn my back on her and keep on walking. I can hear her shuffling behind me.

–What do you dare to care about then? she shouts.

–I don't know yet, I say. Turning to look for her once again amongst the folds of herself.

–I've put too much time into you, she says, not to get any money out of you. I know you have it. I can hear it dancing around in your pocket.

–You care about getting my money then.

–I need your money, she says, I don't care about it. I'm not going to cradle it in my arms and sing it lullabies.

–What are you going to do with it?

–That's none of your business—they say you should give without needing a reason.

–We should do a lot of things, I say, who's they anyway?

–Do-gooders, those people that does good.

–I'm not one of them.

–Neither am I, she says and laughs so hard that she reaches out to me for support.

I don't flinch. I don't feel my hand rise to wipe away hers. Instead, I let her splutter her humour all over me and my heart soars. The roar lost to all that I know now as true.

−What time is it? I ask.

−I don't know, you're the one with the watch.

I show her my wrist, vacant as it is of time.

−How do you know when it's time to put on that suit of yours and go into the office? she jeers.

−How do you know anything about me? I ask.

−I'm smart, she says, there's a clock up in the Brewing District. I'll show you if you give me the money with my name on it.

I turn and keep on walking. I can hear shuffling behind me.

−I can hear you, I shout back.

−You can afford good ears—you're rich.

I keep walking. A man climbs out of the shadows and makes his way to my approach.

−He's my investment, I hear her shout, I'm his bodyguard for the evening.

I smile and keep walking. I can hear her shuffling behind me. The clock adds up the night's traffic. In a free moment, it tells me the time stands at 5.23 a.m.

−Name three things you care about more than yourself, she asks. Shuffling up behind me.

−Love, life and liberty, I say.

She makes a squatting gesture.

−I shit on your ideals, she says, but for the change in your pocket, I'll sit on them and make them hatch.

I laugh. Aloud. It's not a laugh I've ever heard before.

−I got them from an advertisement, I say.

−No shitting me.

−YOU name three things you care about more than yourself.

−My children, my painting and truth, she says.

−You have children?

−Nah. I got them from a film I saw.

I turn and keep on walking. I can hear her shuffling behind me. I see an all-night store open on the corner of the T-junction. I go in and see her skirts follow me from the corner of my eye. I stand in front of the toiletry section.

–You got yourself a little shaving rash, she says.

–Pick out a cream, I tell her.

–Why?

–Pick out a cream, I say. Looking to find her again.

She squirms under the attention and turns away from me.

–I don't want to.

–OK, I say softly enough for her to know that I'm as unsure as she is.

I look around the store, not knowing what to do now. There is nothing I want to buy so I pick up a packet of gum and put it on the counter before a youth that has stopped registering the differences in days. I can hear her shuffling behind me. Her dirty hand partners the gum with a small square box. I pay for them and go back out into the City. I take my gum out of the bag and give the box to her.

She says nothing.

We start walking.

–I need to pee, she says.

–So do I.

–There's there, she says and starts off down a back street. I follow her. She stops at the side of an abandoned building.

–They used to be the toilets for an occupational therapy centre, she says—opening a door into the debris.

–The toilets still flush, and the water's still on in the taps. You go into that cubicle, she orders and I do because I'm in her place now.

I stand above the cracked bowl, dirtied by the years' forgetfulness.

I let it come.

–I can hear you peeing, she says.

–I can hear you too, I say but I can't.

She does not scoff at the premature quip of a ten-year-old. I'm surprised by her silence. I hear her come out of the cubicle and run the tap. She's putting on the cream when I come out. She doesn't look at me. She can't.

–You don't want anything? she asks.

–No, I say. Smiling for myself—through my self.

–You're not trying to get me to do something?

–No.

–A man tried to get me to do things for a film, he said some people like women with no teeth. Are you one of them?

–No, I say. But she sees me look away.

–I have to go, I say and step over a fallen brick to find my way out into the City's morning.

I walk down the alleyway. I can still hear her shuffling behind me. I turn to look at her. This time I find her and she comes up to shuffle beside me.

I keep on walking. I stop when I can see Kitty's on the corner. The lights are on and I think of all the Lost and Forgotten that are brought to her.

–I'll leave you here, she says as if she knows.

–I can smell the cream on my cheeks if I shake my head slowly, she says, showing me. I can smell it anyway. It's what I used to wear.

–I need you to do me a favour.

–Now it comes, she says. Smiling.

–I only thought of it now.

–I don't care when you thought of it, I'll do it if I don't mind doing it.

–I want you to go up to the Assumptia, up there on the hill, and ask for this man.

I give her the Doctor's card.

–Tell him Mr. **** sent you and that you have a message for his father. I want you to meet my father and give him this message. Tell him the tin soldier has stopped fighting the flesh.

She nods.

–I'm smart, she says, I can do that.

She finds me with her eyes. I smile and she smiles back before shuffling into an aging darkness.

I open the door to Kitty's. Gonzo is sitting inside, reading the papers. Kitty is folding a bundle of socks. She says nothing when she sees me. Instead, she smiles softly and walks out to the back room. She leaves the door open. I nod at Gonzo as I shuffle past—closing the door behind me.

12:2: Telephone Transcript

In Search of Infinite Relief, C.W. Sisle
Contracted to Diggin Media Group
Subcontracted to Employee 03
Recorded at 2.13 p.m. on 27/06/****

C78 Hello?

E03 Hello?

C78 Sorry. I don't think I expected anyone to answer. You must be the new man.

E03 The old man really, in every sense. I worked this stint before. What's your name?

C78 Molly. Molly Mae.

E03 Ah yes, Molly. I hope you don't mind. I've listened to some recordings of your conversations with 'Laurence'.

C78 What happened to him?

E03 He went over by all accounts. It happens in this business sometimes.

C78 What does that mean? Exactly.

E03 He began to think of himself as Laurence, began to act like him.

C78 He wasn't acting very like Laurence the last time I saw him.

E03 Yeah. He told me about you. I've been waiting for your call.

C78 Where's he now?

E03 He's gone away for a good while.

C78 Put away, you mean. Did he tell you what he had on the box that night?

E03 Yes. He told me everything. It must have been very hurtful.

C78 Hurtful? He had a six-year-old tied to a chair in front of that shit and a woman locked in the bedroom. Psychotic. Tone deaf. Tell him I said he's tone deaf. Tell him I said literally, too.

E03 OK. How's Daniel?

C78 He's fine. He's still not talking but he will.

E03 And Julia?

C78 She's OK too. Glad. She's glad.

E03 And you?

C78 Fine. Angry. You can tell Laurence as well that he lost the sale. Tell him he's full of shit and I should have known better. Emphasise the 'should'.

E03 That wasn't his shit, Molly, it's not anyone's. It's just something I wrote down.

C78 No offence but I haven't an appetite for any more of it.

E03 I believe it still, despite what's happened.

C78 Good for you.

E03 You can separate the beliefs from the man and from the action. Take them as they are.

C78 I don't want to take them at all.

E03 That's OK, Molly.

C78 I know it is.

(*4 seconds' silence*)

C78 Sorry. I'm still very angry. I don't understand why he did it. Is he a pervert? Is he actually sick? Julia says he's cold.

E03 He was a long way from the good.

C78 What does that mean? What the fuck do you mean by that?

E03 He was a man gone bad.

C78 And now?

E03 And now he's a man that's started on his journey back from the bad. He's a man that's stopped fighting and is turning around. He knows what direction he's supposed to be walking in.

C78 He can keep walking away from me.

E03 You shouldn't feed on anger too long, Molly, it'll ferment into hate.

C78 It already has.

E03 Hate the action, not the man.

C78 I really don't mean to be rude to you, I know you didn't do it but it's hard to listen to any more of this shit. I don't think you understand what he did, even if you have got your three or four eyes.

E03 I understand what he did, Molly. But I don't want you to go on hurting and hating. It's against your nature. I'm just trying to give you a way of understanding everything that's happened. You can throw it all away after if you like.

C78 Go on.

E03 I've hated, Molly. I ran myself into the ground hating. I fed it daily and it took pieces of me away.

C78 Who?

E03 I hated the man who mugged my wife and killed her.

C78 Like the book ...

E03 Molly, I wrote the book. My wife did die, was killed, like I said. I'm not some actor sitting in a cubicle and even if I was the beliefs are still the same. Still there if they help.

C78 I'm sorry about your wife.

E03 So am I. I was a bad husband. I'd a lot of forgiving to do. I think I hated myself more than I hated the man that killed her. I was being a bad husband the night she died.

C78 Have you forgiven yourself and the ...

E03 Yeah, I have. I gave myself away.

(*3 seconds' silence*)

E03 Actually Molly, there's a couple of other things I wanted to say to you. Do you mind?

C78 Let's hear them first, then I'll tell you if I mind.

E03 Firstly I've been listening to your previous phone calls and I was struck by some of the things you said.

C78 You'd no right to listen to them.

E03 I know. I only thought about it that way after I'd listened to them. Before, I thought I was listening to conversations we would have had. I thought I *should* listen to them, but that is probably me being overprotective of the stint. I'm sorry.

C78 Your business is fucked-up.

E03 Maybe. I never saw it as a business.

C78 Doesn't matter. Go on so.

E03 Thanks, Molly. I just wanted to go back to something you touched on with ... before. Need. He was right when he said that need dilutes the working emotional joys of every relationship.

C78 I love people. I want to need them.

E03 The less you need people, Molly, the freer you are to love them more. To need is to expect something of them.

C78 Everybody needs.

E03 I know. I know. But listen, freed from the weight of yourself and with a new understanding of your position in this world, you won't need Isha, Molly. You'll love her more but need her less. You'll free her up a little to travel on her own path.

C78 I don't need Isha that much. You make me sound fuckin' desperate—I haven't got any parents so she's like my mother. And I ...

E03 Molly. Molly. Listen to me. At the moment you need her to understand you, you need her to believe in you, you need her approval. If you're honest with yourself you'll appreciate what I'm saying. And because Isha doesn't understand you as you'd *like* to be understood, you resent her.

C78 I suppose.

E03 Ideally we shouldn't need anything that we can't attain and sustain ourselves. Love liberates. Need conditions.

C78 How long have you been back on the stint?

E03 It's only my second day back. I've been waiting for your call. I want to say so much to you. I think I feel a little responsible for what happened. Even though I know it wasn't my fault, I feel involved. I'm sorry for all of it.

C78 Laurence was good ... or whatever his name was. What did he do? Listen to your old recordings?

E03 Something like that.

C78 Did you make up the spiritual evolution stuff? About evolution taking another new turn, self intelligence and all that shit? We never got to that bit in the book.

E03 I did but I think cynicism found me on my time off.

C78 It finds us all. Just make sure you tell it to fuck off.

E03 Well make sure you tell the Lows to fuck off then. That was another thing I wanted to tell you.

C78 What?

E03 The usual stuff. Where's there's life to be had, live it. That kind of stuff. I do mean it though. Just ridicule those Lows from a height. When the Lows come, before they settle in, I want you to point your finger and laugh at them.

C78 That's a solid plan. I like it. I will. Anything else?

E03 Yeah—you know that feeling you get when you forget yourself, those waves of wantlessness. I wanted to give you a name for that feeling. You'll can't ever possess it but you should spend your life chasing it.

C78 Chasing what?

E03 Humility. I believe it's the only way to lasting happiness. You'd be doing well, my little Molly, to always keep it in sight.

C78 I can't wait to tell Augusta. I suspect she may know it already. Just hasn't put a name on it.

E03 She doesn't need to then.

C78 OK. I'm gone. Thanks for today. I suppose I'll see you somewhere on the horizon.

E03 Absolutely. I'll keep an eye out for the mad girl with the monkey.

End of transcript

12:3: Molly

–Promise you'll never kiss me when I'm drunk, I say.

–I promise, he says.

–Even if I come knocking on your door at three in the morning, tanked up to the hilt and demanding it.

–I'd be too scared to. How about you give me a fighting chance by promising to call here sober or even better still, we'll venture out, take on the real world?

–Yeah maybe. I think I might be ready to grow up—I think I might even give up the drink.

–I don't think we're meant to grow up too much, he says, I'm thirty and I can't even drive yet.

–Isha says you've got to have the head of a grown-up and the heart of a child.

–I think she's right. Does that mean you're going to grow up and leave your Village?

–No, but I'll be considering some properties abroad. I'll be travelling a lot.

–Good plan, he says, I might invest in some *real* estate myself.

I'm about to sprawl myself all over the wordplay when he—wise to my intentions—stops me.

–Close your eyes, he says.

–No, I say. Getting nervous.

A moment swells between us—pregnant.

–Why?

–Because I want to give you something.

–A kiss? I ask. Violently. Challenging him to fuck off with his manly assurance and his dinky one-liners.

–I'm not giving it to you unless you close your eyes, he says.

I close my eyes and my body tightens. My face scrunches up without my consent. I feel his lips on my forehead and when I open my eyes, he's back where he came from. He takes off my scrunched-up expression.

–I'd kiss you if I could reach your forehead, I say. Laughing.

He bends down with mock fearfulness and I place my lips on his wrinkled brow. He smiles at me when he's straightened up.

–I've to go, I say.

–OK, Molly. Isha's going to love her present.

–It's the biggest thing I've ever finished, I say, I'm glad I did. Thanks. And sorry I left it here so long.

I smile at him and walk down the stairs. I feel his eyes on my back and I smile so deeply that I think I might swallow myself. I can't wait to tell Isha that his fingernails look white as seashells. I can't wait to see Isha's eyes roll skywards.

Isha starts laughing when I show her the present. So do I.

–It's wonderful, she says. Taking it over to the kitchen table.

–You're mad, she says, slapping me on the arse. But a good mad.

I open my drawer. I turn back then and slap her on the arse.

–All genii are mad, I say, we can't help it. It's our condition.
Two 'i's, Scribe says.
Good for you, I say.
Isha snorts.

–Have you showed it to Julia? she asks.

–No, she's still sleeping. I think she could be worse than me.

–We'll bring it into Chivers later, Isha says, Puckie's going to break himself when he sees it, especially 'cause he looks so fat.

–I was a little generous all right, I kind of zoned out when I was doing him—I'll tell him I was trying to convey a real sense of his generosity.

–He'll tell you you're full of SHIT, she says. Pushing it out through her teeth, letting it fall on the floor.

–Baby Mac ... I tease.

–Don't mind that mad woman, Isha says to Baby Mac as she reaches down to get him. Don't you mind anything she tells you.

I shiver when Isha calls me a mad woman. I want to tell her how happy I am that she thinks of me as a woman, not as a girl. I want to tell her that I'm ready to grow up. I want to tell her I'm sorry for every hurt I've ever caused her. But Isha doesn't need to hear any of this, she knows everything already. She always did in her own way.

–You should start painting again, Molly or making these yokes here, she says pointing to the sculpture. You could put them up in the hospital. The Doctor won't mind.

–Oh, we're all about the Doctor now, I say. Teasing her.

–I asked him about hanging your paintings. You really should do some.

–Maybe, I say.

–You could earn some extra beer money for yourself.

She says this is a voice I recognise. I look up to find her smiling. I know how it was intended. I know how all her small remarks were. They were never meant to make me feel bad. None of her remarks held court with such empty intentions. Hers belong to a different kingdom, ruled as it is by practical love and real expectations. Isha only wants more for me because she thinks I deserve more for myself. Isha, more than anything else, wants me to be happy. Isha can't say this but she doesn't have to because I don't need to hear it! Mad-glad-not-too-bad-Molly. As lost as the next man but working on a good lead. Sometimes I think me and Isha are like two cows in a field. Bovine, the pair of us, but surviving. I can hear a fiddle somewhere in the Village.

I smile and Isha tells me to stop grinning and go up and put some clothes on.

–I can't look at you shivering there any longer, she says.

I slap her on the arse again as I run past and scream down the stairs that I'm really happy. Just so there's no confusion.

–That's good, Molly, bring down the wet towels from the bathroom when you're coming.

Daniel lets out a squeal when I tell him that the little Boy in the sculpture is him. He throws his head back and laughs. It's still a rusty laugh but it has started to find its form.

–Puckie looks a bit portly, Chivers says. Smirking from the hospital bed.

I try out my line about his generosity.

–That's how fat I would be if I ate all the shit Molly tries to feed me, Puckie says.

I laugh. Long and hard like a machine gun. Unapologetic. Daniel copies me, which makes me worse, and he, worse still. I can hear Chivers scolding Puckie for his foul mouth. I can hear Puckie scolding Chivers for fussing like an old lady. I alight from my laughter.

–I'm going to go up to Augusta.

–Read her more of your mad stuff, Puckie says.

–Excuse me, Puckie Hartly, I've had nurses weeping. That stuff is good SHIT.

–Will everyone stop using that word? Chivers asks as I lean down to give him a kiss.

I thump Puckie in the back and run away.

–Run away off to your boyfriend, he shouts after me.

I go back to the open doorway.

–He's not my boyfriend, I say in a salacious voice I've stolen from the box, he's my lover.

I make a scandalous face and leave again before Chivers starts up about keeping things clean.

I meet the Doctor halfway down the corridor. He nods.

–Molly.

–Doctor, I say. Nodding back.

–I believe Nomoré has you roped in to do some radio with him.

–Scary but true—the Love Hour. I think Puckie's jealous. I'm going upstairs to the station after I see Augusta.

–She'll come through, Molly, she should. Everything seems OK. They did a scan yesterday.

–I know. Time, everyone keeps telling me.

–Time, he says and nods his head.

–I might see you later then, he says.

–Scarier still, you might hear me later.

I make my way down the corridor and smile at the nurse as she presses the button on the lift.

–I like your earrings, I say.

–I have Capricorn ones, she says, they're better. I'm a cusp birth.

Put this on for snoozing, he'd said.

He'd given it to me as my promised birthday present, that night when the Doctor brought us all to the hospital. Everyone cried when we got there, even Isha. She hugged Daniel and half slapped me in frustration. I hugged her anyway, I was beyond caring. And then she hugged me back. That's when she started to cry.

We stayed in the hospital late until Daniel started to fall asleep on his feet. The Doctor let him stay in Chivers' hammock for the night. He's in a new home now. Chivers is happy to know where Daniel is—he's not sad that he can't live with him anymore. Actually, of course he's sad. He's sad that he can't live in his own house again. He's sad that he's getting older and lives in the hospital, but as Isha says he's happy for lots of other things instead. I tell him his legs are getting funnier by the minute. He says they practice their routine every morning—they're currently working on some new material. I laughed loudly at that one too.

Put this on for snoozing, he'd said.

Isha and I had to go shopping for an old turntable to listen to it.

I brought her in to meet my butcher and my cobbler. She said her butcher was cheaper.

We met Serge in town for lunch and I brought them to the bar. Everyone fussed around Isha so much because I'm always talking about her. Everyone said it to her too—everyone said they'd heard so much about her. Isha looked so pleased. No one would let us pay for lunch. J told me about a shop where I could get something like a turntable. He said, –Tell them where you work.

But Isha did, when we got there. –She works in SUCHandSUCH, she said, J sent us.

I told her to stop trying to steal my friends.

She told Serge to put his wallet away, that Molly could pay for her own turntables. But Serge said he was going to put it down as a company expense anyway.

–They're bandits, he said.

–Aren't we all, said the man behind the counter as he came back with a result.

Put this on for snoozing, he'd said.

So I do. I pull the needle over and gently let it down. It has no name, merely a number. Recording No. 19. It's a rich soundscape that drowns out the noises of the now and fills it instead with the soft humming of a place he said to call my own. I can hear the faint undulations of a soft breath, the curved rise and fall of a peaceful chest, but mostly, all I can hear is silence and space.

I snuggle up to myself and heave a sigh of sweet relief. I breathe deep and think nothing. Then an old familiar feeling creeps across my chest and I see her cape from the corner of my eye. She has sniffed out my happiness, she has come to put rights to wrong. I look up to see her rooting through my compliments drawer. I shout at her from the tousled linen of my mind.

Hey Matron! I scream. *You can't touch those.*

She looks around the room for the Lows that should have kept me from screaming, the Lows that should have had me weighted in bed. Lifeless. Careless. Numb.

They're gone, I tell her.

She turns then to look at me and for the first time I see that she has my face. I take my desk lamp and throw it at her. My lamp is not ashamed and neither am I.

Ding-dong! The Matron's dead. Monkey dancing on her head! The Villagers cheer and the Lunatic sounds his fiddle.

IV — The Sigh by Molly-Mae Haeticus

The millions, lost to the weight of life's temper, are
Reclaimed & given back to silence.
The City inhales — the draw of its breath pulls the
darkness down upon it it. Then —
the Laundry Lady sighs, the Drunk sighs,
the Taxi Driver sighs, the Street Children sigh
the Porter sighs, the Neighbour sighs, the
Barkeeper sighs, the Dandy sighs, the Nurse
sighs, the Doctor sighs, the Woman sighs, the
Father sighs, the Old Woman sighs, the Man sighs
the Grandchild Sighs, the Boy Sighs.

} too long Molly!

— The City Sighs — a deep, shaking near endless Sigh of Infinite Relief. It throws the darkness from its shoulders, unravels the knot of existence buried therein and wipes away every empty & aching Want tangled in its living. The monitors flicker & pass over into stillness. The City starts to weep for this moment of sheer wantlessness. Wordless, weightless, wonderful, whole — it rushes to the concrete veins & washes them clean. Life, renewed will have it forgotten but the self will never forget. All this of a moment but where there's men, there lies eternity.
— In memory of Augusta Merrick xx

Acknowledgements

I sincerely love too many people to attempt a comprehensive thank-you list that extends beyond the creation of this book. So many people have inspired me in different ways. I think you all know how much.

As Molly says, 'I think about my life, the people I know, the friends I have ... I get the shivers, sitting there, thinking about every small wonderfulness that makes up my existence.'

And it's true.

 Special thanks to

The people who made a direct and invaluable contribution to this book: Marsha Swan | Barry McCormack | Joe Dixon | Hawkeye | Mike McCormack | Lars from London

The people who put me up, or put up with me, during the writing of this book: the girls in Linen Hall Terrace | the lads in Whelan's | Noni of Hotel Leonie | Ann in the B&B in Bray | the staff of the *Isle of Inishmore* | Marie & JP in Clonakilty | the staff in Crutch's Hotel

The people who made an indirect yet special contribution to this book: Fudge | Michael Diggin | Patsie Prendeville | The Dill | Leagues | Steve Nolan | Mac | Marlene | Clubheadbangers—Keet, Treasa, Amo | Scannell

A Note on the Type

Berthold Imago was designed by Günter Gerhard Lange in 1982. It follows the tradition of earlier sans serifs such as Kompakt-Grotesque and Univers, but with distinctive, slightly squared curves. Lange was born in Frankfurt-an-der-Oder, Germany, in 1921. He fought in World War II and was discharged when he was seriously injured in France, which resulted in the loss of a leg. Before becoming artistic director at Berthold, Lange studied under Georg Belwe, Hans Theo Richter, Walter Tiemann, Paul Strecker and Hans Ullman.

Slimbach was designed by Robert Slimbach in 1987. Born in 1956 in Evanston, Illinois, he grew up in southern California. This was his first font and was inspired in part by German typefaces and the work of Hermann Zapf. He designed Slimbach and Giovanni for the International Typeface Corporation before joining Adobe Systems, where he has been responsible for the development of Utopia, Adobe Garamond, Minion and Poetica font families.

Rodchenko was designed at ParaType in 1996–2002 by Russian type and graphic designer Tagir Safayev, who has created more than one hundred fonts. It is inspired by the works of Russian Constructivists of the 1920s and '30s: Alexander Rodchenko, Varvara Stepanova, Vladimir and George Stenberg, and Gustav Klutsis, among others.